FALLING INTO SUMMER

S. N. CHRISTENSEN

CONTENTS

AUTHOR'S NOTES

This book is the first in the fALLINg series and continues in fALLINg into Senior Year.

Some content in this book may be triggering to some readers.

Trigger Warnings include mention of rape, violence, and the use of drugs and alcohol.

CHAPTER ONE

I savor the scent of baked chocolate chip cookies as they sit in front of me on the table. I close my eyes and hear the commotion of servants packing and preparing to shut down the house for a while. Trying to drown out the noise, I taste the warm gooey cookie and concentrate on my father sitting across from me.

"I'm going to miss this..." my father states in a sentimental voice.

It's been my father and me against the world for many years. Yeah, we have spent a lot of time apart, especially during the summers when he travels for work the most, but during the school year he's mostly around when he's not working. This is the end of how everything has always been. For him, he will most likely be back in a year's time, but for me... I'm pretty sure this will be the last time I sit at this table other than some holidays. I will not be returning to this house next year as I'll be preparing to go to college and starting a whole new life again.

I give him a small smile and say, "I will too, dad, but it's okay. We will both have new adventures ahead of us to keep us busy."

He smiles back and asks, "How did I get so lucky to have you as a daughter? Always looking at the bright side of things. I couldn't do this without you, sweetheart."

My father may not be present as much as a normal kid's parents are, but he has done the best with what he has. After my mother died, he spent every minute he possibly could with me. He hasn't even dated or considered it, that I know of. He loved her, just as he loves me. I couldn't ask for a better father.

His face and tone turn serious. "I want you to know you can tell me anything and call me at any time of the day, okay?"

I give a little laugh and say, "Of course dad, I know that."

He continues, "I'm serious. Anytime. Now, I want you to promise me that if any of the boys do anything at all to upset you or anything else, that you will tell me immediately. Okay?"

My smile fades as I say, "You know I will, but they won't. They never do."

He clears his throat. "Everly, they are all older now and you will be there for a year. All boys want one thing..."

I cough and interrupt him. "Oh no, ew dad please let's not go there. They are basically my brothers, you know that. I'm their little sister and always will be."

He laughs and says, "Honey, I know you feel that way, but you're not a boy. You are beautiful, just like your mother was... They will be thinking about it, and I just want you to be careful around them..."

My voice gets much louder as this conversation continues, "OKKAAAYYY, yep, I get it. Careful. I'll let you know about anything they do. DONE."

I grab another cookie and shove it in my mouth, looking away from my father, hoping he understands now that this conversation is over. I have absolutely no intention of EVER being in one of those boys' beds, in that sense. We have known each other literally our whole lives, and I've spent every single summer staying at the Crawford's house while my dad traveled for their father. The Hale boys live right next door, so they are basically brothers. I'm their sister. Nothing is going to change that.

My father and I finally continue onto other topics like what my plans are this summer before my senior year of high school. My current plan is to relax by the pool with a good book almost every day. After the past couple of years that I've had with my so called "friends" here in Boston, I have no intention of doing anything this summer. Then once school starts back, I have every intention of staying invisible, getting good grades, and going to college as far away as possible from here. One where I won't know anyone.

It is finally time for me to leave for my trip to New York, where the Crawford family lives. I'm excited to start fresh and get away from Boston. These past few years have been rough, and I've found that I can't trust anyone but my dad and myself. Attending a new school for senior year is dreaded by most kids who must do it, but I'm looking forward to the fresh start.

Standing outside the front door saying goodbye to my father is hard, but I keep my emotions in check, mainly for him.

I give him a big hug and he says, "I'm going to miss you so much, sweetheart."

I continue our hug and reply, "I'm going to miss you too, dad. Are you sure I can't come with you this time? I'm starting a new school anyway, why not go to one where you'll be?"

He sighs. "I wish you could, Everly, but there are no good schools around where I'm going to be staying, and it's safer for you to be with the Crawfords. But with that said, please promise me you will take security with you when you go out alone."

"Of course, dad," I say hugging him tighter.

He finally lets me go and I get in the car with my two security guards, who I have had for a few years. They will be driving and staying with me while I'm in New York. Actually, I'm fairly certain they are going to be following me when I get to college as well. I'll be honest, I'm not entirely sure what my father does for work, and I don't really want to know. He has been secretive about it my whole life and just says he's a businessman. I'm pretty sure he is into some illegal stuff, but the less I know, the better, for many reasons.

It only took five hours to get to the Crawford's house from Boston, but I was ready to get out of the car. It's close to dinnertime and I'm starving. Right after dinner, I'll be heading straight to my bedroom to put on my pajamas and continue the book I was reading in the car. While I'm wearing my comfortable yoga pants and a tank top, the pants are too tight for my liking. Nice comfortable pajamas sound amazing right now.

Before my security detail can knock on the front door, Mrs. Crawford opens the door and embraces me in a hug.

"It's so good to see you again, Everly!" She steps back holding me at arm's length to look me over then continues, "My how you have grown in the past year! Come in, come in!"

I step into the house to realize the foyer still looks the same. There's a large chandelier hanging from the ceiling and curved steps on the right-hand side leading to the upstairs. Large portraits of the family line the walls. On the right-hand side are portraits of Mr. and Mrs. Crawford, along with their two boys, James and Benjamin. On the left-hand side there are portraits of the Hale boys, their neighbors and best friends, Sebastian and Jacob. Beside Jacob is a portrait of me, one that Mrs. Crawford insisted on making me pose for last summer. While we are not their children, they treat us as if we are, especially Mrs. Crawford. I'm pretty sure that she always wanted a daughter.

"Everrrlllyyy!!!" I hear coming from the stairs, distracting me from my thoughts.

I look over to find Jacob, aka Jake, sliding down the railing as he's always done since he could basically walk. When his feet hit the floor, he runs up to me, lifting me up in a hug and spinning me around. I laugh as he carefully puts me back down on the floor. I step back to look him over to find he has also grown this past year. He has a lot more muscle, which he is showing off in his tank top and shorts. His face looks about the same, clean shaven, with his hazel eyes and dark brown hair. He has let his hair grow out as it's past his ears and his bangs are pushed to the side, but a piece fell into his eyes.

"Ah, checking me out already? You've gotten HOT!" Jake says while stepping back because Mrs. Crawford slaps him on the arm, giving him a look.

I blush at his statement but smile at how Mrs. Crawford treats him just like her own sons. I hear a laugh come from the stairs again, so I turn to find that sound coming from Benjamin, who stands there with both James and Sebastian behind him. Benjamin, aka Ben, looks just like his mother. He keeps his blonde hair short and has the most piercing blue eyes. He's the shortest of all four boys, but still a few inches taller than me, where I stand at five four.

Ben's brother, James, looks more like his father with the dirty blonde hair and green eyes. He is the tallest of all the boys. I look over toward Sebastian, aka Bash, who looks identical to his brother, Jake. They are both the same height and have the same hair and eye color. Bash's hair is a little shorter, though. Even though they are two and a half years apart, I could mistake them for twins.

I walk over and give Ben a hug, then Bash, and then James. I look back toward the entrance to find Mrs. Crawford has left the room, along with my security guards.

I break the silence and say to them all, "It's good to be back. I've missed you guys."

James pats me on the shoulder. "We missed you too."

"Come on, Everly, we were just playing games in my room. We have a bit before dinner. Come join us," Ben says, already heading up the stairs.

I shrug and follow behind him, then the other three follow behind me. Relaxing in my room with a book sounded good, but now that I've seen them again, I want to hang out. I forgot how comforting it is to be with them. They've always treated me like I was a part of the family, their sister. I'm just hoping the pranks have calmed down as they've aged.

Jake whistles. "Damn, Everly, your ass looks amazing. What have you been doing this past year?"

I quickly put my arms behind my back to hide my butt and blush. Maybe my father wasn't wrong about what he was saying earlier... Jake has always been a flirt, but he has definitely stepped it up and it's usually not aimed at me. Should I be worried?

James snaps, "Jake, come on, she's our sister and she just got here. Leave her alone."

I give him a thankful smile and look back toward Jake, who has a grin on his face and his hands up in the air in surrender. James has always been protective of me. Jake and Ben sit at the end of Ben's bed, and I'm sandwiched between James and Bash on the couch. I decline playing whatever video game they are playing this time because I haven't seen it before. I would rather watch and figure out what you do before jumping in and them ganging up on me.

There is so much laughter, and some arguing because of the game, but I feel at ease. After every summer that I come here, I always forget how much I love these boys and how much fun we have. I don't know why we never seem to keep in contact between summer visits. I send them Happy Birthday texts and they send them to me, but we rarely speak otherwise. Since I'll be here for the next year, I have a feeling our dynamic will change.

While playing games, we catch up with everything going on in our lives. Bash and James just finished their second year at college and are home for the summer. James hasn't had a girlfriend all year and Bash just apparently broke up with his high school sweetheart. I guess the long distance didn't work out for them. Jake and Ben will be starting their senior year of high school with me. Not surprisingly, Jake has been through girls left and right, whereas Ben had a girlfriend who apparently broke his heart a couple of months ago. He's denying it, but the others are relentlessly claiming otherwise.

I didn't give them much detail about what has been going on with me and I don't intend to. This past year especially was the hardest, and I'd like to do my best to pretend that it never happened. That's how I can be so positive and "happy" all the time. If you pretend like nothing ever happened and drown yourself in books of someone else's life, then it's easy to have fun and be somewhat happy when the opportunity presents itself.

After catching up and dinner, I do what I said I would and head back to my room. The same room I've had every summer. It hasn't changed much and still has the pink walls from when I was a little girl. I don't have the heart to tell Mrs. Crawford that it is babyish. I just pretend that I still love it because she does everything that she can to make me feel at home, and I'm usually only here for a couple months a year. There's no reason to make them change something for me when I'm hardly here. Though, I may see about buying a new comforter because the girly pink flowers all over the bed make me feel really young.

I shower in the bathroom attached to my room and get into my comfy PJs. I pull out the book I was reading in the car that only has 26 pages left for me to read and lay in bed with it. I turn off the light in the room but turn on the lamp beside my bed. As I begin reading the first page, the day catches up to me and I slowly close my eyes, falling into a deep sleep.

CHAPTER TWO

I shoot out of bed when I hear loud drumming right beside me. The bangs reverberate in my eardrums, so I put my hands over my ears and stare at Jake, who is drumming on his drum from his marching band years.

I try to yell over it. "What the hell Jake?!"

He continues drumming with a large grin on his face. "Sorry, what was that?"

"Jake! Cut it out!" I yell even louder and jump out of bed to take the drumsticks away from him.

I grab his right arm to stop him from continuing to beat the stupid drum, but he continues anyway. I pull on his arm and the drumstick at the same time, ripping it out of his hand and doing the same to the other. He pushes the drum to his side and tries to grab the sticks back from me. I fall over onto the bed with him tumbling on top of me, almost getting one stick out of my hand, so I throw them both into the corner of the room.

"Oh, it's on!" he says and starts tickling me like he did when we were little.

I can't do anything but curl up and laugh. I try to push off his attack, but he is much stronger than me.

"Jake, what the fuck are you doing?" We both stop in our tracks and look over toward the door where James is standing.

James' face looks angry, but it disappears almost as quickly as the expression was there. He just stares at us, waiting for an answer with his arms crossed at his chest. I look down where Jake's hands are, one is on my hip and the other just below my right breast. With the way Jake is on top of me, this would look like something completely different from what is really going on.

I clear my throat and push Jake off me. He doesn't fight it and stands up, helping me stand as well.

He finally breaks the silence and says, "I was just giving our sister a nice wake-up call this morning."

James shakes his head. "Yeah, looks like it."

I smack Jake's shoulder. "I'm going to pay you back for that. Just wait."

He smirks at me and replies, "Oh, I can't wait."

I smile, shake my head, and start pushing him toward the door. "Okay, both of you out. I'm going to get dressed and I'll see you downstairs for breakfast."

Jake continues to laugh as he leaves my room and before I close my door, I can see James glaring at him. Why is he looking at him like that? He saw him tickling me and there's no way he didn't hear the drumming. He has to know that wasn't what it looked like, but even if it was, what does it matter? Then again, he really has always been my protective older brother. I quickly get dressed and put my hair up into a ponytail since I didn't get a chance to blow dry it last night and it's a mess. I put on the minimum makeup, including foundation and mascara. Since most of the summer I'll be sitting by the pool, there's no reason to be putting on so much makeup.

When I get down to the dining room, only the boys are left eating at the table. There is a large spread of pastries, so I grab a Danish and some orange juice as I sit down next to Ben.

"Good timing, Everly. We were just talking about what we want to do this summer. We just realized it's the first summer that none of us have a girlfriend, well in your case, a boyfriend. We're coming up with a bucket list to complete before the summer ends. Have any suggestions?" Ben asks.

We always come up with a few fun things to do over the summer, but half the time it is only a couple of us together at a time. Last year, Bash and Ben were busy most of the summer with their girlfriends and the same with the previous year. Jake was usually off with someone as well, just not necessarily the same girl each week. James was working a lot with his father, but I spent more time with him than any of the other boys. It could be fun to take advantage of this and have all five of us hanging out together. It would definitely get my mind off the things plaguing me from the past year.

"I love that idea. How about we all have to be present for each item we check off the bucket list? Let's make this summer all about us, like when we were little," I say.

Bash's face lights up when I say that, and he puts his hand out in the middle of the table. James puts his on top, then Jake, then Ben, then I do.

Bash yells, "Yes! Hale, Crawford, Monroe summer!"

We push down and throw our hands up in the air repeating, "Hale, Crawford, Monroe summer!"

Jake has the piece of paper and pen to write the list, and I notice there are already two items on it, so I ask, "What do you guys have so far?"

"So far we have pulling the most epic prank and skinny dipping in the lake," Jake replies

I cringe at the second one because me skinny dipping with four boys? That's not at the top of my bucket list, but I can make it work. I just have to make sure we do it at night in the dark and be the first one in and last one out. I'm good at working around these things.

I smile and ask, "So, who are we pranking?"

We've pulled some pretty epic pranks in the past. I don't know what we're going to have to come up with to top them.

"We're not sure yet, but we'll find someone worthy of our prank," Ben says.

James has been awfully quiet throughout this. Creating this bucket list seems like it's right up his alley, but he looks distracted and maybe a little concerned. I don't think it has anything to do with the list.

"I'm assuming neither of those were your ideas, James. What do you want to add to the list?" I ask, while kicking him lightly under the table to bring him back to the present.

He smiles. "Hmm... There's a lot I can think of, but there's something we haven't done in a while. Paintball!"

"Oh, good one! Maybe this time Everly won't cry," Jake teases.

"Hey! I was only like 12 and you hit me in the face. I had a black eye for weeks," I state, defending myself.

Everyone laughs and we continue going around, thinking of things we could add to the list. I haven't contributed any ideas yet and mainly just agreed to things. I shot down a few ideas, like skydiving and bungee jumping. I wouldn't really mind doing those things, but I also don't have a death wish right now. I always say doing something like that is probably how I'm going to end up dead.

"Alright Everly, we need you to tell us at least one thing you want to do this summer," James says.

I look between each of them and can't really think of anything. I like their ideas and anything I could think of would probably be stupid.

"I don't really have anything I want to do. All of these sound good," I reply.

"Come on, we need at least one thing. What's something you haven't done yet that you want to do? You're about to be a senior. There has to be something," Ben says.

There is one thing that I've wanted to do, but just haven't done it because I've been afraid to get in trouble and just really had no desire to do around my so-called friends back home.

Before I could chicken out, I state, "I want to get drunk."

All four of them stare at me and I feel like that was a really stupid answer.

Bash asks, "You've never been drunk before?"

I shake my head. "Nope."

Jake gives a large grin. "We can definitely arrange that!"

He writes it down on the list. We went around a few more times as we tried to get a decent sized list to complete before the summer ends. When the page is half full, we decide to stop there because we want to make sure we are able to check off every single item on the list. Jake signs his name on the bottom, then Bash, James, and Ben. Ben hands it over to me and I sign my name after reading the list again. We put our hands in the middle of the table, one on top of the other, and yell our mantra when we plan to complete something, "All in!"

Most epic prank
Skinny dipping at the lake
Paintball
Create the beach inside
Ziplining
Get Drunk
Get fake IDs and go to a club
Camping with no tents

Play video games through the whole night

I feel like these are doable bucket list items. I would say that I'm concerned about the fake IDs, but I know James knows someone who will make us some realistic ones. Even if we were to get caught, we wouldn't get in trouble due to who we are. We could even steal a boat and get away with it. I'm surprised that wasn't put on the list, but I'm not about to mention it.

We finish our breakfast and decide that we should knock off an item today by creating the beach inside. This is something that we always wanted to do when we were little kids, but of course, Mrs. Crawford told us we'd be grounded if we did such a thing. We always came up with the idea of buying a kiddie pool and then putting sand all around it, in the bathroom, of course. So that's exactly what we are going to do. It's stupid, but I love it and feel like a kid again.

Ben asks me to go with him to buy the sand and kiddie pool. The others stay home and do who knows what. I hop in the passenger seat of the car with Ben driving. I don't need to take my security guards with me since I'm going out with Ben. All the boys have had training, but I'm a lot safer here than at home. Not many know me here, so they wouldn't know to try anything to get to my dad. I still don't know why people may be after me, but I don't plan to ask since I know it has to do with whatever my father does for a job.

We get to the store, grab a cart, and head inside. We find a blow-up kiddie pool and put it in the cart. I look at all the sand,

and we decide which type of sand we should get. I figure the play sand is probably what we want. I look at the small bag and try to calculate how many we might need to create the beach scene we are hoping for. The description on the bag says it's a 50-pound bag.

I look over at Ben and question, "That bag is 50 pounds? It's so small, there's no way it's 50 pounds."

I lean over to pick it up and my muscles strain as I barely budge it. I don't know what I was expecting, but I wasn't expecting it to be that heavy. "Nope, that's fifty pounds right there."

Ben looks at me and starts laughing, hard. He holds his stomach as he is almost doubling over. "Oh, that was good Everly. You should have seen your face when you tried to lift it. It doesn't look like it would be 50 pounds, I give you that."

Ben lifts ten bags of sand, like they each weigh nothing, into the cart and we're hoping that it's enough to do what we want to. On the way to the checkout lane, we notice a bucket and some sand toys. We pick a couple of those up too so we can have a little fun at our make-believe beach. I feel like a little kid again.

Ben and I go straight home after getting the items we need, so we aren't gone more than an hour. When we arrive, I text the group of all five of us.

I get out of the car and go into the house. Thankfully, there isn't anyone in the foyer. We may get lucky and be able to sneak them all through without anyone noticing.

Jake

Be right there.

Jake and James come running down the stairs and out the door. It only takes a moment before all three of them come back, both carrying two bags of sand each up the stairs like they weigh nothing. I know they train and work out, but man, they are strong. I've seen their muscles and now I'm curious what they look like shirtless. I blush at the thought, especially since instead of being the lookout, I'm checking them out as they go up the stairs. Maybe my father should've been more worried about me than them.

After the last of the sand is brought upstairs, I follow them into Ben's bathroom. We play rock paper scissors to see whose bathroom we will use to make the mess in, and luckily Ben is the one who loses. We plan to clean it all up after, but we all know that sand will be found for eternity in the bathroom after this.

I blow up the kiddie pool and start filling it with water while the boys empty the bags of sand around the pool. We could've used more sand, but this will do. We try to pile it around the pool, but it doesn't really stay and just ends up pretty much everywhere on the floor. While I continue filling the pool with the buckets, which takes forever, the boys go to get their suits on. We switch off and I get mine. I decide to go with a one-piece floral suit since I won't be outside sunbathing.

When I reenter the bathroom, everything is set up, but that's not what I'm focusing on. Not that long ago, I was just wondering what they looked like without a shirt on, and now I know. Each of them is so toned and has a six-pack. James and Bash have the most muscle as they are older, but they all look hot. I can't believe I'm standing here with four of the hottest guys in New York. There are many girls who would kill to be in my position.

"Are you going to stop drooling and join us in making this sandcastle or what?" Jake snaps me out of it, and I look over toward the almost done sandcastle I didn't even realize they started to make.

"Huh?" I answer, as an automated response.

Jake comes up to me and wipes the side of my bottom lip. "You have a little drool there from staring at our nicely sculpted abs."

I blush. "Psh, you wish."

I go over and help build the sandcastle. By help, I mean destroy the progress they made because I'm clumsy and I really have no idea how to make a sandcastle. There is a lot of throwing of sand, splashing in the pool of water, and laughter. James and I are lounging in the pool when the bathroom door swings open. We all pause what we are doing to see Mrs. Crawford standing in the doorway, shaking her head.

"Uh, mom it's not what it looks like," Ben states innocently.

Just when I thought we were about to get scolded, Mrs. Crawford smiles and says, "I expected this to happen ten years ago, not when you all are basically adults. But I'm not surprised. Have fun and you're cleaning up the mess."

She laughs to herself, and before closing the door, she takes a quick picture with her phone. We all stare at each other and burst into laughter.

Chapter Three

I wake up with a smile on my face for the first time in almost a year. I didn't have my usual nightmares that plague my sleep, which typically make me groggy when I wake up. I knew that being here would be good for me, but I didn't realize how good. I've only been here a couple of days, and I've laughed more than I have in over a year. We're acting like carefree kids again, and I'm loving every second.

I grab my phone to find some missed messages. I decide to respond to them before my day gets started because I have a feeling I won't be checking my phone much during the day. The first message is from my dad.

Dad

Hey sweetheart just checking in on you.

I'm doing great dad how are you?

I move onto the next missed message from one of Ben's friends, Alex, who has become a good friend of mine as well over the years.

Alex

I heard you're back in town. Are you really spending senior year with us?

I sure am! You'll have to show me around the school.

Alex

Of course! Hopefully we will have a class together. How are the boys treating you this summer?

Like they always do…

I put down my phone when I hear a knock at the door. Ben comes walking in with a Danish and orange juice.

He puts it on my end table and says, "You missed breakfast, so I brought you something to eat."

It's the same thing I ate yesterday. It's sweet of him to notice. "Thank you. I was exhausted and didn't realize how late it was. I'm grateful Jake didn't give me a wake-up call like yesterday."

Ben laughs. "Jake has been planning that for the past year. He was really excited to finally do it. Jake and Bash won't be here until this evening, but we thought we would knock out another item on the list tonight. Ready for our all-night gaming session?"

A large smile is plastered on my face as I'm excited. "Yes! When do we start?"

Ben laughs again. "Right after dinner. Who knew something so simple could make you so happy?"

I frown. "Well, if you had the year I did, you would understand…"

I trail off, not knowing why I said that. I haven't had anyone to talk to about anything, not even my dad. I really don't plan on telling anyone anyway, so I'm not sure why I just said that.

I try to cover it up and continue, "I mean, I don't even have a sibling, so coming here and having the four of you entertain me is amazing."

Ben frowns at what I said at first but ignores it as he gives a mischievous grin. "Oh, you want four boys to entertain you, huh?"

I throw my napkin at him. "Get out of here. You know what I meant."

He walks toward the door and stops in the doorway. "Well, if you want some entertainment before tonight, you know where to find me."

This time I throw my pillow at him, and he blocks it by closing the door as he leaves. I can hear his laughter echo through the hall. This is going to be a long year with Jake and Ben. Both have been flirting with me since I got here. None of them have ever flirted with me before. I kind of like it.

Something sinks in the pit of my stomach. I thought of my ex-best friend, Kayla, and how these are the types of stories that she would've loved to hear about. I miss having a friend, especially a girlfriend, I can talk to. If only she didn't backstab me and treat me like trash at the end. I hope she gets what's coming to her.

I shake my head and hit my forehead to knock those thoughts away. I'm not like her. I hope for the best for her, and I need to stop thinking about the past and concentrate on the present. We're going to have fun tonight and it's a beautiful day outside. I'm going to get on my swimsuit and head to the pool for the day before playing with the boys all night.

I put on my green bikini and look at myself in the mirror. I decide to not put on any makeup, which I feel like I always look plain without it especially since I'm so pale. My hair is just past my shoulders, brown with a hint of red, and straight as can be. My eyebrows are a darker brown and my small eyes are hazel. My eyelashes are long, but they aren't that noticeable without wearing mascara. The scar on my lip is much more pronounced without any lipstick or lip gloss, but it doesn't bother me like it used to. I fell on a toy and my lip got cut when I was little and we decided not to go with stitches, which ended up leaving a larger scar than my parents had hoped. It's pretty noticeable, but I'm trying hard not to care about these things anymore.

I finish looking at myself in the mirror and am happy with the way my body looks. I'm not really toned since I don't exercise as much as I should, but I'm thin. I would like to be more toned, so maybe this year I'll work out more and join kickboxing or something fun like that.

I put my coverup on over my swimsuit, grab my book, and head out to the pool. It's a beautiful day, and the sun isn't too hot. I lay out on the chaise lounge and put on some sunscreen. I want to have a nice tan, not burn. After getting settled, I pull out my book to finally finish it since I passed out last night before reading it.

After only about thirty minutes, Mrs. Crawford comes out and stands beside me. I put my book down and smile at her. She holds a glass of ice water in her hand and hands it to me.

"Make sure you stay hydrated and keep applying the sunscreen. That sun is stronger than you think," she says with a smile.

"Thank you," I respond while grabbing the glass from her and taking a sip.

I put the glass down next to me on the little table. She sits down on the chair beside me, and I can tell she wants to talk. She's always treated me like a daughter, and I appreciate it because I don't have a mother. She fills that role every summer that I'm here.

She looks me over and clears her throat. "I know your father said he talked to you a little about this from his point of view, but I thought I would bring it up and let you know I'm here to talk if you want to..." She pauses for a good beat. I look at her, confused, and when I don't say anything, she continues, "You're growing up to be a beautiful woman and boys are bound to notice..."

Oh no, are we about to have THIS talk?! It was embarrassing enough with my dad, but even more so with her.

I keep quiet as she goes on, "So I just want to make sure that you know you can talk to me about anything and if the time comes when you want to..."

And here is where I pause her because my face is now bright red, and I can't do this with her. "Mrs. Crawford, thank you, but I get it, I know. You're right, my dad talked to me about it, and I'll be careful around the boys..."

She gives me a cringy smile. "Well, I remember how I was at your age, and I just want to make sure you're prepared. If you decide that's something you're ready for with the right person, then I'll be glad to take you to the doctor and get you on birth control. And you can't be too cautious, so I have condoms..."

At this point, I just feel nauseous as I sit up and stop her. "Oh, thank you, but I don't plan to be doing that anytime soon."

She interrupts me this time. "Yes, well, oftentimes you don't plan for it to happen. It just does."

I want to scream, but my voice comes out almost as a whisper. "I'm already on birth control since last year, so it's okay."

"Oh! Okay, good then, does that mean..." she trails off, waiting for my answer.

"Mrs. Crawford, I really appreciate you for treating me like your daughter, and I'll come to you if I need to, I promise... but... I really don't want to talk about this right now."

She gives me a reassuring smile and pats my leg. "Okay then, enjoy the pool."

I sit there, cringing as I watch her walk away. I'm so embarrassed and deep in my thoughts that I don't hear Ben and James come up behind me.

"Oh snap! Did mom just give you the sex talk?" Ben asks with a huge grin on his face.

I look at Ben, and laugh, embarrassed. James isn't even looking at me. I don't say anything.

Ben continues, "She gave it to us too, before you got here. And don't worry, she also gave us all a bunch of condoms, so none of us will be unprepared when you decide you want us."

I was drinking my water as he said that, so I choke on it and my nose burns as it's trying to come out of my nose. James smacks Ben on the back of his head and glares at him. I can't help but laugh. Ben ignores him and jumps into the pool, doing a cannonball while James sits next to me in the chair. He doesn't say anything, but I can't help but stare at him. He's always been the more serious of the four of them, and the one that I always came to for comfort. He has always treated me like his little sister as someone to take care of, and I've always looked at him like my big brother. Maybe Mrs. Crawford and my dad were right... It must be my hormones starting to act up because I definitely look at James as more than a big brother now. Something stirs inside my stomach as I continue to watch him beside me, putting on sunscreen. I wouldn't mind helping him put it on...

No! I shake my head and concentrate back toward the pool to watch Ben swim. I cannot be thinking like that right now. I blame Mrs. Crawford for putting such thoughts in my head. I have sworn off boys this year and want to get out of high school and start a fresh new life in college. When I get settled there, I can start thinking about those things. Maybe enough time will have passed that I'll want to.

Before my thoughts go any deeper, I force myself up and do a cannonball in beside Ben. James joins in shortly after. We spend a few hours swimming, splashing, and laughing in the pool. I love hearing about their lives this past year. James gives me hope for college and what that'll be like, the new start I'm hoping for. It sounds like he's trying to convince me to go to the same college he is, which I wouldn't mind. I doubt any of the kids from my old school in Boston would be going there. Ben tells me about his high school, and from his point of view, it seems like it will be great. Maybe it's because he's a boy, but it sounds very drama free, which is exactly what I need this year.

After the pool, I go inside to take a long shower and get into my comfy t-shirt and sweatpants for a long night of playing video games. I don't care that I go down to dinner looking like this because it is just Mrs. Crawford, James, and Ben. Mr. Crawford is still away on his trip with my dad. Usually, he's gone for a few weeks with my father, so I don't expect him back anytime soon.

Bash and Jake come over shortly after dinner and join us in Ben's bedroom for our gaming night. He has a nice set up and almost every gaming system there is. I don't usually play video games at home, so the only time I do is when I'm here during the summers. I have no idea what games we have been playing tonight, but the first two were shooter games, which I do the best at. They get angry at me for killing them all the time and claim I'm a cheater. I don't see how I could cheat; they are right there with me the whole time.

"Ah, come on Everly! Stop hiding and come out and fight me!" Bash says, because I keep killing him with my sniper rifle.

"But then you will kill me! The whole point of being a sniper is so I can stay hidden and kill you when you come around."

"Well, use another weapon. Let's have a fair battle." Bash looks at me with a pouty lip.

I laugh. "No way, being a sniper is my fav.... AH! James! You just knifed me! How could you do that to your little sister?!"

James laughs. "Sorry sis, but Bash is right. You've been there too long killing us all. We needed a chance."

There's a knock at the door and Mrs. Crawford comes walking in with a tray of snacks. Usually, the maid will bring up snacks and drinks, but I'm wondering if she just wanted to check to make sure we were all behaving, especially after the conversation that we had earlier.

James pauses the game to help his mom in with the snacks. I know James is close to me in the game, so I grab his controller and quickly unpause it to race to where he is. Mrs. Crawford leaves the room just as James notices what I did.

"Hey! Give me back my controller!"

He runs back to the couch where he was sitting beside me and tries to take it. I'm right up on James in the game, so I throw the controller behind me and sit on it while leaning around James, trying to kill him. James is basically on my lap, trying to get his controller from behind me.

Right before he grabs it out, I was about to place the kill when Jake kills me. "What?! Jake!!! I almost had him!!"

Jake laughs. "Sorry, but you were cheating."

To be fair, I am cheating at this point. When I stop leaning around James to see the screen, I realize he is on top of me, and our faces are inches apart with his hand touching my butt to get the controller that is now pushed halfway down the crack of the couch below me. We both pause what we are doing as we realize the close proximity we are in. James clears his throat and backs off me while I dig my hand between the cushions to get his controller and hand it to him.

Neither of us says anything, but Jake decides it's too good to let go. "Oh, James, you finally realized! You're ready to try to get some action from our hot sis too?!"

James actually looks embarrassed and doesn't say anything, but I laugh it off and say, "Oh Jake, are you jealous?"

Jake gives me a huge grin. "You bet I am! James got to be in your lap and touch your ass."

Everyone but James laughs, and I try to further lighten the mood by getting up to grab a snack that Mrs. Crawford brought in. I pass them out to everyone as we take a quick break from the game. We start playing again and decide on some sort of racing game. I'm not as good at these as the shooting games, but I welcome the change as sometimes the boys get a little too competitive and angry when they keep dying. Especially at the hands of a girl. We continue playing throughout the entire night, and I know we succeed in checking off this summer bucket list item because I see the sun peek through the trees while we are still playing.

CHAPTER FOUR

I wake up stiff with my arm asleep and feeling disoriented. When I fully open my eyes, I realize I'm not in my bed and am facing the tv in Ben's bedroom. I must have fallen asleep while playing because the controller is under my side on the couch. I don't lift my head from its position, but I notice it is moving up and down. Realizing my head is laying on someone's chest, I slowly push off and look down to see James sleeping in a very uncomfortable position on the couch next to me.

I must have fallen asleep and used James as a pillow. Before I get up, I realize someone put a throw blanket over me and my legs are stretched across the couch. Bash must have moved because I find him sleeping in the chair in the corner instead of next to me. Jake is sprawled across the end of the bed and Ben looks like he is sleeping peacefully under the covers in his own bed.

I can't help but smile as I watch the boys sleep all around me. We had a fun night playing video games and these are the memories that are going to keep me going through life. When things get hard, I want to remember this. I pull out my phone and take a picture of them all sleeping. I look at it and smile. I debate laying back down on James' chest and enjoying his comfort, but I know that if I do, it will wake him. That would be awkward because I'd have to explain why I'm wanting to lie on his chest. That odd little butterfly sensation starts again in my stomach as I think about him. I hurry down the hall back to my room to get ready for the day.

When I get to my room, I look back at my phone to see what time it is. Two in the afternoon?! I guess we didn't fall asleep until about 7 in the morning. That's odd for me though, because that's a solid seven hours of sleep without waking up. I don't even remember laying my head on James' chest or anyone putting the blanket on me. I had to have been the first one passed out. Either I was exhausted or just that comfortable being on James because I'm lucky to sleep for an hour before waking up and having to force myself back to sleep every hour after that.

Thinking about how comfortably I slept with James brought back a memory from when I was a little girl spending the summer here. I was maybe six or seven years old. It was after my mother passed away.

I woke up to a scratching sound on my window and it was pitch black in my room. My heart started to pound, and fear crept up inside me. I pulled the comforter over my head and closed my eyes tight to pretend there's nothing out there. When I heard the wind howl, it sounded like a monster trying to get into my room. Maybe there was already a monster in my room, and it was under my bed. I began to panic and cried, thinking about how if I stepped off the bed, the monster would grab my legs and pull me under. If I stayed on my bed, though, it would just come out and pull me off the bed.

I stood on the top of my bed and jumped as far as I could toward the door. I opened it and ran down the hallway to James, who always kept me safe from everything. I opened his door and jumped onto his bed, thinking the monster could also be under his bed and would grab my legs to pull me under. When I was safely on his bed, James sat up and looked at me with the little bit of moonlight lighting the room.

"What's wrong?" he asked as I threw myself into his arms.

He wrapped me in a hug, and I continued to cry.

"What happened Everly?" He sounded concerned, but didn't move from his spot.

"There's a monster in my room!"

James let out a sigh of relief, but he didn't laugh. "It's okay. Monsters don't exist. Nothing is going to hurt you."

I couldn't stop crying, but I felt safer next to him. "But... how do you know? It sounded like there was a monster and Jake told me the boogey man lives under my bed and likes to eat little girls. He said that he would come for me one day and pull me under my bed into his lair to eat me."

James made a groaning sound as he said, "Don't listen to Jake. He's just trying to scare you. The boogey man doesn't exist."

We both stayed silent for a bit until I stopped sobbing, knowing that James was probably right. I was still scared of the possibility it was real, but Jake does like to say things to scare me.

James laid us both back into his bed but kept his arms around me as I had my face against his chest and his arms wrapped all the way around my back, holding me.

"Do you want to sleep with me tonight?" James asked.

I sniffled and nodded my head. "Will you protect me from the monster?"

"I'll always protect you."

The memory makes my eyes tear up at how kind James was even back then and how he has always tried to protect me, at least when I'm here. After that night, I snuck into his room to sleep every night for the rest of the summer. Once I was back home, I had trouble sleeping and stayed in my dad's room as often as he would let me. The next few summers, I would sneak into his room anytime I was upset or scared, and he would always hold me and let me stay. It has been years since I've done that, but I'll always be thankful to him for being there for me.

By the time I decide to leave my room, it's dinner time. All the boys are sitting at the table with Mrs. Crawford. It's nice eating dinner as a large family. At home, it was always just my dad and me. He would try to make conversation with me and keep his phone off, but it still wasn't the same as having so many people around to talk to and listen to their stories. I love listening to other people's stories and about their day.

Mrs. Crawford speaks to me, "Oh Everly, Adam called and said that he is in town this weekend. He said he was trying to get ahold of you but wasn't sure if you were getting his messages. I invited him over for lunch tomorrow. I hope that's okay."

I stop chewing my chicken and want to spit it out. I feel sick to my stomach, like I'm going to throw up the few bites of dinner that I've taken. How did Adam get their number? I figured he would know that I would stay here again, but I made it clear that we were done before I left. My heart beats faster and faster as I think about having to see him tomorrow and in the only safe space that I thought I had from him.

When I don't respond, Mrs. Crawford asks again, "It is okay that I invited him, right? I thought you would be happy to see him while he was here, but if not..."

I interrupt her. "No, that's great, thank you."

It is, in fact, not great, but I don't want Mrs. Crawford to feel bad about inviting him or put her in the awkward position to uninvite him. I still can't swallow my chicken, so I spit it out into the napkin before I really throw up. I sit there with my eyes on my plate and push around my food to make it look like I ate it. Even though I haven't eaten anything all day, I suddenly lost my appetite. I want to go back to my room and stay there forever. I hear the boys all talking, but I don't pay attention to what anyone is saying.

Mrs. Crawford's voice breaks through and says, "Everly, you've hardly eaten. Is everything alright?"

I put my fork down and look at her. "Oh yes. Please forgive me, I'm not feeling that well. May I be excused?"

Mrs. Crawford gives me a concerned look. "Is there anything I can get you?"

I shake my head. "Oh no, we just stayed up all night and the lack of sleep can get to me. I'll be better by the morning, thank you."

She nods as I get up from the table and rush out of the dining room up the stairs. I close the door behind me and slide my back down against it sitting on the floor. It starts to get harder to breathe and tears well up in my eyes. I try to take a deep breath in, but it feels like a stabbing pain in my heart, and I just can't breathe. I sob and my mind just races with everything and nothing at the same time. I put my head between my knees and think about the beach and the calming waves. I try to even out my breaths as I then focus on Jake and Ben's laughter in the bathroom the other day as we brought the beach in there. I smile, continuing to think of that day and all the fun we had. My breaths come easier and then the pain slowly subsides. I continued to push off the thoughts about Adam and thinking about the fun the four boys and I have been having.

I take another shower and get ready for bed, as I figure it would be best to get some good sleep tonight. After I blow dry my hair and get on my comfy pajamas, I lay in bed and pick up my phone to find a message waiting for me from James.

The one thing that I love about James is that he knows when to drop it. I feel bad for not letting him in, but this is a secret that I need to take to the grave with me. In order to do so, I need to face Adam tomorrow. I need to do this for myself, too.

I'm going to be clear with him that I want nothing to do with him anymore and that I've moved on. That he doesn't hold any power over me anymore. He doesn't. I think... no, of course he doesn't. Because I won't let him.

Right before I go to put my phone down, it chimes again with more texts.

Ben

So I'm thinking Saturday we go to the lake house?

James

Sounds good to me.

Bash

I'm in.

Jake

LET'S DO IT!

Sounds perfect, can't wait.

Bash

How long are we staying?

James

Two nights? I have to be home for Tuesday.

Does that mean we can check off skinny dipping one night and getting drunk the next?

Jake

I like your thinking Everly! I thought we'd get drunk at the club but we can do that both times!

Uh I only agreed to getting drunk once…

Ben

That's okay, we can all get drunk at the lake and James can be our DD when we go to the club.

James

Hey why do I need to be the DD?

Because you are the only trustworthy person in this group.

James

Fair enough.

Bash

Hey! What about me?

Jake

Yeah let's not go there.

Laughing Emoji

Ben

Ok I'm getting back to my games. See you guys tomorrow. Feel better Everly.

Thanks, have a good night.

My phone chimes a few more times, but I don't bother looking at it. I'm sure it's just them saying good night or continuing on with the other conversation. While they make me smile with their texts, it's time for me to drown myself in a good book of someone else's drama and go to sleep.

CHAPTER FIVE

I roll over and grab the phone off my nightstand to look at the time. I squint my eyes to see that it is already 10:30 in the morning. I groan, throw it to the side, and roll over. I wonder what would happen if I just stayed in bed all day? If I pretended like I was asleep and didn't answer the door when Mrs. Crawford came to check on me. I let myself feel depressed and wanting to die in this bed for only a few minutes before I force myself to stand up.

A shower will help me feel better. I only have an hour and a half before Adam will be here for lunch. I really need to eat today because the last time I ate anything was the snacks we had the other night while playing video games. Thinking about food makes my stomach growl loudly. Okay, okay. I promise I'll eat and won't let Adam ruin this meal for me, too.

I shower, curl my hair to make it wavy, and put on a good bit of makeup. I even do the contouring thing that I rarely do except for special occasions. I put on a pretty sundress that is fitted in the waist but flares out. It goes to my knees, so it isn't too revealing. As much as I want to throw on a hoodie and sweatpants so Adam can't see any of my skin, I know I will feel better dressed up like this. I don't want Adam to know that he has any power over me anymore. I want him to think that I'm strong and I don't think about him anymore.

I hear a knock on the door and tell whoever it is to come in.

Mrs. Crawford walks through the door and looks at me. "Wow, you look so pretty! Adam should be here any minute. I won't be joining you for lunch today, but I wanted to ask if you wanted to eat with Adam alone? I can set you up for lunch outside so the boys won't bother you."

That feeling in the pit of my stomach comes back, as my whole body just feels sick. "That's so kind of you, Mrs. Crawford, but I don't mind the boys being there. I think Adam would love getting to know them."

She nods, smiles, and walks out the door after telling me to have a good lunch. I hate lying to Mrs. Crawford, but she has been so nice, and I know she was trying to help me. All I need to do is get over this one lunch with Adam and make sure that when he leaves, he knows it's the last time he will ever see me. I already blocked his phone number before I came here, which is probably why he called Mrs. Crawford. I don't understand why he can't take a hint.

Just as I walk down the stairs and reach the foyer, Adam is being let in the house. Looking at his spikey black hair and dark brown eyes makes my stomach churn. He's short, shorter than Ben is. He's not in shape as he doesn't do any sports or any type of exercise that I know of. He's not fat though, just not toned. Similar to me, and I'm going to be remedying that shortly for myself.

Adam smiles at me as I keep a good distance between us. I don't let him say anything before I say, "The dining room is this way."

I walk off toward it, and he follows behind me. All four boys are already sitting in the dining room waiting for us. I sit down next to James, and Adam sits across from me next to Bash. I think self-consciously I sat next to James because I know he always brings me comfort and that he will protect me no matter what. I don't think Adam will try anything stupid while here, but I can't be too cautious.

Everyone introduces themselves to Adam, and I already feel so nauseous. I need to eat, but now I'm not sure I'll be able to.

Adam finally speaks to me as the food comes out. "I've missed you Everly. It's not the same without you around."

My nerves are getting the best of me. I force a smile and say, "It's only been a week since I've seen you, Adam."

He laughs. "Yes, well, it feels much longer than that."

I don't respond as Bash and Jake start talking to Adam about... I don't even know. I can't concentrate on what they are talking about. I didn't realize I was shaking my leg up and down until I feel James' hand on my thigh. He puts a little pressure and squeezes like he is reassuring me that everything will be okay. I stop shaking it and let out a small sigh. He leaves his hand there as I try to eat a few bites of food with him comforting me.

"So, how long are you in town for Adam?" James asks in a non-interested tone.

"I'm here for a couple of weeks. I'm visiting my aunt and uncle," Adam answers.

I swallow hard to keep the bile from rising in my throat. It's going to be okay though. I have a lot of plans to be with the boys most of the summer so there really is nothing to worry about. I'll just have to let Mrs. Crawford know I don't intend to see Adam again and she will make sure that he stays away.

I don't say much at all other than some nodding and answering with a quick yes or no. I'm thankful they are here with me to take over. It feels like we've been here for an hour, and I don't know how much longer I can take of this.

Once our plates are being cleared, Adam speaks to me again. "Mrs. Crawford said there are some beautiful gardens out back. Take me for a walk to show me Everly."

I freeze, and my heart pounds faster. I feel my leg bouncing again, even though James' hand is still on my thigh. Has it been there the entire time?

I respond with the only thing that I know I can, "Okay."

When Adam is demanding like that, there is nothing I can do to get out of what he wants. It wouldn't be bad, though. Security is always watching outside, so it's probably the safest place I could be with him. I also need to get him alone for a few minutes to make myself clear again that this is over, and I want nothing to do with him anymore.

Adam stands up to walk out of the dining room, and James stands up with me.

James grabs my wrist and whispers in my ear, "You don't have to go out there with him."

I give him a thankful look. "It's okay."

He nods, but he still looks concerned. Had I really been acting that off around Adam that I've made him concerned? I didn't want that at all. I don't want him to know what happened between Adam and me. I don't want anyone to know.

I follow Adam out back, and we walk toward the garden. I try to keep my distance from him, but he keeps closing in. I didn't realize with me continuing to move away from him that I was close to the wall of the greenhouse. I hadn't even realized we walked out that far. When I go to turn around to head back a little bit, Adam pushes me against the greenhouse wall.

He stands in front of me, looks me in the eye and says, "You will never get away from me Everly. You can say we are done all you want, but I will always come for you when I want you." He leans in even closer with his face just inches from mine. "Unblock my number and answer me when I call."

It is a threat, one that I know all too well. I try my best to hide my fear from him, but I know my body and face betray me. He knows I fear him, and he knows that I'll do whatever he wants me to do because I have to. His family is powerful, too powerful. I can't put my father at risk. I don't respond to him, though.

He leans back a little to give me some space as he continues, "You see how easily I can get in here? You shouldn't be afraid for only you and your father. Be afraid for your friends, too."

My eyes widen at the threat. I know he sees the fear I have for my friends as well. The bile starts burning the back of my throat as it wants to come up. For a split second I think of letting myself throw up so I can do it all over him, but that would just make him even more angry.

He tucks a hair behind his ear and says, "I sure hope you aren't sleeping with any of them either. If I find out you have... well, you know what will happen."

Yes... yes, I know exactly what will happen. Adam is pure evil, and I hate myself for ever getting myself mixed up with him.

I finally find my courage to speak. "Why do you still want me? What happened to Kayla?"

He laughs. "Oh, I'm still having my fun with her, but there's just something about you I can't seem to forget. Until then, you're mine. Don't forget it."

Adam leans over and places a claiming kiss on my mouth. I don't kiss back, but I don't dare pull away. Thankfully, he pulls away only a moment later and starts walking off with his last words, "See you soon."

Once he disappears around the side of the house, I let my body react the way it needs to after that encounter. I've learned that I need to react and then rein it in, otherwise everything is worse. I look around and don't see anyone, so I let it all go. Tears form in my eyes and my body is shaking hard. That bile that was rising in the back of my throat, I let it out. I vomit in the bushes by the greenhouse and kneel on the ground, continuing to shake. I sob for only a second before I feel an arm come around my waist. I freeze in fear, thinking that Adam has come back.

I turn my head to see James kneeling beside me, and I turn my body to face him. I put my head in his chest as he holds me close, both sitting on the ground now. I want to cry, but I don't because I don't want him to see and know how much Adam affects me. I hope he didn't see me throw up. I can't believe I couldn't at least hold it together until I got back to my room.

James speaks soothingly into my ear, "It's okay, I've got you Everly. Tell me what he did to you."

I choke on a sob and let out one too many before I say, "Nothing, I'm okay."

He groans at my words. "This doesn't look like he did nothing."

I try to force a laugh as I reply, "I'm just sick. I must have eaten something bad."

I feel him shake his head as he pulls me even closer. I love his embrace. He comforts me more than anyone ever has, but I can't stay here with him or else I might just tell him everything that happened with Adam. I can't risk doing that.

I pull away and stand up quickly. "Thank you, James, I'm okay. I'm going to go rest in my room."

Before he can pull me back in, I run in a sprint toward the house. I hear him following me, but I continue running all the way up the stairs until I reach my bedroom. I lock the door and throw myself on my bed face first. I cry and cry for at least an hour. When I have no more tears and feel numb, I pull out my phone to find three texts from James.

James

Please talk to me

Please tell me what's wrong.

I'm here when you're ready to talk.

Thank you, I'm okay. I'll see you tomorrow morning for our lake trip.

I put my phone on the charger and take another shower to clean off my makeup and this awful day. I get in my comfortable silk pajamas that is a tank top and shorts. It feels warm in here, so I need something not so hot. I know I don't have it in me to pretend everything is okay right now, but I really don't want to think about everything that happened and what I'm going to do about it either. So, I'm going to do what I do best and hide from it. I turn off the lights and lay in bed until I fell asleep.

I wake up to that same scratching noise against my window that I used to hear as a kid. I grab my phone off the nightstand to see it is only one in the morning. The wind howls and the scratching increases. I'm not afraid of the monster under my bed like I was when I was a kid, but a chill runs down my spine. I don't want to be alone.

I get out of bed and tiptoe down the hall toward the familiar door like I had done dozens of times in the past. I creak it open, step inside and close it behind me.

"James?" I whisper into the darkness.

"What's wrong?" He sits up in bed and stares at me with the moonlight shining in, only allowing me to make out his silhouette.

"Do you remember when we were little, you told me monsters weren't real? Well, they are real. And they've hurt me." We stare at each other without another word in the silence for a few heartbeats until I ask, "Can I come lay with you?"

He scoots over in his bed and pats beside him. I climb in next to him and we both lay down. I put my head on his chest as he wraps his arms around me and rubs my shoulder.

"Tell me what happened," James says quietly.

I whisper back, "I can't... It's a secret that I'll never be able to share."

He is quiet for a moment until he says like he always does when we're alone at night in his room, "The darkness keeps all secrets."

I feel the silent tears running down my cheeks, and I know he feels it on his chest. He isn't wearing a shirt and I'm pretty sure he only has his boxers on. I let out a couple of sobs and he just holds me tighter, comforting me like he always does. He's telling me he's going to keep my secret, and I know he will. He has always kept my secrets. Maybe it's time I let this one go.

"Adam's family is very powerful, and he knows it. The past year he has been threatening my dad and now he is threatening you guys if I don't... James, I can't tell you. I can't let anyone get hurt," I say as my voice cracks on the last word.

He makes a shushing sound. "No one is going to get hurt, I promise. Tell me."

I take a deep breath and quietly state, "He wants me. This past year..." my voice continues to crack, and I am sobbing, trying to get the words out. I've never said them out loud before, but I force myself to continue, "He's been forcing himself on me whenever he wants me."

I feel James tense and his breathing gets heavier, but he doesn't say anything. I know he is angry, but I wonder if he is also mad at me. That I've allowed this to happen and that I allowed my virginity to be taken away by someone like Adam. I feel disgusted with myself, so it only makes sense he feels disgusted with me.

I break the silence and whisper, "I'm sorry."

He tenses again and says through clenched teeth, "What the hell are you sorry for?"

This time I tense at the anger in his voice and just repeat, "I'm sorry."

James sits up in bed, pulling me with him. He puts his face right in front of mine, holds my face in his palms and says, "Don't you ever apologize for the despicable things he has done to you. Ever. None of this is your fault and you do not have the responsibility to let him do those horrible things to you in order to keep others safe. Trust me when I say that we can handle him. Promise me you will never speak to him again."

I stare into his eyes, which were so angry and hurt. I take too long to respond since he repeats himself louder this time, "Promise me!"

I nod, and he pulls me back into his chest, wrapping his arms around me again. I continue to silently cry as he rocks me back and forth slightly, and I think I hear a sob come out of his chest like he was crying. After a few moments sitting like this, he lays us back down on the bed and he just holds me and strokes my hair. It is so comforting, and I finally stop crying.

When I'm about to fall asleep, I hear him whisper, "I'm sorry I failed you, Everly."

"How?" I whisper back.

"I promised that I would always protect you and I failed..."

More tears slide down my face, but not for myself this time, but for him. "No, it's not your fault, James."

He is silent for a moment. "I failed to protect you."

I snuggle into him even closer. "But you're here now. Thank you."

Neither of us says anything else, and we both eventually fall asleep with the darkness surrounding us.

Chapter Six

I'm startled awake by a gasp and then talking. I can't make out what is being said as my head is pounding and I'm groggy from last night. I move my arm and freeze as I feel myself caressing the abs of a naked body beneath me. I shoot up in bed and so does James. We stare at each other and then toward the door where we hear laughing.

"Ohhh James, you didn't!!!" Jake stands inside the doorway covering his mouth with his hand and wide eyes.

Ben stands beside him, and Bash is behind both of them. What on earth are the three of them doing standing here in James' bedroom? They are all fully dressed and look ready for the day. What time is it?!

James immediately shakes his head and scoots further away from me as I was still pressed against his side. He acts like my touch is burning him.

He quickly says, "No, definitely not."

Bash laughs. "Dude, you're naked and going to tell us nothing happened last night?"

I blush at what they are insinuating and throw back the covers to get out of bed. Clearly, I'm not naked, though this pajama set is probably not the best one to be wearing around boys.

I stand tall and say, "I've always been in James' bed. This is nothing new."

I shrug my shoulders as I pushed past them out the door. I grin as I walked down the hall and hear James continuously denying that anything happened and trying to kick them out of his room. I kind of feel bad for leaving James with that and making it worse, but I needed them to concentrate on him so I could escape and put on some more appropriate clothing and get ready for the lake.

Shrugging on some comfortable clothes for the road trip, I throw a few items in a bag to take for two nights at the lake house. I try to hurry because James and I slept in past the time we were supposed to be leaving. When we didn't meet them downstairs this morning, they came searching for us, which explains why they barged into James' room this morning. I don't think any of them thought they would find us in bed together... with James half naked.

I can feel myself blushing and try to hide my face the best I can while sitting in the back seat between James and Jake. Bash is driving and Ben called shotgun. Two guards from the security team are driving behind us. Our parents wanted us to bring them to be safe. It's only a three-hour drive there, so it shouldn't be too bad. Though the awkwardness between James and I is getting to me. We both know nothing happened, so what is there to be awkward about?

I don't feel like having the others listen into my conversation with James, so I pull out my phone to text him.

> I'm sorry about this morning... I didn't expect them to come in and I panicked and made it worse.

James immediately pulls out his phone to look at his text. I see him lift the side of his mouth in a smirk and start texting back.

James

> There's nothing to be sorry for though you could've gone without saying any-thing.

> Do they really think that something happened between us?

James

> I don't think so but... would it be so bad if they did?

I smile and let out a little laugh before responding. I'm trying not to be too obvious that we are texting each other, but I'm not sure how successful we are being considering both of our phones keep vibrating and the other is texting.

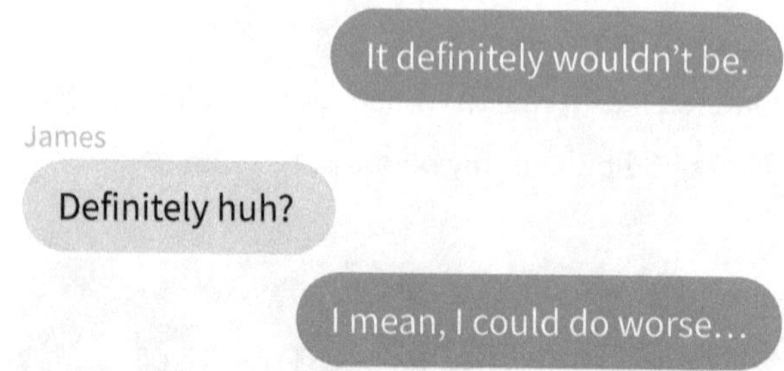

Nausea rolls in my stomach as I sent that. I didn't mean it to sound that way, but after talking about Adam with him last night, the way it sounded crossed my mind. He takes a minute to respond, and I know he's thinking the same thing.

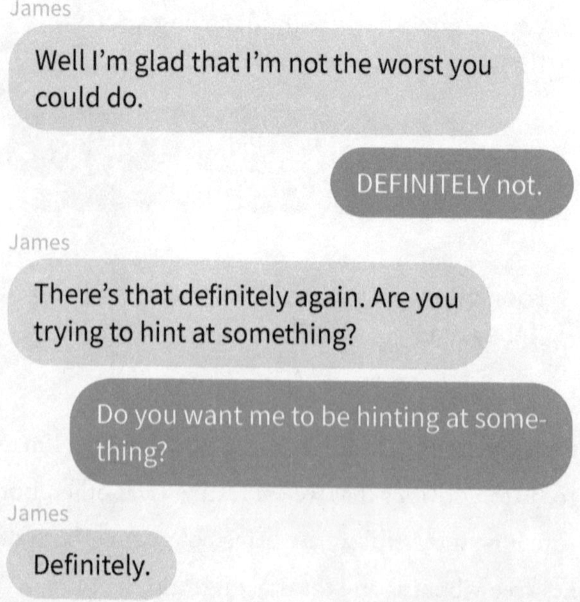

I let out a loud laugh in the otherwise silent car. Everyone turns to look at me except Bash, who looks in the rearview mirror. I quickly apologize and put my phone down.

Jake has an enormous grin on his face. "Is there something you and James would like to share?"

James looks at him innocently. "Huh?"

Jake laughs this time. "Come on now, we can all tell you two are texting back and forth. Is this about last night?"

I would have to think they were stupid to not notice us texting, so I'm not going to lie and deny it. "Of course we're texting about last night. It's hilarious that you guys think we slept together."

James continues after me, saying, "Exactly... I'm her big brother, come on. You guys don't really believe that, do you?"

Jake sits back and sighs. "Yeah, I know, you of all people, James. Now, if she was caught in my bed, we all know there's no denying what happened."

Everyone laughs and I force a laugh. I feel a brief stab in my heart at James' words. I must have been misreading what he was saying, because I felt like he was flirting with me. That would be silly to think, considering he has always made it clear that he's my big brother. He was probably just trying to make me feel better about everything that happened last night and what I told him.

My phone buzzes again. I expected it to be James, but I'm not surprised that it is Jake.

Jake

Did you bring that pajama set you wore last night?

Absolutely not.

Jake

Aw, did you bring anything similar?

I brought a baggy t-shirt and sweat-pants.

Jake

Well why did you do that?!

To keep wandering eyes off me.

Jake

Well we are going skinny dipping. You can just sleep naked.

At this point I would ask if you're flirting with me but I think we both know that answer...

Jake

I can flirt now that I know nothing is go-ing on with you and James.

And if there was something going on between us, then you wouldn't flirt with me?

Jake

Hmm… Fair question. Not sure and I don't have to know since there isn't. But really there isn't right?

There isn't.

Jake

You paused for a minute before answering.

I wanted to see if you noticed. Why are you concerned there is?

Jake

Maybe

Why?

Jake

Because I want to get you in my bed.

At least you're honest.

Jake

I'll always be honest with you.

Jake

This time Jake laughs out loud, and everyone stares at him.

Bash shakes his head. "Come on guys, I can't text and drive, so let's start having some conversations out loud. What are we talking about?"

"Seems like everyone is trying to get me in their bed," I respond.

Everyone laughs out loud this time, but no one says anything else. After what happened with Adam, I would've thought I would have trouble thinking about these things, never mind talking about it with another guy. But these guys are my brothers, and I know they would never hurt me.

It's getting dark by the time we arrive and get settled at the lake house. We each have our own rooms upstairs and the two guards have rooms downstairs near the entrance. We had stopped for dinner on the way here and we are now getting ready for a fun night in the living room.

"Who's up for knocking off an item on the bucket list?" Ben asks, as Bash is the last one to come into the room.

"How about two?" I ask because I was thinking about this and doing both of them at the same time seemed like the best idea. To go skinny dipping, I need some liquid courage. I've also been trying my best to put what happened yesterday behind me so I can enjoy myself, but it keeps slipping through the cracks and bringing down my mood every now and then. I'm great at pretending, but sometimes there's only so much pretending that can be done.

"So, you're needing to be drunk to go skinny dipping, huh?" Bash asks, but we all know the answer to that question.

"Um yeah, it's not really fair that I'm the only girl here and there's four of you," I state, a little embarrassed.

I still can't believe I agreed to go skinny dipping. I mean, it's not necessarily doing it, but the fact I'm doing it with four boys is crazy. I'm also positive that they never would have put this on the bucket list if I wasn't here. What four boys would want to go skinny dipping together unless there's a girl in the mix?

"Orrrr, you're the lucky one because you get to see us four naked," Jake responds, and I should've known he'd look at it like that.

"Hmm... I didn't think about it that way. Four hot guys naked and swimming in the lake with me? Sounds like every girl's fantasy," I tease Jake.

"Exactly what I'm saying." Jake laughs.

The more I think about being here with these four, the more I question our parents' sanity. Looking from the outside, how could you let a 17-year-old girl be around four boys, 17 and 19 years old?! I suppose our parents trust us since we've known each other since we were babies. And we're all about to be adults soon anyway, so we can make our own decisions. I never understood why 18 was when you are technically an adult and can make your own choices. Is there really that much difference from 17 to 18? Especially the day before your 18th birthday. Am I going to magically be more mature within seconds of changing over to 18? Doubtful. But hopeful.

Bash brings out a new bottle of vodka and five shot glasses. He pours each of us a glass and hands it to us. I've had vodka before and wasn't a fan, but I don't think people do it for the taste.

We hold out our shot glasses and Ben makes a toast. "To the best Crawford, Hale, Monroe summer ever!"

We all clink our glasses together and down the first shot. The boys seem like it is no problem, but I choke on the taste and burning in my throat. They all laugh at me, and Bash pours another round of shots. This time when I gulp it down, it doesn't burn as bad, but the taste is still nasty.

"So, are we planning on getting shitfaced drunk before we go skinny dipping? Because I was hoping to remember this part in the morning," Ben asks.

It's only been a few minutes since doing those two shots, but somehow, I already have the courage. So, before I lose that, I stand up and say, "You're right, let's go!"

We all run out the door toward the lake. We don't slow down, and I'm the last one out the door. I watch as they are all pulling off their shirts and shoes as they run toward the lake, throwing them on the ground on the way there. I take a deep breath and follow suit. It's dark so they would hardly be able to see me. I kick off my flip-flops and pull my shirt off, throwing it along with stepping out of my shorts. I only have my bra and panties left, so I wait until the last second to strip out of those and jump into the water with the boys. I'm not paying attention to them as I do that, mainly because I don't want to know if they actually saw me naked. As hot as they are, I don't want to see them naked either. Well... maybe I do a little.

We are all laughing and splashing each other, barely being able to see our surroundings. Bash and James are dunking their younger brothers under the water, and I'm trying to put some distance between all of us. Suddenly, I feel something wrap around my leg and pull me under. I kick at it but miss and it lets go. I emerge from the water out of breath and spitting water out as Jake is directly in front of me, holding me pressed to him. I can feel my breasts press against his chest. I'm embarrassed, but I would be lying if I said I wasn't a little turned on by it.

Jake leans forward and whispers in my ear, "How about you spend the night in my bed tonight?"

I laugh a little too loudly, probably because the alcohol is kicking in and I'm a lightweight. I mean, I've never gotten drunk before.

"What do I get out of it?" I ask.

He smirks and whispers seductively in my ear, "The best night of your life."

"Sounds tempting," I say, and before he can say anything back, James is pulling him away from me and dunking him in the water.

Jake escapes and James gives me a concerned look as he swims off after him. Was James worried about Jake and me being together? Jake is just having fun hitting on me like he does to all the girls. He has nothing to worry about.

After I start shivering, we decide to get out of the lake and head back in. James was smart and put some towels out at the end of the dock for us before we even started drinking. I grab a towel and try to quickly wrap it around me without anyone seeing. I try to avoid looking at them, but Jake is in front of me, and I get a good glimpse of his butt. It is a very nice butt. I feel a twinge in my stomach telling me that I definitely find him attractive.

We gather our clothes on our way back inside and get dressed before meeting back downstairs. I was debating putting on my pajamas, but I really did bring just a loose t-shirt and some sweatpants. I want to look good tonight while hanging out with the boys, so I put back on my shorts and tight short-sleeve shirt. I debated keeping my bra off to be comfortable but think that would be way too inappropriate.

Bash pours us another round of shots and this time, it is much easier to swallow than the last two. I suppose the more you have, the less you realize it tastes disgusting. I'm feeling the effects of the alcohol already, but I can tell the boys are barely phased. I'm pretty sure they have had a lot of practice drinking. Plus, they are much bigger than I am, so I suppose they can hold their liquor better, anyway.

The more time that passes, the more I find myself checking them out. They are all gorgeous. How have I not really noticed before? I mean, I'm pretty sure I've noticed, but like wow, they are hot. I mean, look at James. That sexy hair that falls so perfectly and he's always clean shaven. Bash with his sexy messy hair and the little bit of stubble. He's always so perfectly tan, especially in the summer. Jake has a little bit of longer hair, which I love even more, and he looks identical to his brother except more carefree. Then there's Ben. He's the type of boy that I would go for back in Boston. I'm not sure that he's necessarily my type anymore, but he's still hot.

I guess I was staring at Ben a little longer than I should have been because he calls me out on it.

"You like what you see?" he asks with a smirk.

I can feel myself blush as I say, "I'd have to be blind not to."

I feel like I'd be embarrassed if I didn't have three shots in my system, but I'm definitely not. Flirting is fun. I can see why Jake does it all the time.

Jake interrupts and suggests, "Another round and never have I ever!"

Bash laughs and pours another round of shots. I think this makes four, right? I take it and chug it down like the others do. I've only played never have I ever once before and it was not fun, but I feel like with how I'm currently feeling, it'll be great!

Jake continues, "I'll start. Never have I ever had sex with Everly!"

I choke on my spit and don't raise my hand, and clearly no one else does either. Wait, but if I've masturbated before, does that mean I've had sex with myself? That's what it means, right? I'm confused. I raise my hand anyway.

Everyone stares at me, raising my hand as I say, "I'm not sure? I mean, does masturbating count as having sex with myself?"

All I can do is laugh, and so does everyone else. Yeah, we are all drunk.

"Everly, you are the most amazing girl I've ever known. Okay, sorry, I wanted to make sure James wasn't lying about last night. You go next," Jake says.

I think for a moment. "Hmm, okay... Never have I ever... kissed a girl."

I knew that one would get them all to raise their hands, and I was right. I laugh and Bash says, "Good one!"

James goes next. "Never have I ever kissed a boy."

Obviously, I raise my hand but can't help myself from looking around the room to see if anyone else has, which no one is at least admitting to it. If anyone would've raised their hand, I would think it would be Jake.

I'm not the only one who thought that because Ben speaks up, "Jake, are you sure you shouldn't be raising your hand?"

"Ah nah man, I haven't done that. I don't think. Unless I was drunk and forgot. Who knows," he says, shrugging his shoulders.

Bash goes next and says, "Never have I ever failed a class."

Jake and Ben both raise their hands, and I can't help but shake my head, figuring it would be those two who had failed a class. They are both smart, so they must have been really messing around to fail. I bet it was the same one.

Bash pours another round of shots and tries to hand one to me. I must be really drunk because I miss the first two times as he tries to put it in my hand. I laugh and laugh so hard. I finally get it and down most of it in one gulp. I think. Some, or most, of it spills out of my mouth and onto my shirt, but that's okay.

"I think that's the last one for Everly," James says with a serious face.

"Oh, come on, James, it's actually starting to taste good! Or I mean, not taste like anything. I think. Who's turn is it?"

Ben starts, "Never have I ever peed in the shower."

I raise my hand and continue giggling. The other three raise their hands too and laugh.

"Come on, Ben, you have NEVVEERRR peed in the shower? Like EVER? Not even on accident? Who hasn't peed in the shower?!" I keep asking and rambling.

We continue going around a couple more times with the game and the boys each take another shot or two. True to James' word, they don't give me another shot, but I don't mind. I don't think I could even get it to my mouth this time. It would probably go all over the floor or on someone else.

I really have to pee, so I stand up quickly from the floor and start to fall over toward Jake. Jake stands, catches me, and steadies me.

"Easy there. Where are you going?" he asks.

"I have to pee really bad. I'm thinking of going in the shower instead of the toilet." I laugh, probably a little too loud.

I start walking out of the room when James comes up behind me. "Do you want some help?"

I look at him seriously, but my eyes can't really focus on his face. "You want to help me pee?"

He laughs. "No, I want to help you to the bathroom. You can barely walk."

"I'm fine, thanks. I just needed to get my balance from sitting for a while," I say and walk off to the bathroom.

I sit on the toilet, and it feels so amazing. I really had to pee, so when it all comes out it is such a relief. As I sit here, thoughts of Adam pop into my mind, making me feel sick to my stomach again. Or maybe it's the alcohol. Either way, I shouldn't be thinking about Adam. That's the whole point of drinking. I wanted to have fun and forget about him and everything he did to me. I need to forget about him.

The only times I ever had sex was when he forced himself on me, and he didn't care about me at all. He only cared about himself, and then he'd leave me shortly after. I'm 17 years old and have never had an orgasm given to me by a guy. How lame is that? I bet Jake would never leave a girl hanging like that. Mmm, Jake is pretty sexy, and he's been flirting with me. I bet he's really good in bed. If I slept with him, then maybe I could forget about Adam and how he made me feel. I could concentrate on how good sex actually is and with someone hot and who wants me and respects me. It's not a bad idea.

I leave the bathroom and stop for a moment, considering if I flushed the toilet or not. I think I did. Maybe I didn't. Did I wash my hands? Wait, does it even matter? I laugh to myself and am about to head back to the living room when Jake steps in front of me. I stare at him and can't help but notice how attractive I find him. His hair is all messed up, like he's been running his hand through it. I want to run my hand through his hair.

"I just came to check on you. Everything okay?" Jake asks.

"Mmm, I think so," I say, putting my hand on his chest.

Wow, his chest is rock hard. He really must work out a lot. I run my hand down his chest over, his abs. Oh, it just keeps getting better.

His laughter breaks my trance. "What are you doing?"

I smile at him. "Feeling you up. Is that a problem?"

He hungrily looks at me and growls, "No, that's no problem at all."

The way his voice sounds so pained, like he is trying to control himself, just makes me lose it, if I even had it in the first place. I grab his face with my hands, stand on my toes, and plant a kiss on his lips. He moans, or I moan, or we both moan, I'm not sure, but he pushes me back against the wall and kisses me harder. He runs his hands through my hair, and I do the same to him, messing up his hair even more. His tongue collides with mine and then he moves his kisses down my chin to my neck and sucks. I let out an embarrassingly loud moan, except I'm not embarrassed at the moment. I'm so turned on.

"I want you to sleep with me Jake," I state matter-of-factly.

He groans again and stops what he's doing to look me straight in the eyes. He plants his lips against mine for another minute and pulls back, but still has both hands in my hair.

"I want nothing more, but you're drunk."

I laugh. "So are you."

"I am, but I'm not going to fuck you while you're drunk. Ask me again when you're sober," he says, backing away from me.

He keeps staring into my eyes, looking conflicted, like he wants nothing more than to take me right here and screw me, but his morals are getting in the way. Maybe he just needs another shot or two to get rid of those morals. I want nothing more than to have sex on my terms with someone who cares about me. Personally, I would love to have done that with James, but he's made it quite clear I'll never be anything more than his sister. Jake is hot and seems to have been interested in me for a while. He's also known for his one-night stands with the girls, so no hard feelings will get in the way when it's just this once.

I pull him closer again and try once more by kissing him and running my hands down his abs and into the waistband of his pants. Just before I can go any lower, he grabs my hands and holds them against the wall. He presses his body against mine, showing me the evidence of how much he wants me.

"Please tell me to fuck you again when you're sober," his voice sounds so pained.

I sigh, and he steps away, walking back toward the living room. I follow him and sit back down on the couch where I was sitting before.

"What took you so long, Everly? And why do both of you look like you have I just fucked hair?" Bash smirks at Jake, who just shrugs his shoulders.

I rub my hand over my hair to flatten it down. I run my fingers through it to find it all tangled. How the heck did those few seconds of his hands in my hair turn it into this? I can feel myself blushing, but I'm not embarrassed. I just imitate Jake by shrugging my shoulders too and everyone, but James, laughs.

James leans toward me and whispers, "You didn't really, did you?"

I look at him and say, "Definitely..." pausing for a moment to see his eyes widen and anger growing on his face, "NOT."

I laugh as his expression softens, and he lets out the breath he was holding in. I hate to torture him like that, but it was funny. I know that he doesn't care about me in the sense that he'd really care I'd sleep with Jake. He just cares about me because I'm his little sister and doesn't want me to get hurt.

James decides it's time to call it a night and tries to force me to go upstairs to bed. Of course, me being me, fights him the whole time refusing to leave. He gets impatient, so he lifts me up and carries me up the stairs to my room. He places me on my bed, and I laugh but also am mad, and hit him in the chest for manhandling me.

When he tries to stand back up, I pull his shirt so he can't move and say, "You sure you don't want to stay with me tonight? We could have a lot of fun."

I stare at James' face, and I swear he gives me the same look that Jake did. That hunger in his eyes, along with pain of trying to hold back as he says, "No."

I doubt I saw that right, so just to test it, I pull him a little closer and ask, "Are you sure?"

He cooly replies, "I'm sure."

I let him go, and I know I have a hurt look on my face because that's how I feel. "Of course, because I'm your little sister, that would be gross."

He doesn't say anything as he walks out the door and closes it behind him. As I've known my whole life, James has always only looked at me like a little sister and always will. I never outright admitted it to myself, but I have been crushing on James for years. This heartbreaking feeling is exactly why I never wanted to admit it, and I know I'm going to regret even asking him in the morning. Maybe the alcohol is already wearing off because I'm feeling pretty stupid right now and angry at myself. James is my big brother, and I should've kept telling myself that. But I shouldn't be too mad. Jake is sweet and hot too, and he wants me.

Chapter Seven

I've heard that you sleep better when drinking alcohol before bed, and I've always thought of testing that theory. I've decided that I never needed to test that theory because it is false. I did not sleep much at all last night and feel miserable. I woke up in the middle of the night feeling sick to my stomach. I was somewhat aware of my surroundings, but not at the same time. I think I threw up like 10 times, and I'm pretty sure I made it to the toilet each time.

It's past noon, and I'm still in bed feeling awful. My head is pounding, and I feel so nauseous. I haven't thrown up again since this morning, but I'm pretty sure if I even move a muscle, the rest of the contents in my stomach are going to evacuate.

Someone knocks on my door, and I don't move or respond to it. I'm afraid to talk. Why do people find getting drunk fun? Looking back at last night, I don't remember if I had fun. I remember laughing a lot, but I'm not sure what I was laughing at. One thing I do remember is hitting on Jake and asking him to have sex with me. I cringe and decide I need to stop thinking about that because I'm definitely going to be back in the bathroom sick again.

Whoever it is knocks again and opens the door right after without me saying a word. I open my eyes for only a minute to see James walking in. He looks almost as horrible as I feel. He comes and kneels beside me in bed.

He whispers, "Do you need anything?"

I groan and squeeze my eyes shut. I can't bring myself to say anything because I don't even know what I need.

James moves the hair out of my face and tucks it behind my ear. He points over to the end table where there is a glass of water, crackers, and a banana. When did that get there? Did he bring it in with him?

"You need to drink and eat something," he says, being sweet.

I groan again. "No thanks, I'm just going to stay here and die. I'm not moving."

He laughs. "Hangovers suck. Next time, take it slower and drink water between shots."

I glare at him. "So now you tell me? Where was this advice last night?"

"Sorry, I wasn't being smart either. If I was, then I wouldn't have been struggling this morning and been in here much sooner to check on you," he says like he feels guilty.

He's being so kind to me and always takes care of me. Maybe he just always wanted a little sister to take care of his whole life, too. Whoever he marries will be one lucky girl and so will his children. He's going to be a great father one day.

My stomach churns again and this time I don't know that I can keep it down. I throw the covers back and run over to the toilet. My head is pounding all the way there from suddenly getting up, and I throw up everything that I have left in my stomach, which isn't much. My mouth tastes of bile, but I don't want to move.

James comes over and helps me up and back to bed. He hands me the water and crackers. "Try to eat and drink. Now that you threw up, you most likely won't again right away. Get it in your system."

I sit back on my bed and do what he said. I only take a few sips of the water and eat two crackers. It actually isn't bad, as I feel sick, but not like I'm going to throw up.

"I'm never drinking again," I groan.

James laughs. "Everyone says that when they have a hangover. Don't worry, it'll be better next time because you will remember this and know what to do to mostly avoid it."

I sigh. "Well, yeah, the hangover part is awful, but it doesn't erase the stupid things I said and did last night. Ugh, it's embarrassing."

James looks at me curiously. "I don't think you did anything embarrassing. You were honest, which is always fun. Was there something else?"

I cringe, thinking about Jake. I don't think I can even tell James about what I said to or did with him.

"Did you do something with Jake? You were gone for a while with him last night," he asks with his eyebrows furrowed.

"Yeah, I said a lot of stupid things to Jake, but I don't want to think about it," I reply, not wanting to go into detail.

"Did you do anything?" he asks, and I know he is wondering if we ended up together in bed, considering everyone thought we had when our hair was all messed up.

"You mean like feeling him up, kissing him, and asking him to sleep with me? Yeah, I'm stupid and that's so embarrassing. I don't know what I was thinking." I figure I would just tell him the truth, because why not? And honestly, I wanted to see his reaction to it. I wanted to know if it bothered him at all. I really thought we were flirting in the car, and I want, no need, to know.

James' face is blank and not giving away any emotion. "Did you sleep with him?"

I give a low laugh. "No, after making a fool of myself and kissing him, he turned me away and said I was drunk. I don't want to talk about this anymore."

I really don't want to talk anymore, especially since James is showing no emotion to the whole situation. I was hoping he would care a little bit, but I guess not. I really need to stop thinking about James now, because that's never going to happen. If he can talk to me with a straight face about me hitting on basically his brother, then he has no feelings for me in that sense.

"Okay, well I'm glad that Jake didn't do anything, especially since you were both drunk," he says as he stands up to walk out of the room.

Once he reaches the door, he turns back around and says, "If you need anything, let me know."

I nod and lay back down, closing my eyes, hoping to sleep the rest of the day away and feel better.

Over the next couple of hours, I drink a good bit of water and eat what James brought me. Once I wake up from the little nap, I'm feeling like myself again. It's almost dinnertime, and I wasted the entire day away. I take a shower, get dressed, and head downstairs to see what the boys are up to.

When I get downstairs, everyone is in the living room watching something on tv and eating pizza. When I notice the only spot left is to sit next to Jake, my heart skips a beat, and the nausea begins again. I'm confident that I won't throw up anymore and this is just due to nerves. I think it will make things more awkward if I avoid him, so I figure it's best to just sit next to him and own it if it comes up. I mean, he is hot, and he knows it. I'm sure he will tease me about it later, but I'm really hoping that he doesn't do it in front of everyone else.

When I sit down next to Jake, he grabs another slice of pizza and hands it to me saying, "Welcome to your first hangover."

I give him a thankful smile. "Thanks, it sucked. I feel great now, though."

He laughs and puts his arm around my shoulder, resting it there while eating his slice watching tv. Everyone looks like they are feeling fine from last night and that it's just a lazy night in. Which, I'm good with a lazy night in. I don't think we will be checking off any more boxes from the bucket list this trip.

The movie they are watching ends, and we are all done eating. Ben brought some video games which he decides to set up, but I'm not really in the mood to play, so I figure I will just watch. Jake has to use the restroom. While he is gone, I keep thinking that I should pull him aside to talk to him about last night. Maybe he doesn't even remember it? But if he does, I feel like I need to apologize for how I behaved and thank him for being respectful and not bedding me last night. I wouldn't have blamed him if he had though and honestly, I don't think I would've been upset about it. At least then I could have a good memory when it comes to sex. I am really sick of thinking of it as something horrible because of Adam.

I walk out of the room toward the bathroom to wait for Jake to come out. I need to talk to him, and I don't want to do it in front of everyone else. James knows what happened, but I don't need the others to.

When Jake comes out of the bathroom, he looks at me and smiles. "A reverse from last night. What's up?"

I blush thinking about last night and before I back down, I say, "Speaking of last night, mind if we talk alone for a minute?"

He gives me a wary look, but nods toward the stairs to follow him. He walks up the stairs and into his bedroom at the end of the hall. I walk in after him and close the door behind me, but don't move from the door. Jake stands right in front of me. My heart begins to thud in my chest.

He isn't going to start the conversation, so I finally say, "I'm sorry about last night. Clearly, we were both drunk, but that was wrong of me to hit on you like that."

I don't really know how to put that because surprisingly I don't regret hitting on him like that, but I know that it probably puts him in an awkward position now.

Jake keeps his face straight. "It's cool. Like you said, we were both drunk. If you regret it, we'll pretend it never happened."

I don't want to lie to him, but pretending it never happened sounds like a good idea. "Yeah, that would be good. I mean, I don't regret it, but I don't want things to be awkward between us."

He gives me a mischievous grin and steps closer to me. He pushes a strand of hair behind my ear and asks, "You don't regret it?"

I give a nervous laugh. "Of course not, I mean unless it made you super uncomfortable, then I don't regret feeling you up and kissing a super hot guy." I give him a teasing look.

He leans his face closer to mine and I gasp. My heart skips a beat, and I can feel the butterflies in my stomach. I stare into his eyes to find the same look as last night, just less drunk. He wants me and that makes me feel... great.

I take a chance and lean forward, placing my lips on his. He grabs the back of my head to deepen the kiss and pushes me back against the door. His body presses against mine and his kisses are slow, but intense. My lips part as his tongue tangles with mine.

Groaning against his mouth, we kiss for a few more moments like that and when he finally pulls away, I'm panting.

He presses his body up even closer to mine and I feel how much he wants me. I came here to apologize for last night and move on, but now I'm wondering if I really came here for more. He makes me feel good about myself and he wants me. I can forget about Adam if I do this with him. Would it be wrong?

Before I lose my courage, I look him in the eyes and say, "I'm not drunk. I want you to fuck me, Jake."

He lets out a moan at my words, and his lips are on mine again. He pushes his hand up my shirt and cups my breast while I grab the back of his head to bring him closer. Without breaking the kiss, he moves us over to his bed and lays me down on it, then crawls on top of me.

He pulls away from the kiss and lays his forehead against mine. We are both panting and out of breath as he asks, "Are you sure this is what you want?"

I look him in the eyes and say, "God, yes. But just this once, I know we aren't more than friends. We'll fuck each other out of our systems."

He laughs at my words. "Okay, just this once."

He pulls his shirt over his head, revealing his amazing abs. I can't help but run my hands over his chest before he helps me out of my shirt and unclasps my bra, throwing it to the floor. He kisses down my neck, over my chest until he gets to my breasts where he holds them and takes a nipple in his mouth to suck. I moan as he continues to kiss down my stomach to the waistband of my shorts and he unbuttons them. He pulls those off and my panties with it, throwing them to the floor. I lay completely naked before him.

He leans back, looking me over like he is enjoying the view and moans, "God you're so hot Everly. You're perfect."

I blush at his statement and feel so good. Adam never said anything like that to me. In fact, he would critique every part of me.

Jake takes his pants and boxers off to reveal his hard length. He's ready for me as well. He leans back down and continues where he stopped kissing all the way down. Then he moves to my inner thighs and kisses. I'm getting more and more aroused, wanting him to end the torture.

He finally reaches where I want him to and rubs me for a moment before moaning. "You're so wet for me Everly. Tell me, did you ever dream of me? Or think of me?"

I groan as he puts his finger inside me, already bringing me close. I've never felt like this before, and it feels amazing.

I answer him, "Of course I did."

That answer made him happy, but he stops what he is doing and leans over to his end table to pull something out of the drawer. He opens the foil wrapper and puts the condom on himself. I try not to think about why he has condoms in his drawer here at the lake house, as I'm glad he does.

He crawls on top of me again and starts kissing up my neck, my chin, until he reaches my lips. He kisses me hard, like he can't hold on any longer.

He pulls away and asks, "You're sure?"

I grab his head and pull his mouth toward mine again. Between kisses, I pull away just far enough to say, "Jake, I need you to just fuck me now."

That's exactly what he wanted to hear because the moment his lips find mine again, he enters me. He enters slowly, filling every inch of me. He's acting like he doesn't want to hurt me, but I don't want that. I want him to fuck me like I know he does everyone else. I pull him in deeper and try to help set the pace, so he knows what I want without saying. He understands and goes faster.

"Arg, Everly, I'm not going to last long like this," he groans.

"Me neither," I state.

He continues for another couple minutes just like that and kissing me just as hard as he's fucking me. I'm so close and the moment that I know he can't hold on anymore, I explode around him. We come together as I let out a loud moan and say his name way too loudly. I tried to stay quiet, so the others didn't hear, but it felt so good. After Jake pulls out of me and tosses the condom in the waste bin by his bed, he lays down next to me, cuddling into me. I honestly never took him for a cuddler.

Our breathing is still rapid as we lay there, and he kisses the top of my head. I want to enjoy this for a moment longer. Adam never cuddled after he took what he wanted. He immediately left me in the room like a dirty whore, which is what I was, and he never let me forget. He also never cared about me finding pleasure. I don't think I would've been able to with him, anyway. With Jake, it was easy. He cared for me, and he was good. Surprisingly, it didn't take much for me.

I want to lie there with him for the rest of the night, but I know that we can't. I finally roll to the side of the bed. "We should probably go back downstairs."

Jake sits up and grins. "Unless you want to go for round two."

I laugh while putting on my bra and pulling my shirt over my head. "I told you just this once. It wasn't enough for you?"

His grin doesn't fade as he says, "Mmm, no. Once with you is definitely not enough, but if that's what you want, then it'll have to be."

He's throwing his clothes on too as I pull my underwear and shorts back on. I say, "Well it was amazing, so once was perfect."

He shrugs his shoulders. "Okay then, but there's so much more I could do to you that's even more amazing."

I blush thinking about what he could do. I'm not going to lie, it's tempting to find out, but I need some time to think. This was supposed to be about having a good sexual experience, so I could stop thinking about what Adam did and it wouldn't bother me anymore. It was exactly what I needed, so I don't know if I should continue this with Jake. He's not the boyfriend type. I wouldn't mind seeing where things went with him, but I don't think they could go anywhere. Being friends with benefits just doesn't sound appealing to me.

"I'm going to head back down. See you soon." He winks at me and closes the door.

I go to his bathroom for a minute to fix my hair and make sure I look decent enough to go back down. It's dark outside now and the lights are off downstairs, so they probably won't be able to tell if my hair is a little messy.

I walk downstairs and stop right outside the living room behind the wall to hear the boys talking with Jake. I stand still as I hear what they are talking about, and the bile starts to rise in my throat again. I didn't tell Jake not to tell the others, but I didn't think he would come right down and tell them.

I hear Ben say, "You expect us to believe you and Everly weren't up to something? You guys have both been gone for half an hour."

I hear Jake laugh, but he doesn't say anything.

"So, you did? Does that mean you won the bet?" Bash's voice comes from the far corner.

What bet?

There's silence until I hear a crashing sound and a bang against the wall. I hear James' voice as a growl, "Tell me you didn't!"

I want to go in the room to see what is going on, but my legs are frozen.

"She asked me for it! I asked her three times to make sure she wanted it," Jake yells.

I hear another bang against the wall, and this time I get my legs to move. I round the corner in time to see James pinning Jake against the wall and punching him in the face.

"James!" I yell out, clasping my hand over my mouth.

When he looks over toward me, he's angry, and then disappointment fills his eyes. Why is he disappointed?

Ben and Bash both make their way over to them like they are going to join in the fight against each other, taking their brothers' sides.

James still holds Jake against the wall with his hand clenching the collar of his shirt.

"Let go, James," Bash says in a threatening tone.

"Tell me you're lying Jake!" James screams back in his face and acts like he completely forgot I'm here.

Jake must have a death wish because he smiles and says, "Then that would be a lie. She was great in bed."

James goes to punch Jake again, but Bash catches his hand and pushes him off. Jake slips out from in front of James.

James is so angry, furious as he yells, "Fuck you, man! She was just raped all year by her asshole boyfriend. She doesn't need this!"

My eyes widen and I gasp at what he just said. He has never betrayed my secrets before. How could he tell them that?

They all look over toward me, and I watch as their eyes turn to pity. I can tell James didn't mean to say it as he looks sorry, but it doesn't matter because he did say it. To all of them. I look over at Jake and I can't handle the look he is giving me. I don't even want to know what he's thinking right now. I run as fast as I can out the front door, not bothering to close it behind me. I feel sick, and I want to get away from all of them.

I hear Bash and James yell out for me at the same time, but I ignore them. I keep running until I hit the woods and realize that it was impossible to see in there. I left my cellphone in the living room, so I don't have it to light my way. I go in just far enough to be covered by the darkness, but not too far that I wouldn't be able to find my way back. I lean against a tree and slide down it to the ground. I cradle my knees and let the tears flow silently. I'm angry. How could James betray my secret like that? How could Jake say it in such a way that it was like a game to him? What bet were they talking about? The tears don't ease, and I start full on sobbing in the darkness, alone.

I feel something wet hit my arm and another shortly after hitting the other arm. I lift my head to look up to find it's raining. The rain starts slowly but then picks up into a downpour quickly. I'm still so angry but laugh as I get soaked sitting there. It wasn't supposed to rain for the entire week. Of course, it would start raining right now when I'm outside trying to get a little time alone.

I put my face on my knees again, taking deep breaths to try to calm myself further and clear my mind. I felt what I needed to feel. Now it's time to rein in my emotions. Usually I can do this quickly, but I keep replaying the words in my head that they said. I jump at the feeling of a hand touching my shoulder and look up. It's dark and I can't make out who is in front of me until he speaks, "Everly, let's go back."

Bash kneels in front of me and tries to help me up, but I refuse.

"Leave me alone, Bash," I say weakly.

"I'm not leaving you Everly. Let's get out of the rain and we can talk," he says, trying to coax me to get up.

I came out here so I could get some time alone and away from the boys. I don't want to go back, but I realize that would be selfish because he's having to be out in this downpour as well. I stand up as he's holding onto my arm to steady me. I don't say anything as we start walking forward and I stumble over a tree root that I didn't see. He catches me and wraps his arm around my waist, keeping it there the whole walk back to the house. It feels comforting being by his side until I remember that he now knows what happened with Adam. As soon as we enter the house, he takes out his phone and texts someone. Moments later, the other three come walking into the house drenched as well. Along with my two security guards, who must have been searching for me.

I don't know why I stuck around this long, but I'm not sticking around any longer. I didn't dare look any of them in the eyes as I go upstairs and close myself in my room. I change into pajamas, not even worried about being wet. I think about taking a shower, but I'm honestly too exhausted to do it. I just want to go to bed and start over in the morning. Sleep is always the best cure for me. It makes time pass and allows me a fresh start.

I turn off the lights and curl up in my bed under the covers. I hear a knock on the door and don't respond. I was hoping whoever it is goes away, but I hear the door open and him walk toward the bed. He doesn't say anything as he lays down behind me and wraps his arms around me, holding me. I know it's James and I want to be mad at him. I am mad at him, but I'm always so comforted by his embrace.

"Everly, I'm so sorry," James whispers in my ear.

I thought I was done crying, but after hearing his apology, the tears start flowing again. I'm usually so good at controlling my emotions, but recently it has been impossible. I don't say anything back, as I have nothing that I need to say.

"Please talk to me," he begs.

I don't know what to talk about. He told them something that was supposed to be a secret between us. It's embarrassing, and I didn't want anyone else to know. I didn't even want James to know.

"I shouldn't have told them. I was just so angry when I heard that you and Jake..." he trails off like he couldn't say what we did or for me to interrupt to tell him that we didn't. But we did.

I take a deep breath. "Why were you so angry?"

He hesitates, but he says, "I've been having a hard time not being angry since you told me about Adam. I want nothing more than to go kill him. When Jake said you two... it just set me off and I took my anger out on him. I want to protect you."

I sigh, and it pains me that he's been angry and hurting since I told him. I didn't want that. I respond, "Thank you for wanting to protect me, but I'm okay. I'm the one that approached Jake, and he made sure it was what I really wanted, so please don't be mad at him and take out what Adam did on him."

I feel James tense as I was talking about approaching Jake. I don't think he wanted to hear that we did have sex, but I'm not going to lie to him.

James asks, "Do you love Jake?"

I let out a soft laugh. "No, well, I love him like he's my best friend. I'd say brother but now that's awkward. It was a one-time thing."

"Why?"

"Ever since seeing Adam again, I feel like I'm slowly dying inside. He was the only one that I ever did anything with, and I didn't even want to. It was awful every time. I couldn't stand it anymore, and I knew Jake cared about me and wanted me so I figured if I did it with him once then I would at least have one good time to remember when the bad memories resurface," I say calmly but then my mind starts to drift toward what I overheard them talking about. I have to ask what they meant, so I don't assume the worst.

"What bet were you guys talking about before I entered the room?" I ask before my nerves get the better of me. The longer that James is taking to respond, the more nervous I'm feeling. "James, tell me."

He takes a deep breath and says, "Before you got here, everyone was betting on who you would end up in bed with this summer."

I try not to let that bother me, but it does. I feel angry. I can't believe they would bet on that, and I can't believe James would take part in it.

I ask through clenched teeth, "Did you participate in this bet?"

His lack of response gives me the answer I need. As comforting his embrace is, I push him off me and roll back over to face away from him. He says my name and puts his arm on my shoulder, but I ignore him and shrug it off.

"Everly, it was a stupid guy thing. I'm sorry, I regret it," he states like he was sincerely sorry, but I don't want to deal with it right now.

"So, what did Jake win? Tell me," I demand, while holding back more tears of anger.

He sighs. "He gets a favor from each of us. We all bet it would be him, so none of us lost anything."

I laugh at the stupidity of it, and that's not really how a bet even works. They were just convinced I'd go off and sleep with Jake, but I'm surprised that they made the deal about the favor.

"So, whoever I slept with would've won and got the favor from everyone else? So, you all were trying to get me in your bed then? You too James? For the bet?"

"No," he states sternly.

"So, you didn't want to win the favor? You just resigned yourself to owing a favor to whoever?" I ask spitefully.

"No, I was hoping you wouldn't sleep with anyone," he whispers.

"Well then it sounds like I've done nothing but disappoint you these past few days. I think it's best if you leave now," I state as I curl up more in bed.

"Everly..." he tries to put his arm around me again, but I still push him off.

"No James. I need to be alone. Honestly, I'm pissed about the bet, I'm pissed you told my secret. I'm pissed that everyone now looks at me like I'm broken, and I'm just really pissed at myself. I just need to be alone." I get more and more angry as I speak.

I feel him sit up and get off the bed. "Okay. I'm sorry Everly. Please, if you need me..."

"I don't," I interrupt.

He doesn't say anything back, but I can feel the hurt in the air. I hate that I hurt him, but I'm hurt right now too. I need time to think, or not think. What hurts the most is that I was really liking James. I thought he was feeling the same, but now flirting with me was making more sense. He also wanted to win that bet, even if he won't admit it to me. I want to be mad at Jake too, but honestly, I couldn't be. I knew the type of guy Jake was before getting into his bed. I think that's why I chose him. There were no strings attached. I'd get what I wanted, and he got what he wanted.

I listen for the door to open and close again before I relax and force myself to drift off to sleep.

Chapter Eight

The next four days passed painfully slowly as I did my best to avoid the boys. James left on Tuesday for two days to do something with his dad's business. Ben went to Alex's house, and the Hale brothers didn't come over while they were gone. I mostly hid out in my room reading a book or spent time by the pool when I knew I wouldn't be bothered. Conveniently, it was my time of month, so I used that as an excuse to explain why I wasn't up for doing much when Mrs. Crawford asked.

I've been ignoring my text messages from the boys. James had texted me the most, checking in on me, and Jake was a close second with the number of messages he sent. Ben and Bash sent a few messages, checking on me as well. I didn't respond to any of them. I haven't talked to them since that night at the lake house. The next day, when we were heading home, I drove back with the security guards so I could avoid them. They got home really late that night, so it worked out anyway. I don't want their pity or them being disgusted with me for everything. I don't want to feel angry and get into an argument. I just want time to heal, get over it, pretend, and move on.

Sitting and wallowing is just not something I find worth my time, so today I'm going to suck it up and move on. I'm going to do what I do best, pretend. I'm going to ignore their previous messages and when I see them, just pretend nothing happened. It's the easiest thing to do.

When I check my phone, Jake makes it easy to put my plan into action by texting the group.

Jake

> Checking off paintball today 1 pm. Our backyard.

Ben

> I'll be there.

James

> Count me in.

Bash

> I'm the one that set it up, so I'll be there.

Jake

> The boys will be shirtless so Everly can punish us.

Ben

> I didn't agree to that...

Bash

It's only fair.

James

Agreed.

I can't help but smile as I read the messages. Paintballs hurt and can leave some pretty nasty bruises. As much as getting revenge sounds good, that's not how I want to do it. I don't want to, anyway. I just want everything to go back to the way it was before. So, I decide to join in and message them back.

I'll be there, but you guys are not going shirtless. It would put me at a disadvantage.

Jake

Sorry, would it be too distracting?

Of course it would be.

Ben

Then we could just skip the padding but have shirts on.

I'm not going to be responsible for scarring your perfect bodies.

Jake

Perfect huh?

Anyway, are we doing teams or are we on our own?

Bash

Teams would be uneven

Ben

I could invite Alex

Yes! Tell Alex to come!

Ben

He's right next to me and wants in.

Yay! I want him on my team!

Jake

You seem a little too excited for Alex

Jealous?

Jake

Yes

Ben

I'm on their team

Bash

Suit yourself

You guys think I'll bring down the team, but you're wrong. Let's make a bet for the winning team.

Jake

What does the winning team get?

The losing team has to say yes to anything we ask them to do for the rest of the day. We'll pair off so you only have to be at one person's whim.

Jake

Deal

Bash

Deal

Ben

Deal and Deal for Alex

James

Deal

I confidently walk over to the Hale house and immediately go around back. I'm hoping Jake and Bash told security I was coming because I look like someone about to go rob their house. I'm dressed in my paintball gear with my favorite paintball gun I purchased after making the bucket list. I'm in camo coveralls, a blast face mask, chest pad, and padding for my elbows and knees. With my combat boots on, I'm ready to go. One thing I failed to mention to the boys is that I've been playing paintball for the past few years, so I could have a rematch and beat them. I figured they would underestimate me, since the last time we all played together was when I was 12 and crying.

I stop in my tracks when I arrive in the backyard. Bash has been busy. The yard has been transformed into an arena. It looks like a maze on over an acre of land. There are wooden fences, doorways, and mini rooms all around. I can't see all the way to the other side, but on this side, there is a tentlike fixture with a blue flag in it.

I hear laughter approaching, so I turn around to find all five boys coming out to meet me. They are dressed up in normal clothes, but I can tell they have some chest padding underneath. You can't see any of their skin, smart.

"Everly! You went all out!" Jake laughs while walking around me, patting my outfit and padding.

I lift my mask and smile. "Of course, I'm not letting you all bruise my beautiful face or body this time."

They each grab their own face masks and put them on, wasting no time. I study James, Jake, and Bash's outfits so I don't confuse them with my team. I take a moment to go up to Alex and give him a hug. I'm thrilled to see him again and need to make a point to hang out just the two of us sometime soon. He's one of Ben's best friends and by proxy Jake's. Though I think sometimes Jake gets a little jealous of Alex.

Once everyone is ready, Bash announces, "Alright, you guys are blue and we're red. Get the flag back to your base and you win. Rules are... there are no rules. When the horn blows, we'll begin. Good luck."

The three of them run off to the other side of the arena and out of view. Ben, Alex, and I talk strategy for a moment, and I make them aware of my skills with the paintball gun. I've become a great shot. Alex is a runner, so he will run to grab the flag while I cover him. Ben will stay back to protect our flag. When we get closer to our base, he'll pass the flag to me to run the rest of the way back in hopes the other team thinks he still has the flag, so he'll be the decoy.

The horn sounds, and we all get into position. Ben is hiding with a view of our flag while Alex and I take off running. We dodge around the makeshift walls and houses, which are over six feet tall because neither of us can see over them. We try to memorize the layout for the future and make a note of the little house that we will meet in to hand off the flag. If I take too long, he will try to run it without me. The fun part about our rules is that even if we get hit with paintballs, we're not out of the game. It's just more of a way to slow each other down.

As we near the middle of the arena, I notice some rope hanging from one of the window holes of the little houses. I grab the rope and tie it around my waist to use for later. With no rules, tying down one enemy may come in handy. I'm good at tying ropes, another one of those random skills I've learned this past year. I push down the thought because I don't want the reason to pop into my mind and ruin this fun for me.

It's been about ten minutes and we're almost at the enemy's camp. I'm surprised we haven't run into each other yet, but we must have taken different paths. I'm sure one of them stayed behind to protect the flag, so I'm looking out for him.

As we make it to their side and see their flag, I whisper to Alex, "Stay hidden and let me head toward the flag and create a distraction. There should only be one of them here, and I can take care of him for you to run in after to grab the flag. You'll know when."

Alex agrees and hides back behind a fence. As I walk out into the open, a paintball smacks me in the middle of my chest. I feel the hit, but thankfully there's no pain at all with this chest pad. I duck behind a wooden box and survey the direction the shot came from. Whoever it is must be hiding behind the wall ahead of me, so I aim my gun in that direction and step out again. He peeks his head out and starts shooting at me while I shoot him directly in the head two times. He stumbles back and I take the opportunity to run closer to him and hide behind the opposite side of the wall.

I only see the helmet, but I'm pretty sure it's Jake and that will make this so much easier. He quickly comes out again, shooting me in the arm while I shoot directly at both of his hands, knocking the gun out of his hand. Before he can lean to pick it up, I body slam him into the wall and kick his gun away. I throw my gun away with his and don't move from being in front of him.

"Well, that was not what I was expecting," he says while looking at both our guns laying on the ground too far for either of us to reach.

I can tell by his voice that he is smirking under his mask. He's much stronger than me, so I know he would've been able to easily take my gun and use it against me. Better to have no weapons in this fight.

"Eh, guns are for losers. I prefer hand to hand combat," I say as I'm unknotting the rope around my waist for easy access.

"I can get down with that," he says while trying to push past me, but I step in front of him again, blocking him.

I put my hand on his chest and walk to his side to get a foot behind him.

"Or we can have a repeat of the other night in your bed," I say as seductively as I can.

He laughs. "You're trying to distract me."

I laugh too, while grabbing one of his wrists and rubbing my hand up his other arm. "Maybe. Or I was just thinking how hot it would be to make out here on the paintball field while our friends battle it out for the flag. It's been a long four days thinking about you."

Jake groans at my words and freezes. I know this is my chance, so I quickly grab his other wrist and tie them together in a split second. He catches onto what I'm doing and tries yanking his arms away, but I have him in a good hold and am able to do one small knot. He uses his shoulder to push me into the wall, but I get the second knot in place. As he continues to struggle, we both fall to the ground. He rolls away, but I get the third and final knot, so he won't be able to get it undone with his arms behind him.

He looks defeated as he sits up against the wall. "Aw, you were just distracting me."

I pull his mask off to see his face and lift mine as well. He's smiling, like he's proud of what I just did to him.

I kneel directly in front of him. "I really want you to have to say yes to everything I ask you to do for me today."

He gives a wicked grin and says, "Baby, you don't have to win this for me to do whatever you want."

I laugh. "Well, I have to get going. Thanks for the fun."

I give him a quick kiss on the cheek and walk off. I put my mask back in place and grab both of our guns. I hear him yell after me about how that wasn't fair, but there is no fair when there are no rules.

Alex is long gone with the flag by the time I'm heading back. I'm trying to be careful not to run into anyone on the way to our meeting place, but someone shoots me in the back of my knee and lower back. I quickly duck behind another crate and put Jake's gun down. I figure it's far enough away that if he does somehow get loose, the game should be over by the time he finds and reaches it.

I take a breather before sticking my head out to see where the shots are coming from. The back of my knee is still stinging, and I know that's going to bruise. The moment my head peaks over the crate, three more shots smack into me. Both of them must be together and there's no way I can take them both on. I can try to distract them long enough for Alex to give up waiting for me and head back, but that's risky.

I decide to make a run for it to our meetup place. I'm hit two more times in the back until I duck behind a wall and shoot off at one of them, hitting them in the arm and leg. I continue running and no more shots ring out. They are probably following me. I meet up with Alex in the little house and grab the flag. I tell him to run, so he does.

More shots ring out, hitting the house and following Alex. He leads them in the opposite direction. Before they notice he doesn't have the flag anymore, I sprint out and hide behind another wall. I can see James out in the open shooting at Alex, so I shoot a few rounds at him, nailing him in the head, stomach, and knee. He disappears behind the wall, and I notice he has our flag. I'm closer to our base, so I decide to make a run for it. Ben can help me when I get closer.

Before I can step out from behind the wall, Bash is standing there in front of me. He grabs me by the waist, grabs the gun from my hands, and throws it across the field just like I did to Jake's. He pushes me down and pins me to the ground, grabbing the flag and placing it beside him on the ground.

"Nice seeing you here, Bash," I say.

He lifts his face mask, then mine. He's basically doing what I did to Jake, but in reverse. Well played.

He smirks. "This is what you get for ignoring me the past few days."

He lets me sit up but pins me against the wall. He's too strong for me, so I know that there is no escaping his grasp. I'm hoping if I distract him long enough, then Alex or Ben can come grab the flag.

"Eh, it's all best forgotten," I say, shrugging my shoulders.

His smile fades as he responds, "I'm not letting you go until we talk."

I sigh. "There's nothing to talk about, and we're in the middle of a game."

He laughs. "They can handle the game. Look, I'm sorry about that stupid bet. It was dumb, and I just want to make sure you're okay."

I try not to think about anything, just the words I should be saying. "It's okay, I forgive you. And I'm fine, so you can let me go now."

He doesn't let me go and continues, "I don't see how you're fine. I just want you to talk to me, or one of us, or someone. You need to Everly."

Before I can get out another word, the horn sounds indicating the end of the game. I look down at the flag still sitting next to Bash and I deflate. That means they won. I never even considered the fact that they would win.

"Crap," I say, realizing that now I lost that bet.

Bash laughs. "Sorry you lost."

After a moment of looking me in the eye, his face becomes serious as he puts his forehead to mine, saying, "Everly, we just want to help you. Let us help you."

I give a small smile and nod my head. "Okay."

He gets off me, stands up, and helps me up. We walk up front to meet up with the others.

Once everyone gets there, James, Jake, and Bash high five each other.

I look over at Ben and Alex with an apologetic look. "Sorry I failed you guys."

Ben puts his hand on my shoulder. "Are you kidding me? That was awesome. And I should be apologizing because I let them get the flag..."

Ben's words get cut off by Jake coming over and pushing my shoulder. "Hey, that was just wrong. I can't believe you left me there tied up."

Bash chuckles. "Oh, do tell how she succeeded in tying you up."

"I let her, of course." Jake winks at me.

I respond, "Oh, you wish. You just can't admit a girl overpowered you."

James speaks up, "Well, I also want to know where you learned to shoot like that, because your aim was spot on."

I smile. "I've been practicing to beat you guys."

"Well, it looks like it wasn't enough because we won. Now I think it's time that we collect on the bet…" Bash says with a smirk.

Alex, Ben, and I groan.

Bash pulls out his phone and uses a random matching website to see who will be paired with who. Jake matches with Alex, Bash gets Ben, and James gets me. Of course it would be James, but I don't know that I would've really wanted to know what Jake would have asked me to do if I had gotten him.

Jake complains, "Oh no fair, I wanted Everly."

James spits back, "Too bad. She's mine."

My chest squeezes at the way he said, "she's mine." I know he didn't mean it like that, but I wish he had.

"Alex, go get me a drink," Jake says in a demanding tone.

Alex rolls his eyes and walks off into the house, presumably to get Jake a drink. I hope Jake doesn't push him too much. I feel like Jake has been waiting his whole life to do something like this to Alex.

"Let's go home and change, Everly," James says sweetly.

"Yes, master," I state.

The way he looks at me after I say that stirs something in my stomach and makes me clench my thighs together. I've never seen him look at me like that before. I clear my throat and follow him back to the house.

I go upstairs and change into some jean shorts and a cami. I was sweating in that gear and glad to be out of it. After changing, I go downstairs to get a glass of water and chug it. I hadn't realized how thirsty I was until now.

I pull out my phone and text James.

I put my phone in my back pocket and go straight to his room. I knock before entering and find him sitting up in his bed with a book. When I enter, he peeks over the top of his book, running his eyes up and down my body. I blush, thinking maybe I should've put on more clothes, but it's hot. When he gives me certain looks or says things that could be taken as flirting, it makes me think maybe there could be more between us, but then he makes comments that indicate I'm imagining all of this. Maybe I am.

James puts the book down on his end table and pats the bed next to him for me to sit, so I do. I crawl onto his bed but stay as close to the edge as possible.

James finally breaks the silence. "This isn't how I wanted to do this, but I'd be dumb to not take advantage of the situation..."

My heart races. Is he going to ask me what I think he is?

He must have realized what I'm thinking because he smirks before continuing, "We need to talk Everly, so I'm asking you to talk to me."

I let out the breath I didn't realize I was holding in. Am I really relieved though? What would I have done if he asked me to do that? I shake my head slightly to get the thought out of my head. He'd never ask me to do that.

"Okay, what do you want to talk about?" I ask, knowing full well what he wants to talk about.

He sighs. "You haven't returned any of my messages. I'm really sorry about that night. I hope you can forgive me."

"I forgive you," I state quickly.

I want this conversation over with, but I do forgive him. I know he didn't tell them to hurt me, but I also know that I'm not going to be trusting him with any more secrets any time soon.

He nods and says, "I really want you to talk to me. Or even better, talk to someone, a therapist..."

I interrupt him. "I'm not talking to a therapist, James."

He sighs and continues, "I think you should. It's messed up what Adam did to you, and I don't think you're handling it right..."

I start to get angry, so I interrupt him again. "Who are you to tell me if I'm handling it right?"

He winces. "I didn't mean it like that. I just meant..."

"No, you did mean it like that. Maybe I'm not handling it right," I put finger quotations around the word right, "but I'm handling it the best way I can. You have no idea what it's like to be forced to... it's awful, James."

"I know I don't know what it's like. That's why I want you to talk to someone that can help you. I don't want you to keep making mistakes. I do know what that's like and then you just start spiraling..."

I frown when he says the word mistake. "What mistake are you referring to? Me sleeping with Jake? Because if so, it wasn't a mistake. It was probably the best thing I've done in the past year. I finally don't feel like sex is some awful thing anymore, and Jake helped me with that. Yeah, okay, maybe Jake didn't know and maybe I used him, but clearly, he used me too. It was mutual."

James doesn't say anything back and just stares at me. He is finally at a loss for words. Maybe I am messed up. Maybe he is right, and I made a mistake, but I'm not going to admit it. I'm also not going to spiral and keep making mistakes. That's not who I am.

I sigh. "I'm sorry James. You're right, I probably should talk to someone, but I just can't right now. Okay?"

He nods and scoots closer to me. He puts his arm around me and says, "I want you to know that I'm here for you. If you need to talk about anything, I'm here."

I feel tears well up in my eyes as I respond, "I know, thank you."

"Good, now that's out of the way. I want you to go downstairs to ask them to bring our dinner later to my room. Then I want you to come back here where we can lie in bed the rest of the night and watch videos of people playing video games."

"Yes sir," I say, about to roll off the bed to head downstairs.

James holds onto my arm and groans. "I need you to stop saying that."

I look at him, confused. "Why?"

He groans again. "Just... don't."

"Okay," I say while getting off the bed and heading out the door. The way he was looking at me makes my heart race again and those butterflies reappear in my stomach. I take a few deep breaths and take longer than necessary to get downstairs to ask them to bring our food up later. I need a clear head before heading back to James' room.

When I arrive back, we lay on his bed close to each other, but not touching. He put on some of our favorite videos that always get me laughing. He knew this was exactly what I needed and wanted. He could've asked anything of me, and I'd have to say yes, but he decided to do something for me. This is why I can't stay mad at him, because he's so sweet and considerate to me.

Chapter Nine

I shoot up in bed with the loud clap of thunder waking me. I get up to look out my window, seeing the pouring rain and lightning lighting the night sky every few seconds. I debate lying back in bed, but another loud boom shakes the whole house. I'm not typically afraid of storms, but there's something about this one that's frightening.

I head to the kitchen to make a cup of tea. Usually, that calms me and helps me sleep. I haven't been sleeping great with everything going on as it is. After the talk with James the other day, I've been questioning if I did make a mistake with Jake. I don't regret sleeping with him, but I do regret not being honest. I don't know if it would've made any difference, but it wasn't fair of me to use him like that.

I try not to turn on any lights, not wanting to wake anyone else up. If the storm hasn't already. I walk into the dark kitchen and quickly regret not bringing my phone for a flashlight. The flashes of lightning light up the whole kitchen, and I literally jump and gasp as I see a dark figure sitting at the island.

I put my hand over my heart as a familiar voice says, "Hey."

I start breathing again as I realize it's just James. He gets up and flips the switch for the under-cabinet lighting. It's not much light, but it's enough for me to be able to see James and what I'm doing.

"You scared the crap out of me," I say, giving a nervous laugh and trying to stop shaking.

"Sorry, I couldn't sleep and thought I'd try some tea," he responds while sitting back down at the island.

"That's what I came for too."

"I heated some water on the stove. You're welcome to use it." He points to the kettle on the stove.

"Thanks," I say.

I walk over to the cabinet and pull out a tea packet and a mug. I pour the steaming water over it and let it steep for a minute. I stand there staring at it, not sure what I should do now. Should I bring it back up to my room to drink? Do I sit at the island with James? What's the least awkward thing to do?

I turn around to face him again. Dear God, how did I not notice that he's shirtless? He has on black sweatpants and no shirt. At least he didn't come down in just his boxers, but right now it's impossible not to stare at his chest and abs.

And cue the embarrassment. I notice the smirk on his face, which means he noticed me checking him out. Ugh.

"The storm wake you?" he asks, breaking the awkwardness.

"Yeah, I think so. I haven't been sleeping well lately anyway," I say, sitting down at the island.

I figure at this point it would be rude to head back upstairs. He's making conversation, and I just checked him out, so it's probably best if I sit with him.

"Bad dreams?" he asks.

"Something like that," I say, hoping he'll drop it.

I'm not wanting to say yeah, and I have been thinking about what you said and you're right. I think I made a mistake with Jake. If I tell him that, he's going to push for me to talk to a therapist again, and I'm not doing that.

Thankfully, he doesn't push it, and we continue sipping our tea in silence. I try hard not to look at him, and I wish he would go put on a shirt. I can feel myself blushing. I'm thankful the lighting isn't good.

Another loud crack of thunder sounds through the house, and I jump, spilling some tea on myself. I make a hissing sound as it burns on my skin. James gets up to grab a paper towel and hands it to me. I thank him and wipe up the tea I spilled on myself and on the island.

"You're really jumpy tonight," he observes.

I don't respond and just give him a small smile. What do I say to that?

James looks me over for a moment and then asks, "Want to play a card game?"

I laugh. That's unexpected. "What? Like strip poker?"

His eyebrows raise as he looks at me and takes another sip of his tea. "I was more thinking something simple like Go Fish or War, but sure."

I blush at his response. He's joking, right? He wouldn't play strip poker with me.

"Well, if we did, I have an advantage because you're already half naked," I tease.

"I don't have on much more than you," he nods toward my outfit.

Holy crap, how embarrassing! As I look down at what I'm wearing, I notice my nipples are basically poking through my flimsy night shirt. I never wear a bra to bed, and I didn't think to put one on. I'm wearing tiny shorts as well, though I do have underwear on. I can't tell if he's flirting with me though, so to avoid even more awkwardness, I go ahead and flirt with him.

"True, but I have three pieces you have on two. To make it even, I'll take one off before we start. Should it be my shirt or shorts?"

James chokes on his tea, and I can't help but laugh. He shakes his head and grabs the paper towel I used to clean myself up a minute ago so he can now clean up his mess.

"I think we'll stick to Go Fish," he mumbles.

"Your loss," I say, shrugging my shoulders.

"It is," he says so low I barely hear him.

Okay, he's definitely flirting with me, right?

James gets up to grab a deck of cards in the drawer of the server. He comes back to sit on the barstool right next to me instead of across the island. The island is large, so it would be difficult to reach the cards. As he sits, his knee bumps into mine, which causes a small zing to go through my body.

He deals the hand, and we play a couple rounds of Go Fish. Of course, he wins every round that we play. I don't know how, but James always beats me in cards. Everyone always beats me in card games. At least I'm good at video games.

"Alright, I'm done with this," I say, pushing the cards away from us.

James laughs. "Why? Because I keep beating you?"

"Yes," I say with a groan.

"Well, you have to be bad at something. You always kill us in video games."

So, he noticed that too. Good. I try not to be a sore loser, but sometimes it's hard. Especially when it's the middle of the night, and I haven't gotten much sleep.

The storm seems to have passed, and I can't help but smile, thinking about how James tried his best to distract me. It worked. It's probably best if I head back to bed. Even if I can't sleep, maybe I can read. I don't want to keep James awake more than he already has been.

We both stand up at the same time, probably thinking the same thing. We bump into each other, and I almost fall over my barstool as we collide. James grabs my shoulders to steady me against the island.

He positions himself in front of me, making sure I'm steady. Just when I think he is going to release me, he doesn't. The front of our bodies are flush against each other. He's still holding onto my shoulders as he stares at me.

My heart pounds rapidly in my chest as my stomach has butterflies flapping around everywhere. James leans in closer, which makes me pull in a breath and hold it. I watch as his eyes bounce back and forth between mine and then down to my lips. I can't breathe. Is he going to kiss me?

A stray clap of thunder sounds, startling us both back into reality. We jump apart quickly, and he lets go of my shoulders. He clears his throat, turns away, and takes both of our mugs to the sink.

James turns around and leans his back against the counter. "I'm going to head to bed."

I nod. "Yeah, me too."

We're both silent for a few more moments as we stare at each other. What is happening between us? I'm trying to figure out if he was flirting with me tonight and if he was about to kiss me. I have to be imagining things though, right?

"Good night," he says while finally breaking eye contact and walking away.

"Good night, James. Thank you for keeping me company tonight."

He takes one glance back, nods, and walks away. I give him a few minutes before heading up the steps as well, back to my room. Once I reach my bed, I plop down on it with a sigh. I try to go over everything that happened tonight in my head, but I'm exhausted. I fall asleep with a smile on my face, thinking about what it would be like to kiss James.

Chapter Ten

Another week passes by quickly and I realize that summer is half over. Things have gone back to the way they were before, and I'm trying to enjoy every moment I can with my friends, especially James. Thinking about him going back to college hurts a little bit, even though he will only be an hour away. I've gotten used to having him here to comfort me. As much as I hate to admit it, my feelings for him have grown stronger, too. I've had a little crush on him for the past few years, but this is a full-blown crush now. Maybe it's best that we have some distance between us soon.

Bash, Jake, Ben, and I sit around the pool enjoying our feet in the cool water on this hot summer day. James comes up behind us, holding something out for us to see.

"I got our IDs back from my friend. They look legit," he says with a smile.

I grab mine from him to look at it and he's right. It looks exactly like my normal ID except my age is 21 on here.

Jake looks over his and says, "Alright!! When are we hitting the club?"

"Why don't we do that as the last thing on our list, just in case we get caught? And if we don't, then we end our bucket list with a bang," I say because I was actually afraid of getting caught, and I really didn't want to miss out on the rest of our bucket list.

"Good point," Bash says.

"Alright, so what do we have left on the list? Ziplining..." Jake states.

"And camping without tents..." I add.

"And the most epic prank," Ben answers.

"Have we decided who we are pranking yet?" James asks.

Jake responds, "We haven't... Who deserves a good, old-fashioned prank from us?"

Everyone thinks for a bit, but no one has an answer. I think of Adam for a moment, but he deserves a lot more than a prank. Then I think of Kayla. She was my best friend, but did not act like it last year. Thinking about her brings up a sour memory...

I sat on my bed reading my book when someone knocked on my door.

"Come in," I said.

I looked up to see Kayla walking in. I asked her to come over today because I really needed to talk to her. I needed a friend to talk to about Adam. She knew that we have had sex, but she didn't know the extent of it. Adam told me I couldn't tell anyone, but it was eating me alive not being able to talk to anyone. Kayla was my best friend, so I knew she would keep my secret and understand.

When Kayla sat on my bed next to me, the tears already started falling.

"What's wrong?" she asked, rubbing my shoulder.

I immediately went into talking about Adam before I could back out. I explained how everything was going great when we first met, and he was the perfect boyfriend. Then how he tricked me into having sex with him. I told him I wasn't ready, but he insisted and pushed me. I cried alone so hard that first time. He drilled it into me that I asked for it and wanted it. I started to believe it.

I continued by telling her how he kept forcing me every time he wanted it. I always said no, but he did it anyway. He always made me feel bad about it, like it was my fault. When I started getting more confidence that it wasn't my fault and it was wrong, I confronted him. That's when the threats came in. He threatened to hurt me first if I told anyone. Then he threatened to hurt my dad. Then my friends. I started distancing myself from all my friends so that was one less person he could threaten. I rarely even saw Kayla because I was so afraid he'd hurt her. I tried to break it off with him, but it was the same threats that kept me with him. I didn't have a choice.

When the story ended, Kayla looked at me like she didn't know me.

She asked me, "Are you sure that's what happened?"

I looked at her, confused. What does she mean? Am I sure that's what happened? Of course that's what happened. I was telling her everything that happened.

"Yes, that's what happened. What do you mean?" I asked.

She shrugged and said, "I don't know. That doesn't seem like Adam. You didn't ask for it? I mean, you always flirt with him, and you dress pretty slutty."

I was hurt by her words. I dress slutty? I don't feel like I dress slutty. I dress like normal girls do at 16. And yeah, I used to flirt with him before this started, but doesn't everyone? That doesn't mean I was asking for it. When I say no, that should be respected.

"What are you trying to say?" I asked her.

She sighed. "I'm just saying that maybe you led him on, and he didn't realize you didn't want it."

I got angry. "No, I made it clear I didn't want it. I mean, if he didn't think it was wrong, then why has he been threatening me, my dad, and my friends if I tell anyone?"

She shrugged. "I don't know. Maybe when you confronted him, he got scared. Girls do that all the time. They claim they were raped when they weren't, and the guy gets in trouble for that. It's a serious accusation. Adam just doesn't seem like that type of guy and he's sweet."

I suspected before that Kayla had a crush on Adam, but she was adamant that she didn't. Now that suspicion was proven with what she was saying. She didn't believe me. I was her best friend for five years and she didn't believe me. She'd rather believe that the boy she has a crush on isn't that type of person, but he is. I felt sick.

"Fine, if you don't believe me, then I need you to leave," I said sternly.

"Everly... I'm just saying... maybe you..."

I interrupted her. "Leave!"

She huffed. "Fine. But don't you dare go spreading rumors that Adam raped you because it's not true. Don't ruin his life."

I couldn't help but laugh. I was so hurt that I was laughing at her words. I felt crazy. She got up to leave and when she opened the door, I said, "I never want to speak to you again."

"Fine by me," she said, slamming the door shut behind her.

I'm brought back to reality by James' hand squeezing my thigh as we sit at the edge of the pool with our feet in it.

"Where'd you go?" he whispers.

I've been getting lost a lot in my thoughts around him and he can easily tell now when I'm no longer present.

Instead of answering his question, I speak to the group, "I have someone that I really want to prank."

Jake's eyes light up. "Who? And how far do you want to take the prank?"

I give a wicked smile. "My ex-best friend Kayla. And as far as we can take it."

"Let's meet up tonight to talk specifics!" Bash says while standing up to leave. "I need to do some things, but I'll be back tonight."

I nod as he leaves to walk next door back to his house. Jake and Ben leave the pool too, probably going to play more video games.

I look over at James, who is staring at me with an odd look.

"What?" I ask.

He shakes his head. "Remember how we talked about spiraling?"

I laugh. "I'm not spiraling, James, and I'm not making any mistakes."

He squeezes my thigh. "That's the problem with spiraling and making mistakes. You don't know that you are until it's too late."

I put my hand on top of his to reassure him. "James, I promise I'm not. You don't understand."

"Okay, you're right."

That's all he says, but I can tell that he has a lot more to say to me. I don't give him a chance though as I excuse myself to go change. I have a date with Alex in an hour that I need to get ready for.

I meet Alex at a restaurant close to home. My new home. I don't know when I started considering it home, but I have. Mrs. Crawford always makes me feel part of the family and those boys do, too. One of my security guards came with me to meet Alex at the restaurant since I was going alone. I promised my dad I would take one. It isn't too bad; we always make small talk in the car but nothing more. Whenever we get to the destination, they make sure to stay out of sight and far enough away to give me my privacy.

I walk into the busy restaurant ten minutes late. Knowing Alex would already be there, I walk in and search for him at a table. He is in the furthest booth all the way to the back. I slide into the booth in front of him, and he looks so happy to see me.

"I'm so glad you could sneak away from the brothers to come spend time with me!" he says, giving me a hug across the table.

I laugh. "Yes, they are very demanding brothers. It can be difficult."

Our conversation mostly consists of what we have been up to this summer. I look over the menu and choose the most basic burger when the server comes over to take our orders. Talking to Alex is like talking to a best friend. I feel like I can tell him anything, well, almost. We always got along from day one when Ben introduced us.

"So, how is Tanner doing?" I ask.

He lights up at Tanner's name and says, "He's doing fantastic. We've been able to spend a lot of time together this summer. I think it's the best one yet."

I smile. "Oh, I'm so glad! So, does anyone know yet?"

His smile fades as he responds, "No... I don't plan on telling anyone. Not until at least after high school."

I nod. "I understand. You know your secret is safe with me. And you can talk to me about Tanner any time you need a friend."

"This is why you're my new best friend. Shhh don't tell Ben," he whispers the last part.

I laugh. "Oh, don't worry, I won't tell Ben."

Alex and I had a great meal together, and I haven't felt so free in a long time as I did with him. Maybe it's because he has a secret that I'm keeping. Two summers ago, I caught Tanner and Alex together in his room. Ben and I went over to hang out with the two of them and luckily, I went up first to Alex's room before Ben. When I got there, well, let's just say Tanner and Alex weren't just lying in bed like James and me the day we were caught.

When I saw it, I quickly closed the door and found Ben to distract him while they got themselves together. They met us downstairs afterward, and we all pretended like nothing happened. That night when I was alone with Alex, he told me that he was gay, and he loved Tanner. No one knew, even Ben. I promised him that I would keep his secret for as long as he wanted it a secret. They have been sneaking around for that long, but I'm glad to see that it seems to work for them, and they are happy. I just hope one day he will feel comfortable enough to let his friends know. I know they will be happy for him and not judge him, but I understand why he wants to keep it a secret. People are awful, especially teenagers in a preppy high school.

After finishing our meal, we agree to get together more often, especially once we start back in school. It'll be nice to have a friend outside of Jake and Ben. James and Bash will be back in college, and I'm assuming I'll only hear from them during the holidays when they come back to visit. While I intend to be invisible this year, it would be nice to have a couple of friends.

"So, what does she hate?" Ben asks as we all sit around in James' room discussing our prank. James sits in his bed, leaning against the headboard with his legs crossed. Ben sits on the end of the bed, while Jake, Bash, and I are on the couch.

I grin wickedly as I say, "She has a crazy hatred for dick drawings."

Everyone laughs, but I'm mostly paying attention to Jake because he is the master prankster. I can see the gleam in his eye at this information.

"Okay, so what sort of access do you have to her?" Jake asks.

"I can get into her bedroom easily. I know her security and the blind spots. I also know where her spare key to her car is," I say, like I've already been thinking about doing this.

Bash says, "Nice. So, what are we thinking? A bunch of dick drawings in her room and in her car?"

So, I have really been planning this out all day. The dick drawings would definitely make her cringe and get upset, but I want to do more.

I look around the room at each of them before saying, "So, here's what I was thinking. Yes, the dick drawings in her room and car, that'll definitely make her have nightmares for weeks and she will flip out. I also want to do the hair dye in her shampoo bottle prank. All of them. She hates colored hair. In order to do all this without her knowing, we need her distracted..." I say looking over at Jake, which I can tell he already knows where I'm going with this. I continue, "Jake needs to distract her for a while, like REALLY distract her. Make it look like she's really into him. Then I'd like someone else to be recording and taking pictures of this so we can send it to her boyfriend."

"Wow, what did this girl do to you?" Bash asks, surprised.

"It doesn't matter, but just know she deserves all of it and more," I respond.

My gaze lands on James, and I immediately have to look away as my heart sinks. I can tell by the look in his eyes that he doesn't approve, and he thinks I'm making a mistake. I don't care though, because we need a prank, and I found someone deserving of it.

They all agree to do this prank with me, or more like for me. Jake is going to distract Kayla by flirting with her outside of her thirty-minute yoga class. We will need more than thirty minutes to accomplish this task. Ben is going to record them without her noticing. Bash is going to help me with the dick drawings in her room and the shampoo bottles. I'm going to put the drawings on permanent vinyl to stick all over her walls. James is going to take the car key and put the vinyl in her car, outside her car, and bring the key back as fast as he can. As long as Jake can keep her distracted, which I know he will be able to, then all should go as planned. Bash will later send either the video or photos of Kayla flirting with Jake to Adam. I haven't told them who they are sending it to yet. Bash will use a fake phone number and make sure it can't be traced back to him at all. We plan to do this next week, so we have time to get the right amount of dick drawings on vinyl that we need.

Once everyone leaves James' room, James pulls me aside to talk. I know exactly what it is about.

"James, I told you it's fine. We needed a prank, and I provided a deserving person for it," I say before he can say anything.

He frowns at me. "The drawings and shampoo are fine, but are you sure you want to ruin her relationship with her boyfriend?"

I laugh and answer, "If she loves her boyfriend and is loyal to him, then there will be nothing to send him."

He nods and doesn't say anything else. I excuse myself and run into Jake in the hallway. He's leaning against the wall like he's waiting for someone.

He smiles. "Hey, I was hoping we could talk."

Oh no, not him too. He's usually down for anything that messes with people, so hopefully he's not wanting to talk me out of this or wanting more information on why I want to get back at her.

"Sure, want to go talk in my room?" I ask, wanting to get back to my room to rest. I prefer to be alone, but Jake clearly wants to talk.

He follows me into my room and closes the door behind him. I sit at the end of my bed, and he sits next to me.

"So, what did you want to talk about?" I ask, breaking the silence.

He looks nervous. I've never seen Jake nervous before.

"I've been thinking... about you, us. We never really got a chance to talk about what we did, and I just wanted to apologize because I didn't know..."

I cut him off before he can continue. "No, there's nothing to apologize for. It doesn't matter what you didn't know and know now because I don't regret it. We both agreed to it and enjoyed it, so let's leave it at that."

He smirks and says, "Okay, so you did enjoy it?"

I laugh. "Of course I did."

He lets out a sigh. "So did I."

He stares at me for a few moments before continuing, "Anyway... I was wondering if you wanted to... give us a try?"

I look at him, confused and ask, "Like you and me?"

He laughs nervously before saying, "Yes, us usually means you and me. I really like you Everly, and I can't stop thinking about you."

Wow, this is not where I thought this conversation was going to go. When he said that, I did get the little butterflies in my stomach. Jake is hot, great in bed, and sweet. I'd be a fool not to see where this could go between us. Though he is not known for relationships. I don't even think he has ever had a true girlfriend. The other issue is my feelings for James. I don't know if it would be right to lead Jake on if I am having feelings for someone else.

I think I should clarify what he wants first, so I ask, "So you what? You want me to be your girlfriend?"

"Yes," he replies.

I pause for a moment. "I don't know…"

He interrupts me. "We could take things slow. Honestly, being in a relationship would be new to me, but I want to give it a try if you do. Like I said, I really like you. We'll start slow and take it at your pace."

I think about it and then ask, "So you'd be willing to take me out on dates, hold my hand, and no sex?"

He groans. "Right. I mean, I won't lie I definitely want the sex part, but I can wait until you're ready."

My chest tightens at everything he's saying. It is really sweet of him, and he really does care about me.

"That's really sweet of you, Jake. I just… I need to think about it, okay?"

He nods and responds, "I understand. If you don't want to it's okay. You'll always be my friend, so don't worry about that."

"Thanks Jake," I say, giving him a hug.

Jake leaves the room, leaving me alone with my thoughts. I really like Jake too. I wouldn't mind giving us a try and seeing where we go, but I'm not really sure that we would work out with our personality differences. You don't know, though until you try. My only reservation at this point is James. I need to know where he stands with me. If James feels anything for me, then I know I can't move on with Jake, but if he doesn't... then it's time to move on because I don't want to be stuck loving someone who won't ever love me back. Wait, did I just say love? I don't think I love him, but yeah, it could definitely turn that way one day if I let this crush continue.

I get out my phone and text James. I need to do this now, and I need to do this in person so I can see his reactions and know for sure what he's feeling.

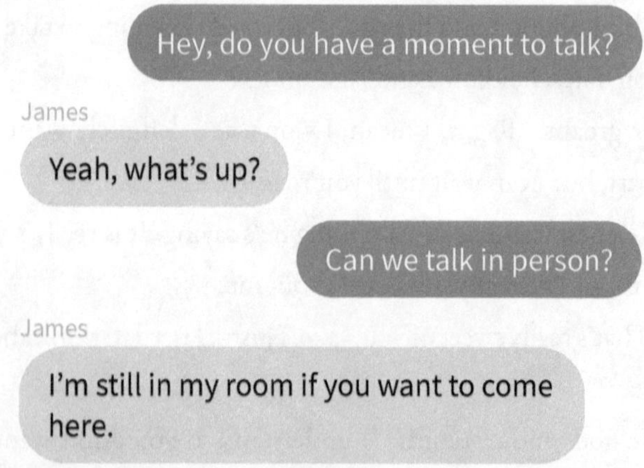

I don't respond and immediately go back to his room. I pause and take a deep breath before knocking on his door. He tells me to come in, so I enter. He's sitting on his bed with his laptop, closes the lid, and pushes it aside when I come in. I sit down on the end of his bed facing him.

"I wanted to get your opinion on something," I say in a casual tone.

"Okay, what is it?" he asks curiously.

I take a deep breath before saying, "Jake approached me, asking me to be his girlfriend..."

I pause there purposefully to gauge his reaction. His eyes grow wide for a moment in surprise, but then his face is completely blank. I can't tell what he is thinking.

I continue, "I know he doesn't do relationships, but he promised me we would take things slow and see where it goes. You know Jake better than anyone. I was wondering, is there any reason you think that I should tell Jake no?"

He looks me over and says, "You're right, Jake doesn't do relationships, but you have a way of changing people. So, he might be serious."

I frown because I really was hoping he would try to give me a reason not to date him. Mainly because I was hoping he would give me an indication that he wanted me. If he lets me date Jake without any reasons why I shouldn't, then I know my answer.

I ask again, "So, is there any reason I shouldn't date Jake? Any reason at all?"

He immediately responds with a straight face, "No. If you want to date Jake, you should."

I expected this to be his answer, but it still hurts. Part of me was hoping he would say yes, there is a reason not to, me. And then he'd kiss me and tell me he wants me to be his girlfriend. Clearly that's not going to happen, and he doesn't feel that way, so I need to let it go. I need to move on, and I think moving on with Jake is a great way to do that.

I stand up from his bed. "Okay then…"

I walk to the door and as I reach for the doorknob, James says, "Everly…"

My heart skips a beat, and I turn back around to face him. "Yeah?"

"You let me know if Jake does anything to hurt you. You understand?"

I feel myself deflate. For a brief second, I thought he was going to let me know that he wanted me, but he didn't. I just nod and leave his room, briskly walking to mine. I pull out my phone to text Jake.

> I want to give us a try too. I want to see where this goes.

Jake

> Good! Do you want to go out with me tomorrow?

> I'd love to.

Jake

> Then it's a date.

Chapter Eleven

I wake to an annoying beeping sound coming from my end table. I swipe my arm toward the direction of the sound and grab my phone, which is vibrating in my hand as it gets louder. I glance at it and it's my alarm going off... at 6:30 in the morning. It's summer. Why is my alarm going off at 6:30 in the morning?

Turning the alarm off, I groan. I relax back in bed for a moment until I realize why my alarm was going off. I groan again and roll to my side. Why did I think it would be a good idea to get up early in the morning to start running? I got it in my head that I needed to exercise to look more toned and lose the bit of weight I've already gained while here. These four boys are gorgeous. I can't be cramping their style by looking pudgy.

I throw the covers off and head to the bathroom to get ready. I put up my hair into a quick ponytail and put on a sports bra, along with tight yoga shorts. It's going to get hot fast, so I don't want to have much clothing on.

I head downstairs to meet with Declan, one of my security guards, who will be joining me on my run. I doubt I will be going far, but I promised my father to always take one with me. I thought he would be driving behind me or something, but he insisted on running with me. I won't lie, I'm nervous because I doubt that I'll be doing much running since I've never done it before.

Before we head out the front door, I hear the door to the basement open and footsteps head in our direction. I look back to find Jake and Ben coming up from the basement, without shirts on and a towel across their shoulders. My eyes wander over their shirtless bodies for a little too long, and I feel the heat rising to my cheeks. How are 17-year-olds so built and good looking?

Jake closes in on the distance, and I have to take a step back to not run my hands over his sweaty abs. I let out an almost inaudible groan just looking at him. Is it possible to have an orgasm by just staring at his body?

He gives me a smirk like he knows exactly what I'm thinking, which he probably does. I'm not being subtle about staring, and I haven't said a word to him.

"Where are you heading?" Jake asks, looking me over.

I clear my throat. "I'm going out for a run."

"You should've let me know. I would've joined you. Ben and I just finished our morning workout," he says, looking at me like he's waiting for an invitation to join. I do not want him to join me.

"That's okay, I'm going to go with Declan. I'll be back soon."

I turn to head toward the door so I can get away from him. There are way too many emotions going on inside me right now to stay standing in front of him.

He grabs my arm and pulls me into his body. Ugh, and this is where I do not need to be.

I try to look away from him, but he leans down to whisper in my ear, "You look hot in your workout clothes. Maybe after your run you can come find me in my room."

I gulp and try to start breathing again because I just realized I'm holding my breath. "I thought we were taking things slow. We haven't even had our first date yet."

He backs up to look me in the eye while he groans. "You're right. I'm sorry, you're just hard to resist."

He leans down and gives me a kiss, holding the back of my head. I want to back away and leave, but my body has a mind of its own. I part my lips for him to kiss me deeper and his tongue meets mine. This time, I let out the groan.

"Ahem…" Ben clears his throat from behind Jake.

Jake lets the kiss go and steps back, glaring at Ben like he was intruding, even though we are in the middle of Ben's house in the foyer.

"I'm heading upstairs to shower. I suggest you two get a room," Ben says as he turns toward the stairs.

I can feel my cheeks blush as I completely forgot Ben was there, and Declan. How embarrassing.

"I'll see you for our date later. Let's have lunch together." Jake takes a few more steps back waiting for my response.

"Okay," is all I can bring myself to say.

That smirk appears on his face again before he turns to walk up the stairs.

After only eight minutes of running, or I should say mostly walking and a bit of jogging, I'm starting to really regret doing this. Why on earth do people like running? This is the most miserable thing I've ever experienced. My heart is beating out of my chest, and I can barely breathe. My throat is burning, and I just feel like collapsing. I'm going to die. I'm going to die right here on this sidewalk and there's nothing my bodyguard can do to prevent it.

I can't take it anymore, so I stop in the middle of the sidewalk and put my hands on my knees, panting. I pull my headphones out, not that I can hear the music over the pounding of blood in my ears, anyway.

As I'm leaning over, I look up at Declan, who is waiting in front of me. "I'm sorry..."

He looks down at me and asks, "For what?"

I let out a laugh. A brief laugh because I can barely breathe. "This isn't really a run, and I'm dying over here. I'm pathetic."

"You're not pathetic. You're actually doing really well for your first time running. The fact you're even trying is great. You will improve the more you do it."

I let out a growl at thinking about doing this again. Why would I do this again? Jake's shirtless body comes into mind. Oh, that's right, I need to look good for him too. Not only that, but I also don't want to be weak anymore. Maybe one day I can earn enough trust from my father to not have someone with me at all times. If I can protect myself and am capable of running, then maybe I can convince him of that.

"Alright, let's head back. No running though," I laugh out, feeling defeated.

Declan walks beside me on the way back. I don't usually have much conversation with the security team, mainly because they are not the chatty type. I've tried to get to know them better, but they usually ignore my personal questions. With his silence, I can't help but study him. He clearly works out a lot as he's fit and looks like he could beat up a guy or two. He keeps his dark brown hair short like he's in the military and has pretty dark brown eyes. He has some facial hair that just looks like he hasn't shaved in a bit, but it looks good on him.

"So, what made you decide to take up running?" Declan asks, breaking the silence.

How do I answer that honestly without sounding even more pathetic? Oh, my boyfriend and his friends are super built and hot, so I want to be as well. Though that is a big reason, it's not the only one.

I stick with the better reason. "I want to be more fit, and I want to be able to take care of myself."

The aching in my chest is starting to be relieved by the walking and the pounding is getting lighter. My heart is happier with me when walking rather than running.

"Getting your stamina up is a good start. Have you considered training in self-defense?" Declan looks at me seriously.

"It has crossed my mind, but I haven't put much thought into it."

I keep my eyes facing forward, looking for the house to come into sight. I'm ready to be home and get a shower. A cold shower because I'm so hot and sweaty right now.

"Let me talk with your father, and we can get you started with some training."

Is he going to be the one training me? Or just setting me up to train with someone? It's not a bad idea.

I nod, mainly because I don't have much energy to talk anymore. I can't believe I've only been gone for about 15 minutes, and I'm already done. I feel defeated.

I study myself in the mirror to make sure I look amazing for my first date with Jake. I put on a short sundress that is yellow with flowers all over it. The dress is fitted in the waist and only comes down to my mid-thigh. It's hot outside, so it's the perfect outfit to stay cool, but look good. I curled my hair to make it wavy and put on a good bit of makeup.

I smile at myself in the mirror, knowing that Jake is going to have a hard time keeping his hands to himself. It might be wrong, but I really want to test him today. What's even more wrong is that I'm hoping James sees me as well.

Before I head out of my bedroom, my phone rings. It's my dad.

"Hello?" I answer on the second ring.

"Everly! How are you doing, sweetie?" My dad asks, like he's excited that I actually answered his call.

"I'm doing great, dad. How have you been?"

"I'm doing good. So, I've heard a few things that I wanted to ask you about..." He pauses for a moment, like he's waiting for my response.

What did he hear? Did he hear about Jake and me? Maybe it's just about the self-defense training. I didn't think Declan would ask him so quickly, though.

"What's up dad?" I ask smoothly.

He clears his throat. "First, I heard you went for a run to-day..."

I laugh. "Yeah, if you can call it a run. I tried."

"No, that's great sweetie. You should be running. Declan suggested you were interested in self-defense training. Is that true?"

I let out a breath of relief. I'm glad that's what this is about because I'm not ready to talk about Jake yet. It's brand new. "Yeah, I think it would be a good idea just to know the basics. What do you think?"

"I think it's an excellent idea. I told Declan that he can start training you as soon as you're ready."

"Great."

The line goes silent for a moment, like he is trying to figure out how to continue the conversation.

"There's one more thing I wanted to talk to you about. How are the boys treating you?" he asks.

Does he know about Jake? Does he know about something else that's happened? Does he know about the bucket list?

I don't want to give up any information that he may not know, so my only response is "Good. We're having a lot of fun."

He clears his throat again. "I'm glad you're having fun. What about Jake? Is there something I should know?"

Crap, he does know about Jake. Declan was standing there this morning when Jake decided he couldn't keep his hands off me and planted a kiss on me. Not that I'm complaining. It was a great kiss. Ugh, I'm going to yell at Declan about not keeping his mouth shut.

I sigh. "Jake asked me on a date. We're actually about to head out now for lunch."

"Is this your first date with him?" he asks, like he's disappointed that he had to hear about our relationship from Declan versus me.

"Yes, it's our first date," I say, gritting my teeth, hoping he's going to leave it at that.

"Well… let me know how your date goes. Remember what we talked about…"

I interrupt before he can continue. "Yes, I remember dad, and Mrs. Crawford had the same conversation with me shortly after I arrived as well. You have nothing to worry about."

"I always worry, sweetie."

"I know."

I hear my dad sigh, and I can't tell what he's thinking until he continues the conversation. "So, you like Jake?"

I laugh. "I think so. I mean, I'm going on a date with him today."

"Alright. Well, I won't keep you from your date. Please keep me updated, though. I want to hear these things from you and not from my security team, who saw you kissing this morning."

I can feel the heat rise in my cheeks and I groan. "I'm sorry, dad. I promise I'll be more open about these things with you. It's just new, that's all."

"You have a good day. I'll talk to you later. I love you," he says and hangs up the phone after I say goodbye.

I put my phone in my pocket before heading downstairs. That's one of my favorite things about this dress. It has pockets!

When I make it downstairs, I don't see Jake anywhere. He should be over here by now. I walk out the front door and sit on the top step, pulling my phone back out. I send him a quick text letting him know that I'm outside ready to go. He says that he is heading over in a minute.

I scroll through my phone on a funny website of memes that I enjoy going through when I have a few minutes to kill. I laugh at one and quickly stop when I hear the door behind me open. I turn my head to find James coming out the front door. My heart skips a beat, and I get excited about seeing him. I want him to see me like this, to see I'm not a little girl anymore.

He smiles when he sees me, and I stand up. I'd say I did it to be respectful, like when someone walks into the room you stand, but I really just want him to be able to see my whole body. Ugh, why am I thinking like this? He made it clear he doesn't care about me in that sense, and I'm with Jake. I'm literally going on a date with Jake right now.

I can't deny how I feel, though, when I notice his eyes skim up and down my body, lingering on my breasts. I made sure to put on my best pushup bra today.

I need to break the silence. "Hey. Where are you heading today?"

"Heading to see Bash for a bit. What about you?"

Before I can answer, Jake walks up the steps. I turn to face him. He pauses on the step below me, doing the same thing that James did. He looks me up and down, but instead of not saying anything, he has the courage to say what he thinks.

"Damn Everly, you look amazing." He steps closer to me and puts his arm around my waist. I smile at him.

"Doesn't she look hot, James?" Jake turns his attention toward James and so do I. I want to know his response as well.

"Mmm," James says with a straight face.

What? Seriously?! Well, that's... discouraging. The more time I spend with him, the more I'm realizing he really does just look at me like a little sister. It shouldn't hurt, but it does.

I look at Jake and ask, "Are you ready?"

He smiles. "Yes, let's go."

We make it down to the last step before James stops us. "Hey Jake."

Jake turns just his head to look at James. "Yeah?"

"Treat her right. If you hurt her, I'll hurt you."

My heart catches in my throat at that, but the hope I had with his statement quickly disappears. That's something a big brother would say, and that's all he will ever be.

Jake laughs and responds, "You have nothing to worry about, James."

We take our last step off the stairs, and he pulls me in closer with his arm around my waist. I pause to turn more toward him, stand on my toes, and kiss him gently. I feel his smirk on my lips before we part and continue walking toward his car. I don't bother looking back at James' reaction.

I have no idea where we are going for the lunch date, but we've been driving for about twenty minutes. I'm running out of small talk with Jake and my nerves are becoming more and more apparent as the time passes. I'm not sure why I'm feeling so nervous when I've known Jake my entire life. We've had one-on-one time many times before and never had a problem.

I take a quick glance at Jake behind the wheel, noticing he looks nervous too. I've never seen him nervous before, but I'm pretty sure that he is. He's tapping the steering wheel to the beat of the music, and he hasn't made many comments to me as he usually does.

"What does NWTF stand for?" he asks out of nowhere while still staring ahead.

I tear my eyes from my window to look at him. "What?"

He nods in front of him. "The car ahead has a NWTF sticker. Like, what are those? Ostriches? Dinosaurs?"

I look ahead to see the decal on the back of the SUV's windshield in front of us. They have quite a few decals, but there is one that says NWTF and three figures on top of it that look like... ostriches like he said? No, I don't think so. Dinosaurs definitely, but the heads are weird.

"Uh, I see what you're saying, but neither of those makes sense. I don't know, maybe... Turkeys? More a turkey than an ostrich."

He laughs. "No, I don't think that's a turkey."

I pull out my phone. "I don't know. Let me look."

I type in NWTF in google to find the answer and read it to myself first.

I smile before saying, "Yeah, those are turkeys. It stands for National Wild Turkey Federation."

"Huh? How are those turkeys? Turkeys don't have little arms sticking out of their chest," he says, trying to catch back up to the car.

I let out another laugh. "What? Little arms. I don't think it had that..."

He drives up closer to the car and thankfully we hit a red light, so we could stop and really take a look at the picture.

"Yeah, it does, see!"

I squint to see better and notice one line by each of their chests. Okay, I kind of see and that's why we thought dinosaurs. But there's only one.

After thinking about it for a moment, it hits me. "Oh! It's probably the gobble thing!"

He leans in closer to see for himself. "Oh! You're right! I can see that. Wait, gobble thing?"

We both make eye contact and start cracking up laughing. I say in between laughs, "Gobble thing… Yeah, I don't know what that's called. I wonder if I can google it."

I type in *what is the gobble thing called on a turkey?* And to my surprise, the exact phrase pops up as someone else asked it. I laugh again and so does Jake, without even knowing the answer yet.

"I typed in what is the gobble thing called on a turkey and apparently I'm not the first person to ask that question." I have to rein in my laughter before continuing. "And the person answering it started with… if you mean…" I continue laughing and then clear my throat. "Anyway, it's called a wattle."

"A wattle, really? What is it for, anyway?"

I keep reading for a minute to see and oh, of course, this is where the conversation would go with Jake. How fitting.

"It fills up with blood and it's used as a sexual display by the males," I explain.

I can see Jake smirking and know that he is holding back, saying something. It's not usually like him to hold back on jokes, but I'm not going to push him on this one because this conversation has gotten interesting fast. I shake my head and smile as I look back out the window.

CHAPTER TWELVE

· · · • · ● · ● · ● · ● · · ·

J ake and I enter a pizza restaurant and are seated by a window. I love sitting by a window in the city so I can people watch. It's one of my favorite things to do.

After giving the server our drink order, Jake smiles at me. "So, what do you think of a pizza place for a first date?"

I smile and my breath catches at remembering a conversation we had last summer.

Jake and I sat on the edge of the pool with our feet in the water. He was telling me about this new girl that he met yesterday. He was going to take her out for lunch and then invite her back to his place. I knew exactly what he was hoping to get out of that date by bringing her home. Jake doesn't date people. He buys them lunch or dinner in hopes to get in their pants afterward. I shook those thoughts out of my head. I hope the poor girl knows what she's getting into with Jake.

"So, what do you think about me taking her to that new fancy restaurant that opened a few minutes from here?" Jake asked, like he actually wanted my opinion.

"Um, the one that every meal is like a hundred dollars or more? I'm not really sure that's a great restaurant for a first date. You guys are 16, what 16-year-old wants to go to a fancy restaurant like that? And what do you plan to do afterward?" I gave him a questioning look.

He smirked. "Well, I was going to just say she should come back to my place to hang out."

I shook my head. He looked me over and asked, "Okay, then what is your ideal first date?"

I smiled and thought for a moment. What would I want for a first date? I said the first thing that came to my mind. "I would love to do something simple. Have good conversation over some cheese pizza and get some garlic knots with it. Then I'd want to walk holding hands to get some ice cream. Chocolate, of course. Then we'd eat it on the sidewalk while watching the people pass by, making jokes about them and trying to figure out their lives. I'd like to be taken home and walked up the front steps to the door. Before opening the door, he'd lean down and give me a sweet kiss and we'd text all night long."

I couldn't help but smile while I was kicking the water below me the whole time. I knew that was not Jake's ideal date, but he asked what mine would be.

Jake laughed. "Well, that is one detailed first date and way too simple. Besides, you forgot the best part."

I looked over at him. "What is the best part?"

He gave a wicked grin. "Coming back to my place to hang out."
He put finger quotations around hang out.

I rolled my eyes but didn't say anything. Yeah, I could never go
on a "date" with someone like Jake.

I'm brought back to reality when the server brings our drinks
and asks if we are ready to order. We haven't discussed what
we wanted yet, but Jake orders for us. "A large cheese pizza and
some garlic knots."

She takes our menus, which I never opened, and walks away.
I look up at Jake, smile, and say, "It's perfect."

Jake holds the door open for me as we walk out of the pizza place. He grabs my hand and walks us down the sidewalk.
"What do you say we get some ice cream?"

"I'd love that." I pull my body closer to his as we walk hand
in hand down the street.

Jake orders for me at the ice cream place as well. Chocolate ice
cream. When we sit outside at a table, I can't help but stare at
him and smile. My chest is tight with happiness and my stomach
has those little butterflies in it. It's hard to believe that I'm
sitting here on a date with Jake. Last year, I said I could never

go on a date with him, but this year here I am. A lot can change in a year.

Jake starts us off with the people watching and making up stories about their lives. Some stories we created were romantic, some tragic, and some just hilarious. I think my favorite one was of this couple that looked so wrong for each other. The guy literally looked like a clown. He had rainbow hair, a nose piercing that was red, and a lot of makeup on for a guy. The girl was beautiful with long blonde hair and the perfect body. They were clearly together, but she kept walking in front of him. So, we decided he was a crazy stalker clown who was following this chick around trying to get her to go on a date with him. We made up all sorts of crazy scenarios where they'd keep running into each other because he was stalking her.

Once we finish our ice cream, we head back to the car. We laugh most of the way home too, and the drive is much more comfortable. We aren't as nervous anymore. He parks his car in his garage and opens the door for me to get out. I can't help but wonder if he is going to try to change the ending to my perfect first date. My heart starts racing thinking about it, but not in a bad way. Honestly, if he asks me to, I think I will. Which again, is so different from how I felt last year. Jake is so easygoing and fun to be around. He's sweet, flirty, and funny. I don't even have to mention how hot he is because I know I have a lot.

When I get out of the car, he takes my hand in his. Instead of walking us toward the door of his house, he walks us out of the garage toward the Crawford's house. He isn't going to try to change the ending at all. He's fulfilling everything. He remembered every detail.

He walks me up the steps to the front door. He leans down, gives me a gentle kiss, and pulls back too soon for my liking.

"I had a really great time today, Everly," he says, looking at me like he doesn't want to let me leave.

"Me too," I say, more as a whisper than I mean to.

I don't want him to go either. I want to just tell him to take me back to his room or come into mine. Would that be wrong?

Ah, what the heck. We've already had sex. Why am I going to make us wait longer? My heart starts pounding. When I open my mouth to ask him to come in, the front door bursts open.

We look over to find Bash standing there. "Oh hey, you guys are back. Great, Jake, I have something I need your help with at home."

Jake nods as Bash walks past us, not waiting. Jake gives me a small smile and I say, "Go ahead, I'll talk to you later?"

He leans down and gives me another kiss and says, "I'll text you later."

I smile and walk into the house, closing the door behind me. I didn't notice James standing by the stairs until now. He must have walked down with Bash as he left.

"How was your date?" James asks with no emotion at all.

"Great." I continue walking up the stairs to my room without another word or glance in his direction.

When I get to my room, I close the door behind me and place my back against it, sighing. I close my eyes. What is wrong with me? Why do I react to James every time I see him? Jake was perfect today. How do I make myself stop feeling something for James?

My phone vibrates in my dress pocket, and I smile as I see who it is. This is how I stop feeling something for James.

I kick my shoes off and lay in my bed with my phone, responding to Jake.

Jake

Hey babe, I miss you.

Its only been like two minutes…

But I miss you too.

Jake

So was our date everything you dreamed of?

It was better. I can't believe you remembered everything I said. I didn't think you were listening back then.

Jake

I listen to everything you say. Always.

Back when we were talking about it did you ever think we would go on a date?

Jake

Honestly? No. I had hoped for it, but never thought it would happen.

Really? Did you ask me back then so you could get in my pants?

Jake

Maybe.

Seriously Jake?!

Jake

I'm glad we didn't back then. I wouldn't have been able to resist asking you to come back to my room, or yours.

Why did you resist today?

Jake

Because I really like you Everly. And I'd like to think I'm more mature now.

I definitely agree you are more mature. But I'm not going to lie I think you're right. I was missing the best part.

Jake

Oh yeah? What was that?

Going back to your place to hang out.

My heart races and I feel nervous as I type that last text out. I don't know what his response will be, but I'm ready for whatever it is. I can tell he's thinking about it because his text isn't coming as fast as the others.

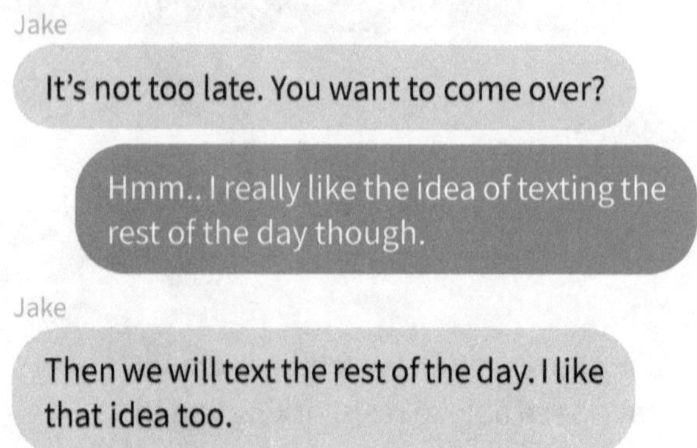

I can't believe he's not pushing it. This is not the Jake that I've known. I like flirty Jake, but I really like this Jake too.

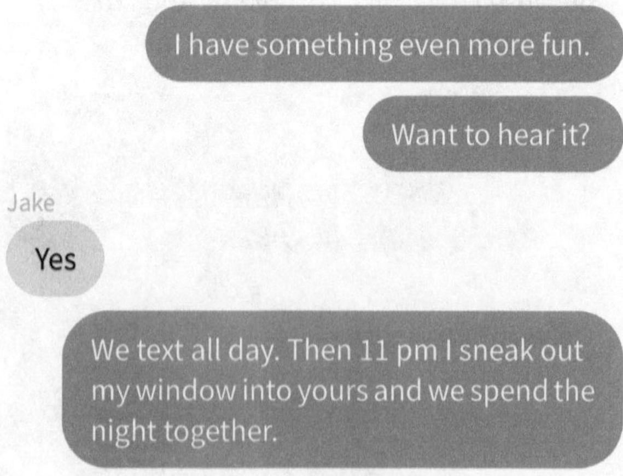

Jake

That's the best idea I've ever heard. Though, shouldn't the guy be the one to sneak over?

Hmm... Probably. But I want to.

Jake

Then I'll be ready for you at 11 pm.

Good. So what did Bash need?

Jake

He needed some tech help.

Did you help him?

Jake

I am right now and he's making fun of me for nonstop texting you.

He has no idea that we are going to be texting for the next... 6 hours.

Jake

Wow, I have to wait 6 hours? You sure I can't just come hang out when I'm done? I mean, I'm right next door...

As tempting as that is, it's more fun this way.

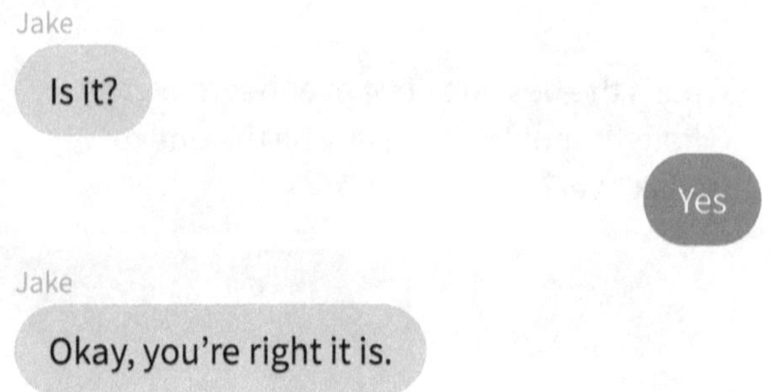

Another text message comes through and it's from Bash. I can't help but laugh.

I set my timer for five minutes and text Bash and Jake when the time is up. Jake, surprisingly, finished in the five minutes that I gave Bash. We texted for the rest of the day except at dinner. There's a no phones allowed rule at their table, which I understand. After dinner, I start getting ready for tonight. I pick out something comfy for bedtime, but sexy. I redo my makeup but keep it minimal because I hate sleeping in makeup at night. I sit on my bed and wait until the clock turns to 10:55 before attempting my escape.

I open my window and step onto the frame. I reach for the trellis and do a quick tug to ensure that it isn't going to break the moment I step on it. We've all done this before when sneaking out, but I'm pretty sure it's been a couple of years, and I was much smaller back then. I take a deep breath and a leap of faith as I swing the rest of my body on it. My weight holds, so I slowly climb down. I jump to the ground when I get to the end. I rub my arms because the plants growing on it scraped against me.

I walk close to the side of the house, hoping to avoid the cameras. I need to make my way to the back of Jake's house because his bedroom is back there. Thankfully, he has a nice balcony, and his trellis should be a little easier to climb to get there.

As I take a step toward their house, I hear a voice behind me say, "Everly, where are you going?"

I freeze, knowing that voice. I slowly turn around to find Declan staring at me with his arms crossed.

"I feel like it doesn't matter where I'm going. You're going to stop me, anyway."

He shakes his head and walks closer to me, standing directly in front of me with only a couple of inches of space between us. "Where are you going?"

I sigh. There's no point in lying. "I was going to sneak into Jake's room for the night."

"Shouldn't he be sneaking into your room?" his face is un-readable as usual.

I let out a nervous laugh. "That's what he said too."

I swear I see a smirk, but that can't be right. It's dark, so I can't see much. "I shouldn't have to tell you this, but sneaking into a boy's bedroom in the middle of the night will give him the impression that... you want to do more than sleep."

Oh! Oh no!! I've done this with my father and Mrs. Craw-ford and now my bodyguard. This is awkward, especially since he's not much older than me, I don't think. Maybe 25 or so? He's handsome too. Well, if he's going to make this awkward and now stop me from doing it, then I might as well continue making it awkward.

"I would hope so. I have a perfectly comfortable bed that I just left that I could've stayed in if I just wanted sleep tonight." I cringe because that didn't come out quite like I wanted, and that just made everything worse. Alright, I should just head back in at this point.

He's definitely smirking this time. I'm glad that it's dark because I can feel the heat in my cheeks, and I know my face is bright red.

"Alright, well I won't stop you under one condition." He let his hands fall to his side.

Did I hear him right? He's not going to stop me? "What's the condition?"

"I never want you sneaking out without telling me where you are going. If you want to sneak off to the Hale residence every night, fine, but you text me. If you are sneaking off somewhere else, I want to know where, when, and with who. Preferably in advance. If it's something that will compromise your safety, I may deny your request. But I will be accompanying you wherever you go, outside of the Hale residence," he states all this professionally.

I'm honestly surprised about this, but thankful. I only have one concern, though. "Will you be telling my dad? Or anyone else?"

He takes too long to answer, which means he's thinking it over. He probably didn't think about this. I don't want him to get in trouble for keeping information from my father, but at the same time, I don't want my father to know.

"I won't tell anyone else unless it's a safety issue, and I'll tell you when that is."

I stick my hand out. "Deal."

He shakes my hand. As I start walking toward Jake's house I say, "Thank you, Declan."

"Everly," he calls after me.

I look over my shoulder at him. "Yes?"

"Do you have protection?" he asks seriously again.

I can feel the heat rise in my cheeks again. I cannot believe I'm having this conversation again, and with my bodyguard. Also, I'm 17 years old! Do they all really think that I don't know how to have safe sex?

"Yes," I answer back. Which isn't necessarily true, but I'm sure Jake does. In fact, I guarantee he does.

"Text me when you're heading back to your room. And I expect you to be ready for self-defense training at 7 am." He walks off in the opposite direction.

I sigh as I finally make it to the back of Jake's house. His light is on in his room and so is Bash's. Their rooms are right next to each other, both with a balcony. I'm glad that I remember which is Jake's because that would be embarrassing to enter Bash's.

I begin the climb, which is much harder than climbing down. They also have a lot more prickly plants growing on their trellis. Once I reach the top, I swing my leg over the railing to Jake's balcony and I swear I pull a muscle. Why do they make this look so easy in the movies?! I should have let Jake come over. Now I have little scratches all over my body, my hair is probably a mess, and I'm out of breath.

Before I can reach his door, Jake opens it and pulls me inside.

"You're late. I thought you were caught." He pulls me into him and wraps his arms around me.

I look up into his face and smile. "I was caught."

"What?"

"One of my security guards, Declan, caught me outside." I make a grunting noise of frustration.

"How were you able to come, then?" He lowers his eyebrows.

"Well, he told me he wasn't going to stop me as long as I text him when I'm going to be sneaking out. He also said he wouldn't tell anyone." I lean into his chest, enjoying his warmth.

He laughs. "Wow, what a cool security guard."

I laugh too. "Yes, so cool that he had a sex talk with me before I came too. He wanted to make me aware that you would be wanting to do more than sleep."

He pulls back a little to look at my face. "And what did you tell him?"

I smirk. "I said I would hope so."

"No, you didn't."

"Yes, I actually did."

We both laugh until he leans down to kiss me. This kiss is nothing like the ones he gave me this afternoon. Those were gentle and sweet. This is hungry. He leads me to his bed without breaking our kiss. He lays me back and lies on top of me, straddling me. I can feel how much he wants me already, as it is pressing against me. My silky shorts and panties are the only thing keeping him from sliding into me.

We continue to make out on his bed for at least thirty minutes. I'm grinding against him, which makes his length press against exactly where I want him. This has been going on too long. I need him. I pull his shirt off and run my hands down his chest and over his perfect abs.

Jake pulls off me and cups my face with his hands. "We don't have to go any further. I enjoy kissing you and will love holding you all night as we sleep."

Yeah, that's not going to happen. I need him now. "That's so sweet Jake, but please fuck me now."

He groans and his face changes into full desire. "As you wish."

He sits me up to pull my top off and then immediately pulls my pajama shorts and panties off at the same time. I lay completely naked below him and he sits back to admire me. He's the only one that has ever looked at me like that before, naked.

"You're so hot Everly." His voice is raspy.

I blush even more. He doesn't waste any more time as he kisses me again and slowly trails kisses down my neck, taking a moment to suck on it. He sucks hard, and it feels so good that I let out a moan. I try not to think about how that's going to leave a mark. He cups my breasts, and he captures my mouth again. Since the last time we had sex showed me how good it can feel, I am not going to be patient tonight.

I pull down his boxers and he lifts his legs to slide them off. I'm hoping he takes the hint.

"You're impatient tonight," he says as a statement, not a question.

"I have been thinking about this since we pulled into your garage from the date, so yes, I'm impatient."

He kisses my neck again. "Then I won't make you wait any longer."

He leans over to his end table and pulls open the drawer. He pulls out a condom, rips the foil, and slides it on. He doesn't wait any longer as he slides into me slowly. He angles my body so he can push in deeper, and he thrusts in and out, getting increasingly faster. I close my eyes with how amazing it feels. Mmm, it feels so good. James...

My eyes pop open as I watch Jake lose himself in me. My heart stops for a moment as I thought of James. Did I really just think of his name? Oh my God, what if I were to call his name out instead of Jake? What is wrong with me?

I shake those thoughts out of my head and Jake's breathing comes even faster. I know he's close. I concentrate on him and his messy hair, his amazing abs. I place my hand on his chest and let it drift lower, feeling him. The pleasure quickly returns as I'm brought close to the edge.

"Everly... It feels so good. I'm going to come." He moans.

"So good," I get out through breaths.

It only takes a few more thrusts before we're both loudly moaning and screaming each other's name as we find our release. He pulls out of me and tosses the condom into the trash next to his bed. He rolls off me and snuggles in beside me, holding me.

We lay like that for a few minutes until both of our phones buzz at the same time. I grab mine and he grabs his. After reading the group text to Jake and me from Bash, we both look at each other with wide eyes and start laughing a little too loud.

Bash

> You know these walls are not sound-proof. Next time give me some warning to put on some music.

Jake

> Sorry Bro

> Who says there will be a next time?

Jake playfully smacks my shoulder and then rolls on top of me again. He brings his face inches from mine and asks, "So no next time, huh?" He kisses me and starts trailing kisses down my neck again. "Are you sure about that?"

He continues to trail his kisses over my breasts, down my breasts, and to my belly button. A moan escapes.

He heard that and then lifts his head up to smile at me. While it would be fun to go again, I need a moment after what I was thinking while doing this moments ago.

"Since we were apparently so loud, I should go wash up and put my clothes back on just in case," I say while gently pushing him off while I climb out of bed.

He looks a little disappointed, but he says nothing as I go into the bathroom with my clothes that I gathered from the floor. I quickly clean myself up, put on my clothes, and go back out. Jake only has on his boxers as he is laying in the bed waiting for me to return. I slide in next to him and let him wrap his arms around me. I'm exhausted, and I know I can easily fall asleep in his arms.

"I love being in your bed with your arms wrapped around me. I can get used to this," I say, while snuggling even closer to him.

"Me too," he says, but he sounds tired.

We are silent for a while, and I'm almost drifting off to sleep when he says, "I have a question for you, and I don't want you to get mad or offended."

"Okay," I say, knowing that I probably will get mad or offended because that's usually what happens when someone says something like that.

"Do you still sleep in James' bed at night?"

Ugh, why is he asking about James? Did I say his name out loud?! No, I know I didn't.

"No. The last time was when you guys saw us, and I was just really upset about... well, you know. I don't intend to do that again, especially while we are together." I hope that answers his question, and he understands I mean it.

"Good." He lets out a breath that I didn't know he was holding.

"Jake, are you jealous of James?" I ask, knowing the answer already.

"Not really. I would be if you were still sharing his bed, though," he says seriously, this time.

I look up at him and kiss him. "The only bed that I want to be sharing is yours."

We cuddle in close again, get under the blankets, and both fall asleep quickly.

Chapter Thirteen

I wake to the sound of my phone buzzing. I reach out toward the end table and pick it up to see Declan's name flash across the screen. My heart pounds as I answer it. "Hello?"

"You're late for your training," he states calmly.

"Crap! I'll be right there." I hang up the phone and toss Jake's arm off me. How is he still sleeping?

I sit up and poke him to wake him up. He still doesn't move. Seriously? I wish I could be that deep of a sleeper. I get out of bed and go over to the other side where he is facing. Leaning down, I place a kiss on his lips. This time, he starts to stir. I continue kissing him and rubbing my hands through his messy hair until he wakes up.

I pull away and say, "Good morning, I have to go."

He grabs my waist and pulls me down onto the bed next to him. "Can't you stay a little longer?"

I laugh. "No, Declan just called me and I'm late for training. I can't believe I forgot to set my alarm. I have to go or he's never going to let me sneak out again."

He groans as he releases me. "Alright, I guess I'll see you later for the party."

Oh wow. I completely forgot about the party tonight. One of James's close friends is throwing a party at his house. I have no idea what it's for, but I'm kind of excited to go. I never liked parties before, but I also never had an actual boyfriend at one either.

Jake pokes me. "What were you thinking about?"

I must have really been spacing out thinking about that for him to notice. "That I'm excited to spend tonight with you at the party."

He smiles. "Me too."

"Okay, I really have to go before I get into trouble." I get off the bed and open the doors to the balcony. I blow a kiss to Jake before I step over the railing and climb my way down. It's much easier to do in the daylight.

I run back toward my house and debate if I should climb back up my window or go in the front door. It wouldn't look suspicious being that it is morning time, and I could have just gone out for a walk, but I am in my pajamas and there wouldn't be any video footage showing that I went out in the first place. I sigh as I climb back up to my window that I kept cracked to make it easy to open.

After I pull myself inside, I'm panting, and my muscles ache. I am so out of shape. I go to my closet and quickly put on a sports bra and some capri yoga pants. As I walk out of my room down toward the gym, I put my hair up in a ponytail. Declan is waiting for me as I enter the room.

"You're twenty-three minutes late," he states matter-of-fact-ly.

I sigh. "I'm so sorry. I forgot to set my alarm last night."

He stands up and walks over to me. He's looking me up and down, and I can't make sense of the expression on his face. Is he trying to figure out how to make me pay for being late? Is he mad at me? I've never seen him angry or have much emotion at all on his face, so it's hard to tell what he's thinking.

"This is the only time I'll let it slide. We are going to train promptly at seven every morning unless I state otherwise. If you are late, then I'll have to find a suitable punishment."

He smirked. Smirked! What did he mean by a suitable pun-ishment? A shiver goes down my spine and I have a feeling I don't want to find out what that means.

"I promise I won't be late again. I already have my alarm set for every day."

"Good. Now let's get started with the warmup." He walks over toward the mat, and I follow.

After ten minutes of warming up and stretching, I'm already feeling sore and sweating. Who knew that stretching could do that to you? I guess that's what happens when you're lazy and do nothing.

We concentrated on only a couple of items during this train-ing. Balance was the first, which apparently, I lacked. I know I'm clumsy, but I could barely stand on one leg for more than ten seconds without falling over. Then we worked on strengthening my muscles by doing simple planks and pushups. Once again, I lacked in this area too. It was quite embarrassing that I could barely do a push up with my knees on the floor. Finally, we worked on some blocking skills. By the end of it, I was completely drained and drenched in sweat while he barely broke a sweat.

After cooling down, I lay flat on my back, never wanting to get up or move again. Declan leans over me and holds out his hand. I really don't want to move, but I don't want to be rude and not take it. I take his hand, and he helps me up as my body protests.

"You did good today, Kid," he says.

I laugh. "I wouldn't say that was good. It's honestly embarrassing."

He looks at me seriously, studying me. "You keep saying it's embarrassing, but it's not. If anything, I admire you for having the motivation to do this and to stick with it. Not many kids your age would even consider it and when it gets hard, they would quit."

I smile. "Thank you for saying that. I just... I don't want to be weak anymore. I want to be able to protect myself. I never want to be a victim again."

I've been thinking about the real reason I've wanted to do all this, and I really believe it has to do with Adam. Yeah, I want to look good, but if I could have protected myself against him, then last year might never have happened. I don't want to be weak anymore.

"What do you mean again?" he asks. Crap, I didn't mean to actually say that aloud.

"Huh?" I ask, playing dumb, hoping that it will work.

"You said you never want to be a victim again. What happened?" he repeats my exact words. How do I get out of this?

"Oh, I didn't mean again. Just that I never want to be a victim." I look to the side before looking back at him. Crap again. I know that is my tell for a lie. Maybe he hasn't figured that out yet. I'm going to be spending a lot of time with him. I need to be careful what I say and do.

"You're lying," he states.

"Why do you say that?" Again, what is wrong with me?! I should've just lied again and said, no I'm not, but no. Now I'm acting guilty, ugh. I've already let this slip to James, which in return slipped to the other three. Being away from Adam has made it easier to talk about it and that's not a good thing. He's still a threat, and I need to remember that.

He steps closer to me, towering over me, and looking down at me. "Tell me what happened."

"I... can't." I try this route because he's clearly not going to let it go easily.

"You can. I'm your security guard, and I need you to trust me. I need to trust you as well. Tell me what happened," he says sterner this time. I can tell he is good at getting information from people. I'm fairly certain I'm about to crack.

"You don't understand. I can't tell you. If he found out…" I pause for a moment. Why is Declan so hard to lie to? "People I care about would get hurt."

He puts his hand on my shoulder. "Will you tell me if I promise not to tell anyone?"

I look him in the eyes and can tell he is serious. That he really thinks he won't tell anyone, but I know better. He is my guard. He will tell my father, and most likely, the other guard, Barry. I can't risk it as much as it would be nice having them look out for me when it comes to Adam.

"I don't think you can make that promise. I think you would have to tell," I say.

His eyes dart back and forth between mine before saying, "I need you to trust me. I promised I wouldn't tell anyone, so I won't. I'm already letting you sneak out, which could cost me my job, so I need you to trust me."

I don't know. I don't know anymore. Should I continue to keep this secret, or should I finally seek help? I need a moment to think. "Can we sit down?"

He nods and we walk over toward the bench at the side of the room. When I sit, I let out a long sigh. I don't know what to do because I want to tell him. I really do. On the other hand, I'm afraid of what would happen if others found out. Adam could seriously hurt my dad, and he could hurt my friends. At the same time, he hurt me for an entire year because I didn't get help. I don't know what to do and aren't we supposed to go to adults when we don't know what to do? Would it really be on me if something happened? Not necessarily, but it wouldn't stop me from feeling that way. I'm so confused.

Declan puts his hand on my knee, which I didn't realize I was bouncing. "Everly, please tell me. My job is to protect you, and I can't do that if you don't tell me."

My emotions are everywhere, and I feel my eyes burning. Silent tears start streaming down my face, and I can't believe I'm still crying over this. When will I get over it? I'm so weak. Physically and mentally. It's frustrating.

"Someone raped me." Those are the only three words I can get out without sobbing. Those are the only three words that I really need to speak for him to understand what happened. I don't need to tell him it was Adam, right?

His demeanor completely changes. He gets tense and his face actually shows emotion. Which emotion, I don't know because I don't know him well enough. If I had to guess, maybe it's pity?

"When?" he asks.

"All last year, my junior year of high school," I say, trying to rein in my emotions. I feel like the older I get, the harder that is for some reason.

"The entire year? It happened more than once?" he asks, like he's just trying to get his facts straight.

I can't speak, so I just nod.

"Who was it?"

I shake my head. "I can't tell you."

Declan gets off the bench and kneels in front of me. He lifts my chin to look directly at his face. "Everly, I need you to trust me. Trust me."

I nod, take a deep breath, and say, "Adam."

His eyes grow wide for a moment, and he is... angry. So angry. He stands up and paces the room for a moment, rubbing the side of his face. I can see the tension in his body and feel the anger coming off him. I shouldn't have told him. What was I thinking?

"I'm sorry," I say quietly, but loud enough for him to hear me.

He turns back toward me and asks, "What are you sorry for?"

"Everything. I'm sorry that I let it happen. I'm sorry I didn't get help. I'm sorry that I told you. I'm just sorry. It's all my fault. But you can't tell anyone like you promised. You don't understand how powerful his family is. He threatened if I ever told anyone that he would hurt my dad. And now he extended that to my friends here. I can't let anyone get hurt because of me."

He kneels in front of me again and says, "Everly, I never want to hear you apologize for this again. It's not your fault. But I need you to tell me. Do you have any contact with him still?"

"No, I blocked him. But when he came here, he told me I needed to unblock him. I didn't. I'm afraid he might do something, I don't know. I was hoping moving here would be enough to end what was happening." I'm rambling, so I stop talking.

"If he contacts you, I need you to tell me immediately, okay?" I nod and he continues, "Everly, I'm so sorry I let this happen. Fuck." He looks away from me, and I can see the anger rising again. "Don't ever keep something like this from me again, do you understand? I can't believe I didn't see it. How many times did it happen?"

I look away. He's blaming himself. He doesn't need to know this. I know he just wants this information so he can punish himself for letting me get hurt, but it wasn't his fault. There was no way he could have known. "It doesn't matter."

He shakes his head. "It matters to me. How many times?"

I sigh. I really don't have the energy for this anymore. "I don't know, a lot. Like once a week. Sometimes more."

Declan looks so upset. I don't want to hurt him. This is why I should've kept my mouth shut. What is wrong with me?

"It's okay. It wasn't that bad, and I got used to it. Honestly, looking back, I deserved..."

Declan cuts me off. "Fuck Everly. Don't you ever say you deserved that. No one deserves that. Damn it." He leans in and hugs me tight. It takes me a second, but I hug him back, leaning into him and feel... comfort and relief. It's just like when I told James. It's nice not having to bear this alone anymore. Is it selfish of me to think that way? Because I've clearly hurt both of them by sharing this information, but I'm relieved. Maybe I am a terrible person.

He lets go of our hug and leans back, looking at me again. "I need to ask you this, and I need you to tell me the truth. Okay?"

I nod.

"Is Jake forcing you to…"

I interrupt him this time. "No! Dear God, no. I had to beg him the first time because I wanted to experience it for real. I needed to forget…" I clear my throat. I'm giving up way too much information. "He asked multiple times to make sure it's what I wanted, and no, he didn't know about what Adam did. I would not have snuck over to Jake's house otherwise. I avoided Adam as much as I could. We never went on dates, and I only saw him at school and when he forced me to see him. It's real with Jake, and it's my choice."

He nods, but he doesn't look any happier. I don't know why I went on that long tangent about it. I guess I wanted to make sure I convinced him that what I have with Jake is nothing like Adam.

"Thank you for telling me and trusting me with this. I want you to be able to tell me anything. I'm going to be around for a long time, so we need to trust each other, okay?" he asks as his anger fades, or he is just better at hiding it.

"Okay. Thank you for being here for me and for everything. For being willing to train me and let me sneak out. Thank you for being my friend." I smile up at him.

When I'm leaving the room, I notice he stays behind and walks over to the punching bag. The moment I'm out of the room, I hear him punching it. He must be taking his anger out on it, and I feel bad that I angered him and hurt him. I think he's right, though. I need to trust him, and he needs to be able to trust me. I really like him as my guard, and I don't want anything to happen to him.

I make my way upstairs to shower and get ready for the rest of the day. As I'm showering, I can't help but think about Jake and tonight. Going to a party with my boyfriend is exactly what teenagers do. It'll be nice to feel normal for once. I turn off the shower and search for the sexiest party outfit that I can find in my closet.

Chapter Fourteen

I t's too early to get ready for tonight, so I put on some comfy shorts and a tank top for now. I grab my phone off my desk and look at it to find a message from James.

James

> I'm going to Dillon's house to help set up for the party. His sister is in your grade at the same school. Do you want to come with me?

Is James trying to set me up with a friend for the new school year? That's what it sounds like, and it sounds pitiful, but the thought behind it is sweet.

> Sure! What time are you leaving?

James

In thirty minutes

Are you coming back before the party?

James

Probably not, but if you need to come back I can bring you.

That's okay. I'll bring my stuff so I can get ready there. Meet you downstairs shortly.

I grab a bag and throw my dress, makeup supplies, and shoes in it. I hope his sister is nice and not some stuck up girl. Pretty much everyone in my last school was like that. It would be nice to have an actual friend, that's a girl, in school. I love the boys, but I'm really needing some girl time.

I meet James downstairs and we head outside into his car. I text Jake the plans and he agrees to meet me there shortly before the party begins. I also text Declan, letting him know. Since I have James with me, I don't need a guard to come, but after everything, I feel like I should let him know where I'm going to be.

James and I don't say anything to each other as we drive to his friend's house. I feel like things have been a little awkward since Jake and I have made it official and gone on a date. Maybe I'm imagining things. Regardless, the silence between us is killing me.

"So, how do you know Dillon?" I ask.

"He's a buddy from college," he replies.

"That's good. What is his sister like?" I ask, hoping that he knows a little about her.

"She's nice. Her name is Ashley. I think you two will get along," he says in a hopeful tone.

The silence continues, and it's deafening. James and I have always been able to fill it up with conversation, but something is different. I stare out the window, tapping my fingers against my leg, trying to think of something to talk about.

"How was your date with Jake yesterday?" he asks out of nowhere.

"It was actually really great. He was sweet. Apparently, he remembered from a year ago that I told him what I'd want my first date to be like and he did it," I say while keeping a close eye on him to see his reaction.

Of course he doesn't react. "Well, that's nice. I never thought anyone would describe Jake as sweet."

I laugh. "Neither did I."

Thankfully, we get to Dillon's house shortly after that conversation. His house is big, but not as big as the Crawford's house. The outside is made of brick and looks like it's an older house, but the inside is modern, like they recently remodeled everything. It's beautiful. Dillon meets us downstairs and gives

James a pat on the back with a side hug. "Hey man, thanks for coming."

James smiles and says, "No problem." He leans toward me, putting his hand on my lower back, introducing me, "This is Everly."

I smile at Dillon and try to ignore the feeling of James putting his hand on my back that arises in me.

"Nice to meet you." I hold out my hand and Dillon shakes it.

He smiles. "My sister is upstairs in her room. She said to send you up when you got here. Second door on the right."

I nod and head for the stairs. I can feel my chest tighten as I'm getting nervous with every step I take. I hate meeting new people, and I'm stuck here for the next few hours until the party begins. I can get along with pretty much anyone, but it doesn't mean I enjoy it.

I walk up the steps and count the doors. One... Two... The door is closed. I knock and someone answers, "Come in!"

I open the door and step inside. I take a quick glance around and it's nothing like what I'm expecting. Not that I was expecting much, but this never crossed my mind. Posters hang on the walls of bands and actors. Really hot, shirtless actors. I don't watch tv often, so I'm not sure who they are. There are books basically in every corner of the room, not just on the bookshelf. Her desk, which she's sitting at, is messy with papers and more books.

She turns around when I walk into the room, and I close the door behind me.

She smiles. "Hey! I'm Ashley." She stands up and walks toward me, putting her hand out.

I shake her hand. "I'm Everly. Thanks for having me over. I don't mean to interrupt if you're busy." I nod toward her desk where she was just working.

"Oh no, not busy at all. So, you're going to be attending Terion High School this year? As a senior, right?" she asks, as if she doesn't already know that.

I look her over for a moment before answering. She looks nice enough and doesn't have that stuck up attitude. She seems down to earth, and she's pretty. She has thick, dark brown hair that looks like it's naturally wavy. It goes down to the middle of her back. She has beautiful green eyes that are cat-like. She barely has on any makeup, and I'm not sure if it is because she is waiting to get ready for the party, or if she likes to not wear much makeup. Regardless, she doesn't need it.

"Yeah, you're a senior too, right?" I finally respond.

She nods. "Do you want to sit out by the pool?"

"Sure." I step to the side of the door to let her lead the way.

We walk downstairs toward where I came in at. We turn in the opposite direction from the front door, which leads us toward a huge living area and kitchen. The whole back side of the house is two stories tall, with large windows. It's beautiful and lets in the natural light. We step out the back door by the kitchen, which leads to a sunroom filled with more windows. Then we make our way out toward the large pool.

We slip off our sandals and stick our feet in the water. Feeling the sun beat down on my bare skin feels amazing, as does the coolness of the water against my feet.

I look toward Ashley, who was leaning back on her hands, slowly kicking her legs in the water. "So, tell me about the high school."

She looks over at me with a strange expression. "It's an expensive private school with kids who think they are invincible and own the world."

I laugh a little too hard at that. With the way she described it, I can tell she is nothing like them. I can see us being friends.

"That sounds exactly like my old school, so nothing new. It's only one year though, so I intend to stay invisible," I tell her.

She scrunches her nose. "I hate to say it, but you're the new kid. It's going to be impossible to stay invisible. Especially since you're living with the Crawfords."

I furrow my eyebrows at her. "Why does that matter?"

She sighs. "Alright, you want complete honesty?" She pauses like she is waiting for my response. I nod so she continues, "The Crawfords are well known here, so everyone is going to want to know the guest staying with them. Ben's ex-girlfriend is also super jealous, so I have a feeling she will not be happy with you being there. They are good friends with the Hales too, which you clearly know. Jake has slept with a lot of girls at that school who will be jealous of your friendship as well."

I must have made a face because she pauses, looking at me like she's trying to figure something out. Did I really just give away with my face that I like Jake? I mean, who wouldn't feel jealous of someone telling them their boyfriend slept with a lot of girls at the school?

"Well, Jake is currently my boyfriend, so it sounds like I'm going to have a lot of enemies," I say with an unsure laugh.

Her eyes go wide. "I'm so sorry. I shouldn't have said that like I did. I mean, I don't think he's slept with THAT many girls..."

I interrupt her. "No, it's okay. I knew that he was a man whore before getting into this relationship."

We both laugh and continue swirling our legs and feet in the water. This feels good. Not just being outside like this, but being with another girl who I can see becoming a friend. I've been stuck with boys for the past few weeks and while they are great, there's nothing like being able to talk to a girl.

"So how long have you been dating Jake?" she asks.

"A couple days. We just went on our first date yesterday and it was really sweet. If you would have told me last year that I would have gone on a date with Jake, I would've laughed in your face." I smile, thinking about our date yesterday.

She laughs. "Yeah, honestly, he doesn't seem like the boyfriend type. He must really like you if he agreed to be your boyfriend."

I shrug my shoulders. "Yeah, I'm pretty amazing."

She rolls her eyes. "I can see that. So, what's it like living with the Crawfords? Ben and Jake are the two most popular in school right now. I'm pretty sure any girl would kill to be in your situation."

I raise my eyebrows at her and joke, "Would you kill to be in my position?"

"Absolutely… not. Honestly, I'm into older guys. Boys, our age are too immature."

I smirk. "I honestly can agree with you there, but some are really hot and it's nice to have fun."

Her smile widens. "So, by fun, do you mean you and Jake…?"

I laugh again. "Apparently, he has slept with half the school. What do you think?"

"I'll take that as a yes."

I nod. "Anyway, to answer your question, it's a lot of fun living with the Crawfords. I've spent every summer there almost my whole life and Mrs. Crawford is like a mother to me. The boys are… boys. We have fun, but honestly, being here with you is even better. I haven't had girl time in a long time."

"Well, I'm glad I can help. Let's head back inside before we burn and get ready for the party tonight. We'll also exchange phone numbers. Let's hang out more this summer. I have a friend, Lauren, who moved here in the middle of last year. I moved here at the beginning of last year, so we both know what it's like going into that school as a new girl," she says, standing up and not bothering to put her sandals back on. I follow her.

Before getting ready, we sneak around to spy on James and Dillon. They are getting things ready for the party, mainly the alcohol. They mostly have snack foods, so it looks like that was quick and easy for them to put out.

James seems so at ease when he's hanging out with Dillon. He's laughing and making jokes. Watching him like that does something to my heart and I try to push the feelings down, but I can't help but smile at him. After a few more minutes, I have to pull my eyes away from him because this isn't helping with my feelings for him, clearly. I look over toward Ashley to find her watching me instead of them. She nods for us to head back to her room, and I follow.

After she closes the door and locks it, she says, "You have feelings for James."

It was a statement, not a question. How does she know?! "Why do you say that?"

"I saw the way you were looking at him. You were so happy seeing him happy. So, you do like him?" she asks this time.

I sigh. "He's like my big brother. I'm his little sister that he looks out for."

She frowns. "That didn't answer my question."

I roll my eyes. "Fine. Yes, I've had feelings for him for a while. He doesn't feel the same way about me, so I'm trying to move on."

"By getting in bed with Jake?" she asks, but it doesn't sound like she's being judgy.

"There's a lot that led me to Jake. I really like Jake."

She nods like she understands. "Well, maybe one day you can tell me everything, but I don't blame you. You're young, have fun. I can't wait to see you and Jake together tonight."

I want to change the topic. "So, what about you? Do you have a boyfriend?"

She laughs. "No. I'm not the type of girl boys at our school are interested in."

"I highly doubt that. They must all be blind then," I say, meaning every word. She's beautiful. There's no way not a single boy is looking at her.

She shrugs her shoulders and moves toward her closet. "Alright, let's get ready for tonight. Do you have a dress?"

I nod, pull my dress out of my bag, and get ready for the party.

We wait until the party gets started before we go downstairs. We both have similar dresses, which means we have similar tastes. Short, fitted, spaghetti strapped dresses. My dress is black and sparkly, just the way I like it. Her dress is green, like her eyes. I don't know how she doesn't have a boyfriend, but I can guarantee she's going to be hit on tonight.

The music is already going, but it isn't so loud that you can't talk over it. People are already making out on the couch and in corners. Drinks are everywhere, which isn't very smart. Rich people equal drugs. It's so easy to drug a drink.

Ashley pours us both some punch. I take one sip to realize it's spiked with alcohol. Or should I say, the alcohol was spiked with punch. "So, do you think there's any punch in this alcohol?"

Ashley laughs. "That makes for the best punch. Look, don't drink more than two unless you want to be throwing up in the morning."

I'm thankful for the warning. I don't want to be doing that, especially since I'll be training with Declan at 7 am. I have a feeling he won't be taking it easy on me. Plus, I really don't feel like getting drunk after the last time.

My phone buzzes in my hand to see Jake texted me.

Jake

Where are you?

By the alcohol spiked with punch.

Two seconds later, Jake shows up beside me. He wraps his arm around my waist and kisses my temple. It feels good being in his arms and that was such a sweet gesture.

"Hey Jake, this is my new friend Ashley," I say, gesturing toward her.

"Ah, yes. I believe we had history together last year." He nods to her.

"We did. I hate history, but you always made it entertaining."

They both laugh like they are remembering the same thing. I smile, hoping that I will have a class with each of them. It would be nice having someone I know in my classes and, by the sounds of it, Jake would make a class interesting.

"I'm going to find my friend Lauren. We'll catch up in a bit?" She waits for me to respond.

I nod and she walks off. I look over at Jake and ask, "So, how was your day?"

He frowns. "Horrible."

"Why?" I ask, hating to hear he didn't have a good day.

"Because you weren't part of it. You left me early this morning, and all I wanted was for you to stay in my bed."

I laugh. "Jake, there's more to a relationship than making out and sex."

He gasps. "What?! What more can there be?"

I slap him on the arm and down the rest of my drink. I don't want to get drunk, but I would like to get tipsy. I pour myself one more cup and decide I will take Ashley's advice and stop at two.

Jake leads me outside and he sits in a chair facing the yard where a few Cornhole games are being played. I go to sit in the chair next to him, but he grabs my waist and pulls me onto his lap.

"I need you on my lap to cover what that dress is doing to me," he whispers.

I gasp when I realize what he's talking about. I can feel his erection below me, pressing into my thigh. Jake starts kissing behind my ear and down my neck. Goosebumps erupt all over my body at how good it feels.

He stops on a sensitive part of my neck and sucks. "I see I left my mark last night and you're trying to cover it up. Why are you hiding it?"

I shiver as he continues to suck and lick at the spot where he left the hickey. I did cover it up with makeup because I didn't want anyone to see it. As good as this feels, I quickly remember there are a lot of people around us. I don't mind public displays of affection, but I'm only willing to go so far. I pull away and place a quick kiss on his lips.

"Jake, I don't want to do this here," I whisper.

He smirks. "No one's paying attention to us, but if you prefer, we can go find a room."

I smack his arm again. "I'm not hooking up with you at a party in my new friend's house!"

He laughs. "You're no fun. I told Ben I would catch up with him and some buddies. You okay if I do that real fast? I'll come find you in a bit."

"Yeah, that's fine. I'll go find Ashley," I say, a little disappointed.

I get up and we walk back inside together, but he isn't touching me anymore. He walks off toward the stairs and I lose sight of him with so many people around. I begin my search for Ashley, who I find talking with a girl in the corner of the kitchen.

"Hey!" I say over the music.

"Hey! Everly, this is Lauren," Ashley says, introducing us.

"It's nice to meet you, Lauren." I shake her hand, and she repeats it back.

Lauren has short, dirty blond hair and hazel eyes. She's thin and tiny. She can't be more than four foot ten. She's cute.

We spend a little time just chatting in the corner, eating food, and finishing our drinks. I finish the second one, and I almost regret drinking the whole thing. How much alcohol was really in that? I grab some water and down it in hopes it will counteract it.

Lauren seems nice, but more reserved than Ashley. It doesn't seem like this is her scene. She's kind of acting like she shouldn't be here, or she will get grounded. I wonder how strict her parents are because most rich kids don't have strict parents at all. It's not that they don't care, well some of them don't, but they are just never around to know what their child is really doing.

"Do you want to go upstairs and watch the guys play pool?" Ashley asks.

Lauren and I both nod in response as we follow her upstairs to the poolroom.

It's a large room with a pool table, two dart boards, a couple of couches, chairs, and a large television. It looks like it's a gathering place during football games and stuff. We sit down on the couch and watch the guys play. Jake is in the corner playing darts with Ben and another guy. James is playing pool with Dillon, Bash, and someone else. There are a couple of girls stationed in every corner of the room ogling all the guys. Maybe that's what it looks like we are doing.

I watch Jake for a moment, and he clearly knows how to play darts. It's hot watching him. My attention gets drawn away from him as I hear James and Bash laughing. James is holding his pool stick close to him, leaning on it. He's talking with Bash as the other guy is taking a turn. I can't help but smile, watching him smile. James has been pretty serious this summer, so seeing him have fun is a treat when it happens.

Right before James is about to take his turn, we make eye contact. His face is straight in concentration until he notices me. He smiles and doesn't take his eyes off me until he leans down to take his shot. It's a perfect shot where the ball goes into the hole. He moves around the table with his back facing mine as I watch him lean over. He has on tight jeans and a fitted button-down shirt. His butt looks amazing bending over like that and his muscles are showing through his shirt. I feel my heart start pounding. When he stands up, he turns his head behind him to see if I'm still looking. Spoiler alert, I am.

I jump as someone whispers in my ear, leaning in from behind me. "Are you checking out my brother?"

I turn my head to find Ben leaning over the back of the couch, his face inches from mine. "What? No..." That's a lie.

He laughs. "I don't know. You have some drool right here." He wipes the corner of my mouth with his thumb.

I go to say something but he has Ashley scoot over so he can jump the back of the couch to sit beside me. He leans forward, looking at me and says something, but I can't hear him. My focus is no longer on James or Ben, it's on Jake, who is in the corner leaning toward a girl a little too close for my comfort and smiling at her.

Ben sits back up, blocking my view, and says, "So?"

"So what?" I ask, trying to lean to look around him, but he follows my moves, continuing to block my view from Jake. Is he doing it on purpose?

"So, do you want to go downstairs and get something to drink with me?" he asks.

I hear Jake and the girl laugh. I stand up and so does Ben. He grabs my arm and says, "Let's go downstairs."

I nod and let him lead me toward the door. My chest aches thinking about what's happening. I take a glance back before leaving the room to see Jake whispering in her ear now. I never saw him look my way. Does he know that I'm here? Even if he didn't, why is he flirting with another girl when we came to this party together? When he's supposed to be my boyfriend?

Ben links his arm with mine as we walk downstairs, and he lets go, only to pour us each some punch. I know I shouldn't take it, but I do and gulp a good bit down.

"What's going on, Ben?" I ask, glaring at him.

His eyebrows furrow, and he looks like he's pitying me. Really? "Look, Jake already had a good bit to drink before we came here and then had some more. He gets flirty when he drinks. It doesn't mean anything."

"So, you took me away, so I didn't have to watch him flirt with another girl? Why not stop your friend instead?" I ask, a little more accusatory than I mean to be.

He sighs. "Everly, I'm sorry. I did try, he just... he's Jake. You know how he is."

I do know how he is. I mean, really, what was I thinking would happen when I started dating Jake? I mean, I thought he would look at me and only me. That I'm his girlfriend and he wouldn't want anyone else. My stomach twists in knots.

I sigh and walk outside, back to where Jake and I were sitting earlier. I sit down in the same chair and will the tears forming in my eyes not to fall. I'm being a hypocrite, right? I was staring at James. I have feelings for James. There is a difference, though. I'm not flirting with him openly in front of Jake, or at all. I'm not going to take him to bed. Oh my God, is he going to take that girl to a room? I turned him down, so he found someone else? My heart pounds faster, and I gulp the rest of my drink down.

Ben sits beside me. "Hey, what are you thinking?"

I look at him and I feel one of the tears slip down my cheek. "Is he going to sleep with her?"

His eyes widen. "No! No… I don't think he would do that to you. He just has a flirty personality, that's all."

He looks away for a moment and I don't believe him. "You don't believe that, do you?" I ask.

He sighs. "Look, he's never had a girlfriend before, so I don't know what's going on in his mind. But you're right. I'm going to go back up there so he doesn't do something stupid. You good?"

I nod, and he leaves. So, what do I do now? Do I just sit here and wait for him to come back down? Should I go find Ashley and Lauren again? I don't have to sit long and decide because

Ashley and Lauren come outside and directly toward me like they are looking for me.

"Hey, are you okay?" Ashley asks as she stands in front of me.

"Yeah, I'm fine," I say, but I know it's not convincing.

Ashley and Lauren exchange looks. A look that I don't need to know them to know what it means. They are debating telling me something.

"What is it?" I ask.

Ashley kneels in front of me and puts her hand on my lap. "Jake left the room with that girl, but I didn't see where they went..."

My heart stops for a moment and then I want to scream. Seriously?! We've been dating for a couple of days, and I said no once and he's already off with another girl? I grab my phone and text Jake, asking where he is. There's no response.

"Do you want to go hang out in my room for a bit?" Ashley asks.

"No, I'm going to go find Jake," I say, standing up.

I search around the living room and kitchen but don't find them. I go back upstairs and don't find them in the hallway. Those stupid tears are now unwillingly falling from my eyes, and I can't stop them. I go back to the pool table room and scan it, not finding him or the girl there either. I must have opened the door a little too hard because all eyes are on me. Crap.

I run out of the room and stop in the hallway to take a few breaths to compose myself. I also feel very lightheaded and a bit dizzy. I drank too much. I look down the hall and try to remember which room is Ashley's, but I can't even remember that. I don't want to walk into the wrong room and find Jake screwing that chick.

I walk off toward the stairs when I feel a hand wrap around my wrist. I turn back to see James looking down at me with concern.

"What's wrong?" he asks.

Oh, come on. Why does he always have to look at me like that? Why does he always have to find me when I'm at my worst?

"Nothing." It comes out as barely a whisper.

He doesn't say anything as he pulls me down the hall a few more doors and knocks on one. When no one answers, he opens it and takes me inside, turning on the lights. I look around and realize this must be Dillon's room. It has a couple of computer monitors on a large desk and some sports stuff on the walls. James locks the door behind us.

He sits me down on the edge of Dillon's bed, which I would've thought was awkward if I wasn't drunk and upset. Why am I upset again?

"What happened Everly?" he asks.

What did happen? Oh, that's right... "It's nothing. It's late. I'm going to text Declan to come get me."

I take out my phone and notice I still don't have a text from Jake. He's probably screwing her right now in the room next door. I clench my fist around my phone, thinking about that and release it to text Declan. He responds immediately and is on his way.

"Everly, tell me what happened," James demands again while rubbing the side of my arm. It feels so good. I lean into his touch and let him comfort me. I start to relax. That is until my mind reminds me of what Jake did. Stupid Jake. Maybe I should tell James and he'll hit him again.

"It really is nothing. I just saw Jake flirting with that girl by the dartboard. Ben took me downstairs to distract me, but now we can't find Jake or that girl. I mean, we all know what they're doing. I told him I didn't want to come up to a room with him, so he found someone who did." I shrug my shoulders like it's no big deal.

Maybe it isn't. I kind of feel numb now and not so upset anymore. Maybe the alcohol is kicking in more. I stand up, and that is definitely the right assumption because I stumble forward. James catches me.

"How much have you had to drink?" he asks seriously.

I smirk. "Only three cups of that punch. I meant to stop at two, but I was mad or sad. Or I don't know. Why am I mad and sad?"

James' face still looks serious and concerned. Also, angry. Why does he always look like that around me? He never laughs with me. It's not fair.

I reach my hand up to his face and caress his cheek. Or at least I try to. "Why do I always make you mad and sad? I like it when you smile. And when you laugh... You're so hot when you laugh, speaking of hot... when you were playing pool... now that... was hot!"

Wow, wait, what did I just say? Eh, whatever, it's all a dream, anyway. Right? Oh wait, no. I'm just drunk. Oh well, he won't remember it in the morning. Wait, that's me who won't remember it. Oh man, I hope I don't throw up again.

"Everly, you're drunk. I'm going to take you downstairs to wait for Declan." James wraps his arm around my waist and leads me toward the door.

"I like it when you wrap your arm around me and when you touch me." I stop us in our tracks so I can face him again. You know, when you're drunk, it's a good time to get all those stupid things off your chest that you're too embarrassed to say when you're sober. I'm going to just do it.

I continue, "James... you know I like you, right? Why can't you look at me as more than your little sister? Do you think you ever can? You know I've had this stupid crush on you for years. I thought it would go away, but you just keep being all you... and sexy... you're beautiful... and..."

Before I can embarrass myself more, James stops me. "Everly, you're really drunk, and you're mad at Jake. Let's go."

He leads us out the door and down the hall. I turn to ask him, "Why won't you answer my question?"

His lip twitches up in the corner and he says, "I'm not entirely sure what your question was, but ask me again when you're not drunk, and I'll answer."

Oh, okay. Yeah, that makes sense. I think. Who knows? James helps me walk down the stairs and doesn't let go of my waist at all. We finally make it outside just in time for Declan to pull his car up. He parks it in front of me and gets out of the car.

Declan walks over, looks at me, and grabs me from James. They exchange some words which I don't really hear or don't want to. I'm tired now.

Declan helps me into the car and before he closes the door, I hear Jake yell, "Everly, wait!"

That wakes me up. I'm not tired anymore. I look at him and his hair is a mess. Why is his hair a mess? I feel my heart racing again and the anger rising. Did he really sleep with her? You're kidding me.

I see James step in front of Jake and place his hand on his chest, shaking his head no. Declan closes the door and gets into the driver's seat and drives off. I don't look back.

"What happened Everly?" Declan asks but keeps his eyes on the road.

"Why does everyone keep asking me that?" I ask, still fuming with anger.

"Because something happened, and you called me for a ride home."

I look over at him, and he doesn't wear any expression on his face. "You're my guard... My very good-looking guard... I needed a ride, so I called."

Wait, did I just say that out loud, too? Okay, no more drinking. Never drinking. What is wrong with me? He is good looking, but I don't want him or anything. What am I doing?

I see him smirk before he says, "You're definitely drunk."

"And everyone keeps saying that too," I pout.

"Because you are. So, tell me what happened. You promised to trust me," he reminds me.

I sigh. I don't want to talk about it anymore. "It doesn't have to do with my safety. Just stupid teenager stuff."

"I happen to like hearing about stupid teenager stuff, so tell me," he says, keeping his eyes on the road.

I groan. "Fine, just so you can leave me alone and I can go throw up in peace and die tonight. I caught Jake flirting with another girl and then they went off for a while to who knows where. Well, we all know where." Those stupid tears appear in my eyes again. "But it was my fault... He wanted to take me to a room, and I said no. Why did I say no? I don't even remember, but I said no. So, yeah, he found someone to say yes. See, my fault."

I glance at Declan and his expression changes to anger. "Why do I always make everyone so angry?" I ask him.

He looks at me for a second before looking back at the road. "I'm not angry at you Everly. I'm angry at how boys are treating you. And stop blaming yourself for their choices. You had every right to say no, and there's no reason he should have cheated on you. That's not your fault. I'm sorry."

The tears run down my cheeks for a little longer, but they finally subside as I feel numb again. This emotional roller coaster is getting old. Now I'm starting to feel nauseous, and I really hope I'm not going to throw up in Declan's car. I close my eyes to keep the nausea at bay.

Chapter Fifteen

I wake up to my head pounding and an awful taste in my mouth. I roll over to reach for my phone to see what time it is. Eleven in the morning. I put my arm over my eyes and groan. Why do I feel like crap? I search my memory for a moment to remember the party last night and getting drunk. How did I get home and into bed? That's right, Declan drove me home. I must have fallen asleep in the car. Did he carry me upstairs?

Crap! Declan! It's four hours past the time we were supposed to meet for training. I promised I wouldn't be late again and here I am, late. I squint at my phone again and immediately open his texts, ignoring all the others on my phone.

I'm so sorry I missed training!

I can't believe I already broke my promise of not being late!

It's okay. I turned off your alarm. Rest today.

Well, that was not what I was expecting. I turn my alarm back on, so I won't miss tomorrow's training. I look at the rest of my texts and calls on my phone. Ashley texted me, asking if I was okay. I send a quick text back explaining I went home and passed out. James texted asking if I made it home okay, so I text him back too. It's time to deal with the ones that I was avoiding. I also have five missed calls from Jake.

Everly, it's not what you think please call me back.

I'm so stupid I should've never left you. Call me!

Everly I didn't sleep with her!

Please just let me explain.

My chest tightens as I read the messages. What should I do? Do I text him back and let him explain? It would be the right thing to do, but I don't want to get hurt again. It sucked watching him flirt with that girl. I'm not the type of girl that can handle seeing her boyfriend do that. I sigh and figure I might as well text back.

> You're right, you are stupid.

> What is there to explain? I saw you flirting with that girl even Ben took me away so I didn't have to watch.

His text comes back almost immediately.

Jake

> I was being stupid and flirting, you're right, but I didn't sleep with her.

> Look, I don't want to do this right now and especially over text.

As much as I do want to hear his side in hopes nothing happened, I need to see him in person. It's a lot easier to lie over text than in person.

Jake

> Can I come over?

> I'll meet you out back in 30 minutes.

I didn't look at myself in the mirror before hopping in the shower. I was still in the same clothes that I wore last night, and I'm certain my makeup is a mess. The shower feels good for a few minutes, but the steam starts to get to me, or the memories from last night. Either way, I feel nauseous, so I turn off the shower. I wrap a towel around myself and sit down at my vanity to avoid feeling like I'm going to throw up.

I don't bother blow drying my hair and put it up in a ponytail. I also put on a minimal amount of makeup. I force myself to go downstairs to the kitchen to get some water, medicine, and crackers.

Right before walking through the kitchen door, I run into Mrs. Crawford. I love her, but I do not want to see her right now.

"Oh Everly, I heard what happened last night," she says with pity in her eyes.

How did she hear?! And why…

When I don't respond, she puts her hand on my shoulder and says, "Come sit with me in the kitchen."

I don't argue, and I still have almost ten minutes before Jake meets me outside. Though, I don't particularly care if I'm late meeting him. She leads me to sit at the island in the kitchen. She goes around it to get me a glass of water and some crackers like she reads my mind.

She sits down beside me. "First, I want to say I don't condone drinking alcohol underage, but I know all teenagers do. I'm glad that you were responsible and called your security team for a ride home. I want you to be able to talk to me about anything, you know that. Are you okay? Do you want to talk about it?"

No, not really. I don't even know what's happening with Jake and me yet. "I'm okay."

She shakes her head. "You must be feeling awful about what happened last night. I'm sorry. Boys this age are... I'm not sure what the correct word here is..."

I interrupt her. "Stupid?"

She smiles. "Yes, that's one way to put it. They don't think about how their actions affect others."

I nod. "How did you find out what happened?"

Her eyebrows furrow and she looks at me like she isn't sure if she should tell me. I mean, there's only a select few people who could have told her.

"James told me, but before you get mad, I didn't leave him a choice. He came home... not himself, so I forced him to tell me what happened. I know you might not want my advice, but I think you should talk with Jake and tell him how you're feeling. I support you in whatever decision you choose with him," she says, being the supportive mom she always is to me.

I smile. "Thank you, Mrs. Crawford. I'm actually meeting him out back now to talk."

"Good, good. I won't keep you then. Like I said, you can talk to me about anything. I'll always be on your side, no matter what."

That makes me feel really good to hear. Like she really does love me like a daughter. I give her a hug before heading out back to meet with Jake, who is surprisingly already there.

He is sitting in a chair by the fire pit and stands up when he notices me coming out. I don't say anything to him as I sit in the chair across from his. I stare at him, waiting for him to start the conversation. He looks horrible, like he had way too much to drink last night and has a hangover.

He rubs his hand through his hair. "Everly, I'm so sorry."

"For what?" I ask calmly.

"For everything about last night. I never should have left you alone at the party, and I definitely shouldn't have flirted with someone else. I don't even like her. It was stupid," he says quickly.

Well, I'm not sure that makes me feel any better. "So, if you liked her, then it wouldn't have been stupid?"

His eyes widen. "What? No! I... ugh... this is all coming out wrong. I don't know what to say, Everly. I've never had an actual girlfriend before. I'm not used to this."

I sigh. "Yeah, I know Jake." I mean really, what can I say? We all know this isn't going to be a one-time thing. Jake's personality is to flirt. Some guys are just like that. I don't want to change who he is, but my personality has way too much jealousy in it to be with someone like him.

"Everly, James said you thought I slept with her. I didn't. I didn't touch her. I don't want to sleep with anyone other than you," he says seriously, and I believe him.

"Okay," I respond, but feel pretty emotionless right now.

"Okay?" he asks.

"Okay. I believe you," I elaborate.

His shoulders relax as he lets out a breath like he's relieved. "So, we're good?"

I'm not sure exactly what he means by that, but I say, "Yeah, we're good. But Jake, I don't think I can do this."

He tenses again and looks like he just wants me to continue.

"Jake, you're sweet and I really like you, but I don't think I can be your girlfriend. Your flirty personality is what makes you... well, you. I don't want you to change that, but if I'm being honest, I'm not the type of girl that can handle that. Also, I think we both deserve better than each other."

He looks defeated. "Everly, it's only been a couple of days. Please give me a chance..."

I interrupt him. "No, I don't think you understand. It's not just the flirting and how I feel... It's... you deserve better than me, too."

He gives a sad laugh. "Why do you say that?"

Because I'm in love with James... Wait, did I just think that? Love? That definitely isn't right. I can't go from a crush to love. Especially when James doesn't even like me. Right?

I sigh. I need to tell him the truth. It's only fair. "Jake... I really like you and enjoyed the little time we spent together, but it's not fair to you that I'm not all in. I... I think I'm in love with someone else and have been for a while..."

I stop myself there because that's all the information that he needs to know, especially since nothing will ever come of it.

He looks down at the ground. "Yeah... I know."

Wait, what? He knows? "What do you mean, you know?"

He laughs, but it sounds forced. "I mean, I suspected as much. It's James, right?"

My eyes widen. How could he possibly know that?

"Why do you think that?" I don't deny it.

"I see the way you look at him every time he enters a room. Your eyes light up and you just look... happy. I also see the way you watch him when you think he's not looking. You and James always just had this... bond. So... you love him?"

I shake my head. "I... It doesn't matter because he doesn't feel the same way. I'm just a little sister to him, but that doesn't change the fact it's not fair to you that I'm in love with someone else. You deserve someone who is all in and only thinking about you. And I deserve the same as well."

Jake stares at me for a moment before responding. "Are you sure about that?"

There were two things I said there. Which is he referring to? "Sure about what?"

"Are you sure James doesn't feel the same way? Have you asked him?"

I think about it for a moment and then reply, "Well, not in so many words."

He shakes his head. "You need to ask him. If he feels the same way, then that solves your problem. If he doesn't, then you can move on. I can be the one you move on with."

This time, I shake my head. "No. I'm not doing that to you Jake, it's not fair. You deserve to be with someone who wants you first, not just as someone to move on with."

"I'm okay with that. It wouldn't be long for you to move on and want me first." He winks at me.

I laugh because that's the Jake I know. I do really like him; I just don't love him. He might be right, and I could fall in love with him, but I still don't think it's fair. It's not right to be thinking about someone else while I'm with him, even if I can never have James. With how horrible I felt watching Jake just flirt with that girl, I can't imagine how he would feel knowing that I want someone else. Plus, there's still the issue that he's going to continue flirting with others because that's just who he is, and I really don't want to change that.

"You might be right about that, but I still stand by what I said," I say, smiling.

He stands up, and I follow. He looks serious. He closes the distance between us to where there are only a few inches keeping us apart. He stares in my eyes, grabs the back of my head, and kisses me. Hard. I kiss him back, groaning. God! Why does this feel so good when it is so wrong? I part my lips and let him deepen the kiss and our tongues collide. I grab the back of his neck and run my other hand up his chest.

He finally breaks the kiss and trails kisses down my neck, stopping at the same point he always does and where the hickey is that he marked me with. I didn't cover it up today. He moans when he sees it and then sucks on it again.

I push on his chest to break us apart. My teenage hormones protest, but my brain knows better. Thankfully, my brain wins.

Jake leans back and smirks. "See, I told you that I could be the one you move on with. Go talk to James and let me know what you decide."

I roll my eyes. "Jake, I'm not going to ask James if he wants to be with me and then, if he says no, come crawling back into your bed. That's wrong on so many levels."

He laughs. "I mean, I won't protest. Sometimes when it's wrong, it's right."

Alright, I need to get out of here. I'm glad this is settled, and I really feel like Jake and I are in a good place. I don't have any hard feelings about what happened, and I hope he doesn't either.

I put my hand out toward him to shake as I ask, "So we're good? Best friends again?"

He grabs my hand and pulls me into a hug. He whispers in my ear, "We're good. Any way we can change best friends to friends with benefits?"

I roll my eyes. "Sorry Jake."

He pulls back and shrugs. "It was worth a try."

I leave him standing there and don't look back when I go into the house and up to my room. Jake is right. I need to talk to James, but now isn't the time. I go to my room and crash on my bed to relax, like Declan recommended. I've shared enough of my feelings for today, or more like a lifetime.

Chapter Sixteen

$\bullet \cdot \bullet \cdot \bullet \cdot \bullet \cdot \bullet \cdot \bullet \cdot \bullet \cdot \bullet$

Of course, we pick the night that it's going to be in the 50s to camp outside. It's the middle of summer, so the thought of it being cold out never crossed my mind. While 50 degrees isn't necessarily cold, it's not a comfortable temperature that I prefer to sleep in.

We're camping out in the backyard of the Crawford house because Mrs. Crawford denied us going elsewhere overnight. After we all got drunk at Dillon's house, the trust has been fractured. Plus, I haven't been forthcoming with anyone about my relationship with Jake. I just haven't felt like talking about it with anyone, so I let them think whatever they want. Which means Mrs. Crawford thinks we're still together, so she probably doesn't want us sleeping anywhere that she can't keep tabs on us. It's hard to do anything when you have cameras on you all night.

"My parents have some little propane heaters we can use. I'll see if I can find them," Ben says, heading off toward his house.

I follow behind him. "I'll help."

We walk into one of the garages and I can honestly say I don't remember ever coming in here before. There are three cars here, but it looks like they could fit double that amount easily. There's a nice workstation, like a whole room, toward the side of the garage. Ben leads us toward that and starts looking around in large drawers.

While he's searching for the heaters, I notice a lighter sitting on the workbench. I grab it since I know we're going to need it to light them. Ben finds two that are about the size of my arm. They're small, but I know they will work to keep us warm. If only his parents would've let us use the firepit or let us leave the house and go to a campsite. I suppose that's what we get for almost setting their house on fire a couple of years back when we wanted to make s'mores.

I walk toward Ben and hand him the lighter. He picks up one of the heaters, turns it on and tries to light it. He keeps trying, but nothing is happening. "Do you think it still works?" I ask as he keeps trying.

"I'm not sure..." he says but stops as the heater lights and flames erupt all around it.

"Is that normal?" he asks as we both stare at the flaming propane heater.

"I think so..." I state in automatic response to the shock of seeing the flames surround the whole heater.

We both look at each other, and I can tell we realize at the same time because both our eyes widen. "No! No, Ben, that's not normal! Turn it off!"

"I'm trying!" he fumbles with it and brings the flaming heater closer to his face so he can see what he's doing. Once it's off, he sets it back down on the workbench and we both turn to each other. His mouth lifts into a smile and I lose it. Seriously? Did we just have a flaming heater in front of our faces, and he asked me if it was normal, and I told him I think so?! What is wrong with us?

I can't breathe because I'm laughing so hard and can hardly keep myself upright. I'm leaning on Ben, who is laughing just as hard, holding onto my waist to keep me upright and himself steady. He continues laughing which in return makes me laugh harder. My stomach is in physical pain from laughing, so hard, and I can feel the tears forming in my eyes.

Neither of us can stop laughing even though Jake, Bash, and James all walk into the little room in the garage and just stare at us.

"What is happening?" Jake is smiling, laughing at us because we can't stop laughing.

"I... Ben..." I can't get out any words because just thinking about having to tell and relive the story makes me laugh even harder.

Ben attempts a few words as well, but nothing comprehendible comes out. I straighten up from his grip and take a deep breath in and out, trying to rein in my laughter. Ben does the same and we both get it under control and stop laughing.

The problem is, I look at Ben's face and can tell he does not have it under control. I burst out again and mock what I'm thinking about in a very high-pitched voice, trying to get the words out. "Is that... normal?... I think so!"

We both can't contain it anymore, and I fall to the floor. It physically hurts, and I don't think I've laughed this hard in a long time. If ever. Ben follows suit and sits next to me.

"Have you guys been drinking?" James asks, trying to be serious, but that gleam in his eye and the smirk he's holding back shows he finds this quite humorous himself.

Both Ben and get out a no. Bash decides to throw in, "Drugs?"

"NO!" I yell out and slowly my laughter begins dying down again. If I stop thinking about what happened, then I can stop laughing. Laughing fits should be a legit torture strategy because they are painful. And it is awful not being able to control yourself when you're in one, especially when you have to pee. I feel like I'm going to pee my pants.

Once we both finally settle down again, Ben stands up and holds his hand out for me. I take it and when I stand up, I notice something odd on the top of his head. My eyes widen at the realization of what it is.

"Oh my... Ben!!!!" I pull off a piece of singed hair to show him. Most of the bangs he has in front of his head are scorched and gone! I pull out my phone's camera and let him use it to look at himself. He reaches up to his bangs and swipes them off the top of his head. His eyes meet mine and he starts laughing again, which in return, makes me start.

I'm so glad that he's not mad because I'm pretty sure I would be devastated if I lost some bangs.

"Oh, come on guys, again? Alright, let's just grab the heaters and head back outside," Jake says, walking forward.

Both Ben and I yell, "NO!" at the same time. Jake pauses from moving forward to grab them.

"We don't need the heaters, right Ben?" I ask, still trying to hold in my laughter.

"Right, not necessary." He clears his throat.

We all walk out of the garage and back to where we are going to be camping out for the night. I have to say it's really chilly out, but not enough for me to attempt lighting one of those again. Plus, it probably wouldn't even be safe. I still can't believe we lit it inside an enclosed space like that.

Ben is able to get out the story to tell the others what happened, and they all laugh too. Thankfully, my laughing fit subsides.

"Okay, you two are no longer allowed to do anything together. That was so dumb on so many levels," Bash says as his laugh dies down.

"Bash!" James says, trying to scold him while reining in his laughter.

I smile at James. "No, it's okay. He's right, and that's why I was laughing so much. That was the stupidest thing we did. And the fact that he asked if it was normal... and I said I think so..." I clear my throat a few times trying to contain the laughter again.

Jake shakes his head, but I can't help but keep my eyes on James. I don't think I've ever seen him laugh like that before or look at me like that. It's like he's enjoying himself watching me laugh. It does something inside me... No, I can't think like this anymore. I still haven't talked to him, but that's only because I already know how he feels and don't want to hear him say it.

Jake speaks up again, "Man, this is no fun. I can't believe we're not allowed a fire in a fire pit. I mean, come on, you two almost just burned down the garage because we can't use one."

"You're right, this really isn't fun without it. Let me go talk to Mrs. Crawford myself and see if I can convince her..." I say, but James interrupts.

"She won't let us. Trust me, I tried every argument." James is still looking at me the way he was earlier. I take my gaze away from him and stand up.

"Well, I can be more convincing. I'll be right back," I say as I walk toward the house. I'm going to convince Mrs. Crawford to let us use the fire pit, but first I need to use this as an excuse to finally go pee in case I do laugh again tonight. I don't need to pee my pants in front of these boys for them to forever make fun of me about it. I've given them plenty of ammunition this summer without adding that to the list.

The moment I walk into the house, I run into Mrs. Crawford. It's like she knows that I'm coming in to talk to her. I really do have to go to the bathroom, but I figure I will speak to her first, so I don't have to go find her later.

"How's everything going out there?" she asks with her motherly smile on her face.

"We're having a lot of fun… but… I was wondering if there was any way I could convince you to let us use the fire pit tonight. It's really cold for it being the summer, and I don't want to look like a wimp to them." I give her a small smile and the look of pleading.

Her smile falters as she responds, "James already tried to talk me into letting you guys use it, but do I need to remind you what happened last time?"

I shake my head. "No, I remember, and we truly are sorry. We learned our lesson and promise that we will be more careful." I have to stop myself from saying more because I start thinking about what just happened in the garage. If she knew what happened, then it would be a definite no. In fact, I'm pretty sure she would tell the maids to lock up every lighter and match in this house.

"I'm sorry Everly…" she starts, but I interrupt.

"I'll have Declan light the fire. I'm pretty sure that's where we went wrong last time." And this time with the heater. "I'll even have him watch out with a hose or something on hand. Please, Mrs. Crawford. I'll owe you one if you let us do this," I continue to plead with her.

She sighs. "Alright, have Declan watch out for you and start the fire. I'll bring out the stuff to make s'mores. But I have one condition."

I squeal and throw my arms around her in a hug. She laughs before I ask, "What's the condition?"

"You have to tell me what happened with you and Jake after you talked. It's been almost a week, and I have no idea where you two stand."

My smile falters, but she's right. I need to tell her what happened. "We're good. We decided it would be better to remain friends, though. I think we were always meant to be just friends."

She nods and pats me on the shoulder. "Thank you for telling me. I'll go get those s'mores."

She steps away, heading toward the kitchen. I quickly make my way to the bathroom, text Declan, and head back out to the boys, who are eagerly anticipating my news.

"So, what did she say?" Ben asks.

I sit down in our circle between James and Jake. "What do you think she said?"

"I told you that you wouldn't be able to convince her," James says with a sarcastic grin.

I give him a grin back. "Well, thankfully for us, you were wrong, James! Declan is going to light the fire for us and she's bringing out stuff for the s'mores!"

"No way!!" Jake exclaims, and he looks proud of me.

We get everything settled for the night while Declan lights the fire and Mrs. Crawford brings out the s'mores. We sit in the chairs cooking the marshmallows over the fire. There are a few times they catch fire, and I'm sure that something is going to happen to ensure we are never allowed to use the firepit again, but thankfully it doesn't. Eating burnt marshmallows, though doesn't taste the best.

"Alright, we've gone all summer without doing this game and now's the perfect time..." Jake says, and my heart starts pounding knowing exactly what game he's talking about. We play it every summer and it wouldn't be a summer without it, but I'm really nervous this time.

"I was thinking the same! One condition this time... You have to do one of each at least," Ben says.

No... Ugh, I can handle truth, but I'm really afraid what a dare from these guys is going to be.

I look over at James, who looks like he has the same concern as I do.

"Look... we can skip this tradition this summer. It was fun when we were little, but I don't trust you guys..." I say, being serious but trying to joke at the same time.

Bash laughs. "Oh, come on Everly. Look, we promise no one will get naked. Deal?"

I laugh. "Okay, fine..."

"Everly, you can start. We will go to the right of each other," Jake says.

I sigh. I looked over at Bash, and he cocks his eyebrow. "Truth or dare?" I ask him.

He smirks. "Truth."

I grin. "So, you don't trust me either. Hmm... This was easier when we were kids... How many girls have you slept with this summer?"

"Really? That's what you want to know?" he asks.

I laugh. "I don't know. It's the first thing that came to mind. I don't really care, but you have to answer now."

He shrugs his shoulders. "None."

I lean forward, surprised. "What? Really? None?"

Jake laughs. "Seriously? What have you been doing, bro?"

Bash cocks his eyebrow at Jake this time. "Well, obviously not Everly like you have..."

Well, this just got awkward, and I feel like I set that one up.

"Alright Bash, your turn," I say, trying to move this along.

"Dare," Jake says.

"Post on your Facebook page that you're coming out of the closet," Bash says.

We all laugh so hard. Poor Jake. That's a good one.

Jake laughs as he pulls out his phone. He takes a selfie of himself in front of the fire and then types something. "Done."

I pull out my phone to look at what he put. I open his page to see the photo of him with the caption, *I'm coming out of the closet. I'm flaming!*

I can't help but die of laughter with that. He never shies away from anything, and he just nailed that post.

While we are all looking at his post, he goes to Ben next to me and whispers something to him. I see Ben smile and nod, but I have no idea what he said.

"Alright James, truth or dare?" Jake asks.

James sighs. "I hate this game, so might as well go with dare to start."

Jake has a huge grin on his face as he looks at me and winks. Oh no.

"I dare you to make out with Everly, right here," Jake says.

WHAT?! No. Absolutely not. "Wait, wouldn't that be like a dare for me too, then? That's not right..."

"No," James says sternly.

"Hey, we said no one would be getting naked, that's it. We never back down in this game. Ever," Jake says, and he's right. How many summers have we done this, and we haven't ever backed down?

What is Jake thinking? He knows that I haven't talked to James yet. Does he really think this is going to help? Well, it's not. If anything, it's going to make everything worse. I don't want to kiss James. I mean, that's the problem, I do, but I don't want to because I don't want to fall more than I already have.

"Everly, just pretend you're kissing me," he says, puckering his lips at the end.

I roll my eyes and say, "No thanks, but I'm fine with it. If that's really what you want to dare James to do. You're strange."

"Jake, what the hell? Aren't you with Everly?" Bash asks.

He didn't tell him? I thought he would've told them all.

"Nah, Everly and I broke up a week ago. We're just friends," he says like it's no big deal.

They all look at me like they are waiting for me to confirm, so I say, "Yeah, we're much better off as friends." I shrug my shoulders.

"Jake…" James starts.

Jake interrupts. "You picked dare. Come on, I know you want to know what it's like to kiss her. She's pretty amazing."

"What's your definition of make out?" James asks.

"At least thirty seconds and with tongue. I'll set the timer."

"Can we go elsewhere?" he asks.

"Nope. Right here in front of us all. You two would chicken out and lie about doing it. Don't trust you, sorry." Jake smirks.

James just stares at me, and I roll my eyes. I get up out of my chair and sit on his lap. On the outside, I know I look like this is just another normal dare, but on the inside, my heart is about to pound out of my chest.

"Jake's not going to let this go, so we might as well. It's thirty seconds," I say, shrugging my shoulders.

James put his arm around my waist to hold me steady on his lap. He looks at me like he really doesn't want to do this, which makes my heart sink. I hate Jake for this.

I whisper to James, "Look, if you think kissing me is that awful, then I'll be the one to deny it since it's not my dare…"

He slams his mouth against mine and holds my head steady with his other hand behind my neck. My heart soars and I feel a spark. No, I feel those fireworks everyone talks about. Holy crap. I part my lips and James' tongue tangles with mine as he kisses me even harder. I can't think and can't breathe. I put my hand behind his head, pulling on his hair. He groans in my mouth, which in return makes me moan. My other hand goes to his chest. He removes his hand from my neck and brings it to my stomach under my shirt. I'm completely lost in him and forget anyone else is there until an alarm goes off.

He keeps kissing me for a few more seconds, like he forgot this was all a dare and his friends are sitting there watching us. I gasp when we pull away from each other. He's staring at me... like he wants more? That can't be right, but if he felt what I did... I definitely want more. Need more.

Before I go down that rabbit hole, I jump off his lap and walk back to my chair. As I sit down, I say, "See, that wasn't so bad, was it?"

James doesn't say anything. He just looks straight ahead into the fire. Jake breaks his attention away by saying, "Whoop whoop! See, man, I just wanted someone else to know what it was like to make out with her. Amazing right?"

James shakes his head and moves on to Ben. "Truth or dare?"

"I'm picking truth after that one." Ben laughs.

"What's the biggest mistake you've ever made?" James asks.

Ben thinks for a moment and says, "That's deep... Biggest mistake... probably getting so drunk that I passed out at a friend's house and didn't notice they drew dicks all over my face and body."

We all laugh hard. I can just imagine that happening, but I'm honestly surprised Ben got that drunk. He doesn't seem the type, but what do I know?

"Alright Everly, truth or dare?" Ben asks.

"Well, I feel like I already took an extra dare, so I'm going with truth," I say.

I see Jake smile and then realize this must be what he was whispering about to Ben earlier. Crap.

Ben asks, "Who is the better kisser? Jake or James?"

I look at Jake and narrow my eyes. "Seriously? I know you put him up to that one."

Jake puts his hands up like he's innocent. "Remember, it's a truth. You have to be honest."

I roll my eyes, but I'm not sure that he can see it. "Sorry Jake. James wins."

I see James smirk at my answer, and Jake looks offended. "What? Really? Are you just saying that to get back at me or do you really believe it? Why?"

I laugh. "I'm not just saying it to get back at you. He really was. It was hot."

I don't want to, but I can't help but look back at James. He isn't smirking anymore. He's intensely staring at me. Like he has hunger in his eyes. I stop breathing for a moment as our eyes connect.

I break our eye contact and look over toward Bash. "I guess yours is a dare this time... I dare you to give your phone to James and he can send a text to whoever he wants."

James knows Bash better than anyone, so he would know who to send a message to that would make Bash squirm.

"Oh man really, Everly? That's cruel." He takes his phone out of his pocket, enters the passcode, and hands it over to James.

James is smiling as he scrolls through his phone and starts typing. He gives it back to Bash. Bash looks down at the message and laughs hard.

"Who and what does it say?" I ask.

"James sent a message to my other best friend saying that James is indeed my best friend." Bash chuckles.

We all laugh because we know that James and Bash's other best friend have this ongoing thing about who the better friend is. That's one way to end the debate.

Bash moves on by saying, "Alright Jake, yours is truth. So, you and Everly broke up, but are you really over her?"

Jake's smile falters for just a moment that I don't know if anyone else caught it. He gives a laugh, but it was more like a nervous laugh as he says, "I don't see how anyone could ever be over Everly. She's amazing."

My heart stops for a moment at his confession. That was... sweet, and it's terrifying at the same time. Does he really mean that or is he just saying it?

"I didn't ask about anyone. I asked about you, Jake," Bash says.

Jake rolls his eyes. "Everly and I are friends, but I would be lying if I didn't say I wish we were more than friends. So, yeah, I screwed it up and regret it because, like I said, she's amazing." Jake looks over toward James as he says, "And anyone who likes her would be stupid not to go for it and not fuck it up."

James looks over at Jake and they make eye contact for a moment before Jake looks back at me, smiling. Oh, Jake... I don't even know what to say or think about any of that.

Bash clears his throat. "Alright, moving on."

Jake looks at James and says, "So your truth, man. Since we're on a streak making Everly blush, how did you feel about that kiss with her?"

Jake's right about me blushing. I feel the heat in my cheeks and it's not from the fire in front of me. What are you doing, Jake? Is this why we played the game? You're trying to find out how James feels about me? Are you doing this for me or for yourself?

James looks me in the eye for only a moment before leaning back casually. "She's a great kisser."

Wow, really? That's it? How vague.

Jake laughs. "Well, we know that, James. I asked how you felt about it?"

James squirms. "Like she said, I thought it was hot."

Jake looks like he was about to say something else, but James cuts him off. "Alright Ben, your turn for the dare. Talk in a British accent until your next turn."

We all laugh as Ben tries to talk in a British accent, and I'm trying to understand what my dare is.

"Go ask Declan out on a date and tell us what he says," Ben says in his best British accent. It is actually pretty hot.

"Wait, he's my security guard. Seriously? What is with you guys this year?" I ask and they all just laugh, including James.

Well, if James thinks it's funny, then I guess it's alright. I get up and walk over to where Declan is sitting in a chair next to the house. He has his arms crossed and is watching us the whole time, like I promised Mrs. Crawford.

"Hey," I say, sitting next to him.

He cocks his eyebrow. "What's up?"

I shake my head and hold in a giggle. "Do you want to go on a date with me?"

He stares at me for a moment, looking me over like he's trying to figure something out. "Have you been drinking again?"

I can't contain my laughter. "No, and I don't plan on it anytime soon."

He smirks. "I'm not going on a date with you."

I pretend to gasp and put my hand over my heart. "You wound me!"

I get a smile out of him. "It doesn't sound like you're too hurt by that. And I saw you making out with James."

I shake my head. "We're playing truth or dare. They dared me to ask you on a date."

"So, you wouldn't have asked me on a date if you weren't dared to?" he asks, feigning to be hurt as well.

"Look, you're hot and all, but you're also, like, ten years older than me and my bodyguard. Awkward." I grin.

"I am not ten years older than you," he states seriously.

"Wait, really? How old are you?" I ask.

"Seven years older than you," he replies.

"Ohhh... That's not so bad. In that case, I definitely am asking you on a date," I joke.

"Well, I'm definitely saying no."

"Ouch, turned down twice. When I'm eighteen, should I ask again?" I tilt my head to the side, looking at him.

He shakes his head. "Sure, but it'll still be a no."

"Twice turned down today and once turned down in the future. You're cruel."

He laughs. "I think you should get back to your game. They are waiting for you."

"Thanks for the self-confidence boost, Declan," I say over my shoulder as I walk back to the group.

"So, what did he say?" Ben asks, continuing with his British accent.

I pout. "Yeah, not ever happening. He turned me down twice. It's okay, I've already come to terms with being a crazy cat lady in the future since no one wants me."

Jake shouts, "Hey! Don't you dare be a crazy cat lady. I want you."

I laugh. "Okay fine, since no one except for Jake who wants any girl that walks in front of him."

"That's not true." Jake frowns and I think he really means it. I didn't mean to hurt him, but it does kind of feel like it's true.

We continue around the circle for a couple more rounds. The boys finally leave me alone with the date, kissing, and love stuff. Ben was only supposed to continue with his British accent until his next turn, but he's having too much fun with it, so he continues for the rest of the game. It's getting late, so we all decide to lie down in our sleeping bags on the ground.

I'm laying between James and Bash, and we are close together, but not touching. I'm looking up at the stars, smiling. Being here with them makes me happy, even though they push my buttons sometimes. The sky is clear so I can see the stars easily even though we are technically in the city. Thankfully, we are more on the outskirts because I can't imagine not being able to see the stars. I'm also thankful we didn't pick a night that it was supposed to rain.

I start to drift off to sleep when I feel something on my right arm. I think it's my sleeping bag at first, but when I pull my arm out, I see a giant spider walking along it.

My heart leaps out of my chest as I try to swipe it off, but it doesn't budge. I panic, scream, and try to get up out of my sleeping bag, but I trip as I get up on my knees, rolling over toward James.

"Oh my God, get it off!!" I yell as the dang spider still stays on my arm.

I can't breathe and almost start crying. It crawls up my arm and is now on my right breast. James sits up steadying me, trying to figure out what is going on.

I give up on trying to get it off and rip my shirt over my head, still screaming and throwing it. My shirt lands on James' head, and I panic more, thinking that maybe the spider fell off while I was taking off my shirt and it's in my hair. I'm shaking and rubbing my body and hair all over, trying to see if it's still on me until I notice that it's still on the shirt, which is now on James' lap.

"What the hell is happening?" Bash asks as he's now standing along with Ben and Jake.

James finally sees the spider on his lap as he swipes it off quickly, and it lands on Jake's foot.

"Holy shit!" Jake kicks his foot, which makes the spider come flying back at me. Thank God it lands in front of me and not on me. I run away and Bash stomps a few times on it. We all look down to realize it's dead.

"Okay, that thing was huge," Ben says, grossed out.

I'm literally shaking, and I don't know if it's from being creeped out by the spider that attacked me or because I'm now shirtless. I really don't care that I'm only in my bra, in front of them. I'm thankful I have a bra on.

Declan comes out of nowhere and stands in front of me. I can't see the others anymore. "What happened?"

"A tarantula attacked me," I say, still shaking.

Declan continues to stand in front of me as he turns toward James, who has my shirt. James hands Declan the shirt and he turns it right side out, shaking it. He puts it over my head and helps me get it back on. I don't even question that he is doing it, I'm thankful.

I shiver and look up at Declan as my shirt is now completely on. He has a gleam in his eye like he finds this amusing. Really?

"Are you laughing at me?" I ask.

Declan is holding back a smile and a laugh by biting his lower lip. "Never."

I can't help it. Maybe it was from the adrenaline rush that's wearing off or the embarrassment, but I burst out laughing and so does Declan. Everyone else joins in, too.

Before Declan walks away, he whispers in my ear, "You really shouldn't throw your shirt at a guy. It'll send mixed signals."

I slap his arm as he walks off. "James, I'm sorry I threw my shirt... and that spider at your face..." I say while cracking up again. Oh my God, I threw my shirt at James' face.

James is dying of laughter too. "That was a huge spider, Everly. I didn't mind the shirt, but please never throw something like that at me again."

Once we all calm our laughter down at the stupid situation that I just put us in, I'm more concerned about the spider again. "So... do you think that it has a family? Is it going to come for us in the middle of the night? I don't know that I want to sleep here anymore..."

Ben agrees with me. "Look, camping in the open sounds great, but I agree. I don't do spiders."

The look on Ben's face makes me think he is more afraid of spiders than I am, which is shocking. I really thought that I was going to have a heart attack with that spider crawling on me.

"Well... our bucket list says camping with no tents... we didn't say it had to be outdoors, right?" Bash asks.

"Right!" I immediately throw out there because I really do not want to sleep outside anymore. Not only is it cold, but I don't want any more bugs crawling on me.

"Why don't we move into Ben's room, then? We'll still be camping... just inside. And we can play some video games to calm us down." Jake suggests.

Sounds good to me. I'm the first to pick up my sleeping bag, and I shake it out for good measure. Everyone follows my lead. I quickly tell Declan our plan and he puts the fire out. At least now he doesn't have to stay awake all night watching us to ensure we don't burn down the house.

Ben and Jake set their sleeping bags on the bed, which I don't think is fair. That's not really camping if you're on a comfy bed, but I'm not going to argue because at least we are safe inside.

Bash quickly throws his on the couch. Jerk.

James and I lay ours out on the floor. I open mine all the way up to inspect it to make sure there aren't any other spiders or creatures crawling around in it. Hopefully, everyone else did the same because I don't want to wake up to anything else on me.

Jake and Ben are sitting on the bed starting a video game. I don't feel like playing and convince them to turn off the light so I can try to go to sleep since I have to be up and training by 7 am. I'm not going to miss another training session.

James follows my lead and tries to go to sleep as well. He's much closer to me since there isn't much room on the floor between the couch and the door. I try not to think about how close he is and about the kiss we shared tonight. It was just a dare, and it meant nothing. To him.

Chapter Seventeen

I groan as I reach over to turn my phone alarm off. I must have hit the right button because it stops making that annoying sound. I snuggle into my pillow more, wanting a few more seconds before getting up. My eyes pop open as I realize the pillow I'm caressing with my hand and laying my head on is hard. That is not a pillow.

I shoot up and realize I'm laying on James' chest. What am I doing?! I push off him and try to stand, but stumble as my foot gets caught on something. I slam into the side of the couch and almost fall on Bash. Crap. I forgot we were "camping" in Ben's room last night. If my alarm didn't wake anyone up, surely my stumbling around did. I hope that James is still asleep and didn't notice me caressing him. It's not the first time I've woken up doing that... Ugh, what is my problem? I'm so embarrassed but so turned on at the same time.

No one says anything, so I fumble for my phone and turn the flashlight on so I can leave the room. I leave the sleeping bag there and will get it later. I run down to my room and quickly throw on some workout clothes. By the time I get down to the gym, it's two minutes before seven. At least I made it early. My heart is already pounding, so I don't need any cardio this morning.

Declan walks in at exactly seven. "You're on time," he observes.

"I figured I couldn't be late again after the past two days and how lenient you've been with me." I smirk.

He laughs. "Well, I'm glad to see you are also fully clothed."

I don't know why, but I look down to see what I'm wearing. I do have a tank top on with my workout bra and my capri leggings. It's chilly this morning, so I figured more than just the sports bra was needed. I can always take the shirt off if I get too hot, but after last night I feel like I need to keep my shirt on.

"Ha ha, very funny," I say sarcastically.

We start warming up and stretching. After we finish, he says, "We'll continue to work on balance and getting your strength up, but I want to work on some more self-defense, too. Let me show you how to throw a punch without hurting yourself."

I cock an eyebrow at him. Really? Without hurting myself?

"Form a fist," he says.

I do and then show it to him. He grabs it and says, "No. If you throw a punch like this, you're going to break your thumb." He grabs my thumb and places it on the outside, resting below my first and second knuckle.

"Now I want you to stand with your left foot in front and have it at an angle toward me. Then take your right foot behind you and point it away, keeping it open." I do what he says, and he leans over, pointing my back foot out a little more. "Good."

"Now take your right hand and tuck it against your chin and raise up your left hand." He pulls my arms into the positions he wants them to be in. "You want to keep this hand up at all times so you can block anything coming your way." He taps my left arm.

"You want to keep your knees bent, don't lock them. Keep your balance and use your lower body to power your punch." I follow his instructions and keep my knees bent.

He steps back and looks me over. "Good, make sure you keep your left arm up, though. Don't drop it. Now throw a punch at my hand."

He holds out his hand, and I take my right arm and punch it. He barely moves and laughs.

"What's funny?" I ask, pouting.

"That was so weak, Everly. You can do better. You didn't even use your lower body like I said. Don't just twist your shoulders, use your hips and push into it. Come on, try again."

I bounce on my legs two times before leaning forward to punch his hand again. It's still weak, and I know it. I step back and do it again, this time harder.

"Good! That was perfect. I want you to do that for a few minutes at the punching bag," he says, leading me over toward it.

I follow him and get into position. I throw a few punches, and he keeps correcting my stance and holding my waist, pushing on it to show me how it should feel when I use my lower body to punch. We do it over and over until my knuckles start to hurt.

"Shouldn't I be wearing some gloves for this?" I ask, rubbing my knuckles.

"We will next time we work out more with this, but I just wanted to do it a few times to show you what you're doing."

We go back over to the mat, and he has me working my leg muscles out more and they are burning. Bad. I can barely balance, and they feel like jelly by the time we're finished. He even has me doing some pushups and planks, which I still fail miserably at. My arms are weak as well and I'm sweating like I just got out of the shower.

"Alright, that should be good for today. You did good," he praises.

I roll my eyes. "I appreciate the compliment, but we both know that was far from good."

He looks at me seriously. "Everly, we talked about this. Seriously, you did good. You're already improving, and you have punching down. I am confident that if you have to throw a punch in the future, you will not break your hand or thumb. That's important."

I laugh this time. "Well, thank you. I'm glad I won't hurt myself, but I think I need to work more if I want to hurt the person I'm punching."

After showering, I look at my phone to see missed messages from the boys' group.

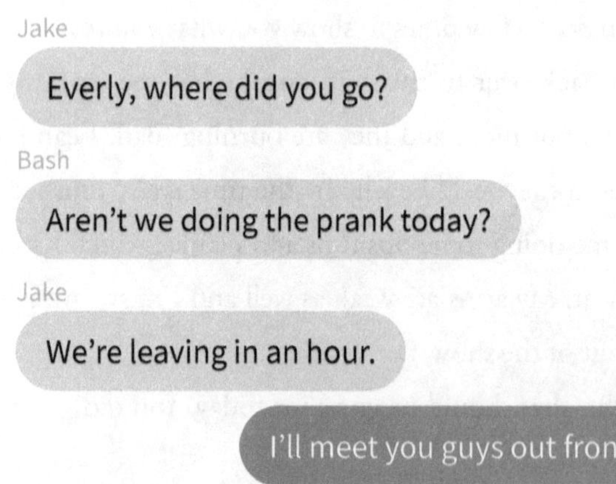

Why do I keep forgetting what we are doing every day? This summer is seriously flying by, and I feel like school is about to start. I'm not ready for that, but I am ready for this prank. I quickly get dressed because they sent those messages thirty minutes ago. I put on a black tank top and black leggings. I tie my hair up into a bun and throw on some sunglasses. If we're going to be doing illegal things, I should be dressed like I'm about to do illegal things.

I meet the guys outside and they are all ready to go. Jake looks really good, especially in his tight t-shirt. Wow, I told him to look good so he can seduce Kayla, but dang.

Jake smiles as he walks up to me. "Like what you see?"

I grin. "I don't think Kayla is going to be able to resist you."

"I take that as a yes." Jake winks.

I see James roll his eyes. I'm not sure he meant to do that.

"Alright, let's go," I say, and we all get into two separate cars.

Jake and Ben get in one car so they can go distract Kayla and take the video. James, Bash and I get into another car so we can go to her house. I'm going to throw Kayla's car keys at James so he can go put them in her car while Bash and I put the permanent vinyl dicks all over her room along with switching out her shampoo.

It takes us almost six hours to get to Boston with the traffic. James, Bash, and I are sitting outside of Kayla's house waiting for Jake's text that he has eyes on Kayla at her class. It should have just started. We barely made it on time. I sit in the front seat, staring at my phone as the text comes through.

"Let's go," I say as we get out of the car quickly.

We need to do this faster because we were hoping to have more time. Thankfully, I already told them exactly where the camera blind spots are so we can hurry this along. No one is outside, so we move fast. Her bedroom is on the first floor at the side of the house. Kayla always forgets to lock her window, so we're banking on that, but if not, we have another plan to get in.

Sure enough, once we get to her window, it's already slightly cracked. She must have snuck out last night. I push the window open, and we climb in. I dig in the bottom drawer of her end table near her bed and grab her spare car key. I toss it out of the window to James, who catches it and runs off. This should be a lesson to all, to never backstab your best friend. If you want to make enemies, make sure it's someone who doesn't know all your secrets.

Bash starts placing the vinyl dicks on her walls while I head to the bathroom with the shampoo with hair dye in it. I look in the shower and notice her shampoo bottle and thankfully she is still using the exact brand as when I was friends with her. I grab it and switch it out for the one with the hair dye in it. I go into her cabinet and switch out the others as well. I toss hers in the bag to take with me. That was too easy.

I go back out to her room and start putting the dicks along the opposite wall from where Bash is putting them. I look up at the ceiling and smile.

I whisper, "Hey, can you reach the ceiling?"

He looks up and smiles, too. "Yeah, I think so."

He stands on a chair and barely reaches, but he does! I giggle quietly to myself. She's going to have to get a ladder to remove them. Man, I wish I could see her reaction.

A text comes through to my phone and I read it.

Jake

Class just ended.

Well, that felt like a short class. We still have like fifty of these to put up. I get on the floor to put some under her bed where she would least expect to find them. I place a couple down, finding her journal sitting there. It's tempting to take it, but I decide not to. I take a peek though at random pages.

One that catches my attention is dated before our fight.

I'm in love with Everly's boyfriend. I liked him long before she did. Do I go for him or try to forget about him? I've been trying to forget, but it's hard. I think he has been flirting with me. I don't want to lose my best friend, but I also really like Adam. I'm torn.

I continue to the next page.

So, I flipped a coin, and it decided for me to go for Adam. Everly has been bitchy lately and complains about him. Clearly, she doesn't love him the way I do. He was definitely flirting with me in class today and he made me feel so special. Now I have to decide if I should tell Everly or just see him behind her back for a while after making him break up with her.

I really should stop spending time reading this, but I'm getting so angry and need to see where this is going. What kind of journal is this? A write a paragraph on how I can be the worst friend ever each day?

Today showed me that I made the right decision about Adam. Everly and I got in a fight because she was claiming he has been raping her! She's such a slut, how can she claim something like that? Clearly, she has been wanting it. I won't feel bad for a moment for taking her boyfriend. She doesn't deserve him.

What a bitch! Man, I'm so glad that we're pranking her. My heart is racing with how angry I am. I'm still laying half under her bed reading with my cellphone light. I turn to the last page she's written on.

I'm pretty sure that Adam is cheating on me. He's been avoiding my texts and calls the past few days. I saw a Facebook post of him hanging out with another girl at the lake. I've never seen her before, but they looked pretty cozy together. It hurts…

I hate to say it, but… good!! She deserves it! Ugh, I shouldn't be like this, but she makes me so angry. What kind of friend does this? What did I do to deserve her to treat me like that? I feel like I was nothing but a good friend and she backstabbed me.

My phone buzzes, and James is back with the car. I throw the journal down and put two more stickers down before coming out from under the bed. One of those stickers is placed on the front of her journal.

"Let's go," I say to Bash.

He jumps off the chair and pushes it back where it was. We jump out the window and run down to where James is waiting with the car. I get in the back seat and Bash gets in the passenger seat as James drives off. By the time we get to the restaurant, we planned to meet at for dinner, it's already 6:30. I'm really happy with what we accomplished, but I'm exhausted.

Shortly after we arrive, Jake and Ben sit down at our table. Ben sits next to me, pulling out his phone.

"I think I got a good one." He smiles.

I take the phone and watch the video. I know that Jake accidentally ran into Kayla and spilled something on her shirt, but at the angle Ben took this video, that is not what it looks like happened. It looks like Kayla walked up to Jake and stopped to talk for a second, and then Jake was feeling her up. He then led her away with his arm around her waist. It looked so natural. Ben pulled up a second video of them coming out of the coffee shop they went into. They both had coffee in their hands, and she was looking up at Jake, laughing as he had his arm around her shoulders and the video ended there.

"Wow. You guys really made it look like she was cheating on her boyfriend. This is amazing," I say, impressed.

Ben sends it to Bash, and I approve for it to be sent to the phone number I gave him. Apparently, he's already able to send it. I thought he would have to upload it to a computer or send it from a special place or something for it not to be tracked, but I guess not. He knows what he's doing and can make it untraceable.

"Man, I wish that I could see how all this turned out, but knowing what she's about to be walking into when she gets home is good enough for me," I say, smiling and proud of what we accomplished.

"Yeah, pranks are a lot more fun when you can see the reaction from the person, but this was still great," Jake agrees.

"So, what do you think her boyfriend is going to do when he sees the videos?" James asks me.

I smile. "Knowing Adam, he's going to flip his lid. Kayla has no idea what she's in for."

They all just stare at me. Did I say something wrong?

"Did you say Adam?" James asks.

"Yeah, why?" I question, confused why they are all looking at me like that.

"Everly, you didn't tell us that Adam was her boyfriend. He seems... dangerous. Are you sure that was a good idea?" Jake asks.

Wow, even Jake? "It's fine. He'll just break up with her and make her feel like crap. Besides, he's cheating on her. I doubt he even likes her."

"Well, it's done now," Ben says with a shrug.

We all eat our dinner and laugh about the dicks we put everywhere. James took pictures of her car and Bash took some of the room before we left. That's going to be fun for her to try to get the permanent vinyl off. She's going to be scraping for days and probably will have to repaint her room.

Before we leave the restaurant, Jake asks, "Do we want to drive back, or should we get a hotel for the night?"

I'm exhausted, but spending the night in Boston is honestly the last thing I want to do, but I'm not the one driving either car, so I stay silent.

"Nah, we can drive back. We should be back by one in the morning or so. There shouldn't be much traffic at this time," Bash says.

We all agree to go back home and go our separate ways in the same cars we came in. I take the back seat with Bash driving and James in the front seat. I sprawl out and get comfortable sleeping behind the driver's seat while James put his seat back to try to get a nap in. Bash drives for a couple of hours before pulling over to switch with James. I move to the front seat because Bash wants to lie down.

I can't fall back asleep once we get moving again. I guess that nap was enough for me.

"Not tired?" James asks as we continue driving.

"Not really," I say, looking at him.

I see him look in the rearview mirror like he's trying to gauge if Bash is asleep or not.

"We haven't had a chance to talk about last night," James says.

"What about it? The fact I threw my shirt at you with a spider on it? I already apologized," I say jokingly and laughing.

James smirks and says, "No. Not that part."

Okay, so which part? The part where I molested you in your sleep when I woke up this morning? The fact I even cuddled up to you without even knowing? Or the fact that Jake made us make out in front of our friends? There's a lot that happened last night between us.

"Then which part? A lot happened last night," I say, trying not to blush, thinking about all those things.

"The kiss," he adds quietly, like Bash wouldn't be able to hear it if he was still awake.

"Ah, yes. That. What about it?" I ask.

I'm not going to be giving up any extra information than necessary on that. I honestly thought that he would just pretend it never happened and move on.

James is quiet for a bit before answering. I try to study his face to figure out what he's thinking, but his face shows nothing. Or I just really don't know how to read him.

"Do you regret it?" he asks.

"What?"

He gives a nervous laugh. "The kiss. Do you regret it?"

What do I say to that? This can go two ways. I can pretend like it meant nothing to me, and we can move on like the friends we are, or I can most likely make a fool of myself by telling him I loved the kiss because I love him and then he gets freaked out. Which path do I choose? I remember the question that I asked him the night of the party.

"Well, first you have a question that you didn't answer from the other night," I say.

"What is that?"

"Can you ever look at me more than like a little sister?" I ask the same question from the party that he told me to ask again when I wasn't drunk.

Once again, he's taking a while to respond. I'm not the only one deciding what to say and trying to figure out how it will affect our friendship. But I'm pretty sure that he's just trying to figure out how to make me not feel bad about what he's going to say. I wish he would just spit it out already.

"Yes," he answers.

Wait, what? "Yes?" I ask back, trying to remember how I phrased the question and what that means.

"Yes. I can look at you more than like a little sister," he says with a straight face.

I look down and think about that for a moment. Does that really mean what I think it means? That maybe he does like me? But he says he can, not that he does. Why did I even ask the question like that? You know what? Screw it. Maybe it's because I'm tired or because I'm stupid, but I'm just going to throw this out there.

"No, I don't regret the kiss. It was amazing and I wish it would happen again," I say with my heart pounding. I can't believe I actually just said that.

I watch his reaction, and I see his lip quirk up. Okay, at least he's not disgusted by what I just said, but I need a little more than that. I literally just told him I want him to kiss me again and he hasn't said anything. I shift in my seat, trying to hide how uncomfortable I am now.

He still hasn't said anything and now I'm feeling nauseous thinking about what is going through his mind. Why did I say that? As I'm working up the nerve to ask him to say something, I hear Bash stir in the back seat.

James and I both look at each other and back at Bash. He sits up and says, "I have to pee. Can we pull off?"

"Yeah, I actually just saw a sign for a rest stop a mile ahead. You're lucky or you'd have to pee on the side of the road," James responds.

Sure enough, there's a rest area directly ahead. James pulls off and Bash gets out of the car. To avoid being alone with James, I get out too and go inside to pee. I'm glad that I do because the moment I sit on the toilet, I pee for what feels like an eternity. While washing my hands, I look at myself in the mirror. My hair is all messed up, so I put some water on it and fix it up a little, even though it's dark out and no one can really see me.

When I come out of the bathroom, I see James leaning against the wall like he's waiting for me.

"Is Bash out yet?" I ask.

"He's back in the car," James answers.

"Okay. Why are you waiting here?" I ask, and my heart rate picks up. What is wrong with me?

He looks at me and says, "I wanted to make sure you were safe. It's late."

Oh... Right... He's my big brother, of course he's going to make sure I'm safe.

"Thank you." I say, feeling a bit disappointed with his answer.

When I walk away, he grabs my wrist and pulls me back toward him. My breath hitches as I look up at him and he's staring down at me. I can tell he's debating something. Is he debating on kissing me again?

"James…" I say but get interrupted by his lips slamming into mine.

I close my eyes and savor how amazing it feels. I can feel the kiss all the way to my core. It's gentle, sweet, and passionate all at the same time. I've never felt like this before kissing someone. I moan, which makes him moan in return.

The kiss ends sooner than I would like, but we are in the middle of a rest stop, and we need to get home. When we part, I look up at him and smile. He smiles back.

"I want to kiss you more, Everly," he says with a rough voice.

"I'd like that." I blush as I reply.

He grabs my hand and leads me back to the car. Bash looks like he's already asleep in the back seat. James walks around to the passenger side and opens the door for me. I get in and he closes it. I can't help but smile at how sweet that was and how much of a gentleman he can be.

We don't say anything for the rest of the way home, but halfway back, he grabs my hand and holds it for the rest of the drive. I can't keep the smile off my face and the butterflies in my stomach won't go away. I can't believe this is happening, and I'm hoping that this isn't just a dream that I'm going to wake up from soon. After all these years of having a crush on James, he finally likes me back. I think. Right?

When we make it home, Bash goes back to his house, and James walks me upstairs. James stops me before I go into my bedroom. He pulls me into him and kisses me again. This one lasts much longer than at the rest stop. I want to tell him to come into my room with me to continue kissing, but I have a feeling we should really take this slowly. Whatever this is.

He pulls away and says, "Good night, Everly."

I reply breathlessly, "Good night, James."

When I enter my room, I plop down on the bed with a loud sigh and a smile on my face. It doesn't take long for me to fall asleep to dream about James.

CHAPTER EIGHTEEN

After training with Declan, I plop myself back in bed without even showering. I only got about five hours of sleep last night from getting in late and waking up in the middle of the night thinking about James. I'm nervous because I don't really know where we stand. I'm assuming that he likes me if he's kissing me, but I feel like we need to have a conversation about it.

My phone vibrates. It's a text from an unknown number.

My heart races because I know who this is from. Adam. What does he want? Does he know we played the prank on him and set up Kayla? Why is he in New York again? What do I do? I reply "okay" to the number just so he knows I intend to show up. But do I tell Declan? James? No. I definitely can't tell the boys. I don't want them getting hurt because of me. Declan should be able to take care of himself if I tell him, but what if something happened to him? I would never be able to forgive myself.

I go to shower and then look up how far that location is from me. It's a pizza place. Are we really going to be eating lunch in a pizza shop? Why does he want me alone? I know why...

My heart continues to race as I think about what I need to do. I can't bring anyone with me. If I get hurt, then that's okay. I can't let anyone else get hurt. I've dealt with Adam for a year. I can handle another day. I doubt he will really hurt me, other than what he's done before. After I see what he wants, I can talk with Declan, and we can figure this out.

I quickly sneak out of the house and call for an Uber down the street. I don't have a car here, nor do I really want to be driving in New York by myself. Is it sad that I would rather see Adam than drive in New York? Maybe I wouldn't. I don't know, my mind isn't thinking clearly right now.

The Uber pulled up to the pizza place in what feels like record time. I'm ten minutes early. It took almost thirty minutes to get here. What am I doing? How could I have just left and come here by myself? Am I that stupid?

Before stepping out of the car, I quickly send a text to Declan.

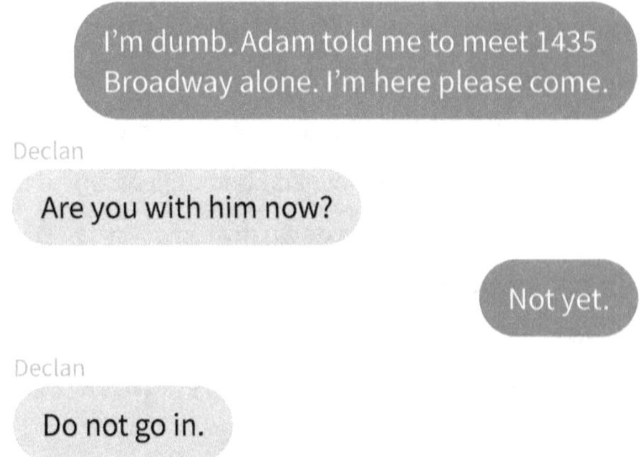

When I think about turning around to go into another business, it's too late. Adam's coming around the corner and he definitely sees me.

Too late

I put my phone in my pocket and don't bring it out again. I don't want him to know that I was texting someone else.

Adam walks up to me and puts his arm around my waist, leading me into the pizza place. My stomach turns.

We sit in a booth, where he puts me on the inside against the window and sits on the other side of me instead of across from me. Clearly, he doesn't want me to escape.

"So, you really did come alone? Does anyone know you are here?" Adam asks.

"No," I say nervously.

He grins. "Good. Because I have four friends over there ready to hurt anyone who you might have brought."

I look over to the table he points at and sure enough, there are four very large men sitting there and one smiles at me when he sees me looking. A shiver runs down my spine.

"What do you want, Adam?" I ask, trying to get to the point.

The server comes over and asks for our order. Adam orders us pizza without even asking me and when she leaves, he takes out his phone.

He pulls something up on it. "You know, I got this very interesting message yesterday. It was a video of my girlfriend cheating on me."

He shows me the video of Jake with Kayla from yesterday. I watch it like I have no interest at all in it.

I say, "Kayla isn't very loyal."

He smirks again. "You're probably right about that, but her cheating on me isn't what interests me the most here. You see who she is with? You know, from the angle it's hard to see the guy, but I've actually met him twice now. Once, when having lunch with you. Honestly, I might not have remembered him just from that. But the second time was when he and his three friends decided to corner and threaten me a few weeks back."

My eyes widen at what he's saying. They did what now? When did they do that? Why would they do that?

"They what?" I ask. I don't even have to pretend I didn't know.

"Oh, you didn't know? Well, you did know that you told them what I did to you, right? What did I tell you would happen if you told anyone?"

My heart begins to pound out of my chest again and I feel my throat tighten and the tears in my eyes form. "Adam, I didn't... I didn't mean to tell anyone..."

He interrupts me. "Oh no, I think you did mean to tell them. You felt like you were safe, right? Because you are no longer in Boston? Well, I have some bad news for you. I have a lot of friends here in New York. You see, I visit quite often. I also have friends at the high school you will be attending. Terion High School, right?"

I feel like I'm going to throw up. He's right. I did think I was safe. I can't say anything, so I just shake my head.

"Well. This is rather unfortunate for you and your friends. Possibly your dad too, I haven't decided yet. Either way, I'm going to be very nice and give you another chance. Would you like that?" he asks, as if he's giving me the best offer of my life.

"Yes," I say, but it comes out in a whisper.

"Good girl." He pats my thigh, and I gulp. "So here is what's going to happen. You're going to tell your friends that you made a mistake. You were mad about me dating Kayla and lied about what happened. They are going to drop it and you are going to continue having a good time with me when I want you to. You're very pretty Everly, and I just can't seem to get you out of my mind."

He leans over and brushes my hair behind my ear. After he does that, he pulls my head toward him and kisses me. It takes every ounce of energy I have to not throw up on him. I feel sick, but I don't know what to do. If I pull away from him, then he's going to hurt my friends. I just sit here and let him kiss me while tears silently run down my cheeks.

Thankfully, the server comes back with the pizza and places it in front of us. I turn my head toward the window so that Adam nor the server, couldn't see my tears. I quickly wipe them away, but more fall in their place.

Adam grabs a slice of pizza and hands it to me. He then grabs one for himself and takes a bite out of it. "Mmm. Everly, the pizza here is really good. Take a bite."

I shake my head because how can I eat? I can't even think about food right now with how sick I feel.

Adam lifts my slice up to my mouth and demands, "I said, take a bite."

I take a bite and roll it around my mouth for a bit, trying to keep my nausea at bay before swallowing. I can't believe this is happening. Why is this happening? What did I do to deserve him to treat me like this?

It feels like we are sitting here for an eternity, but it can't have been more than thirty minutes. And how do I know this? Because Declan comes walking into the pizza place. He scans the room and notices me. I make eye contact with him, and my eyes grow wide. I try to subtly shake my head no and glance over to where the four men sit at the table near us. He looks over in their direction. I hope he understands what I'm trying to tell him.

Declan walks over anyway, and I don't think that my heart can pound any harder, but it does. Is it going to pound out of my chest? Is this how people have heart attacks?

Declan smiles at me as he reaches our table. "Everly, is that you? It's good to see you!"

I'm not entirely sure what he's doing, but I feel like I need to do my best to go along with this. "Hey! What are you doing here?" I try to make myself sound excited and shocked to see him.

"I'm in town for the day and I came by for some lunch. Do you guys mind if I sit?" Declan sits before he even finishes his question.

He reaches out his hand for Adam to shake it and says, "I'm Mario."

Adam shakes his hand. "Adam, her boyfriend. How do you know Everly?"

"Oh, my sister and her are friends. We've met on occasion," Declan, or should I say, Mario says.

They make small talk for a moment, and I'm not sure what Declan's plan is here. I'm not sure he even has a plan until he starts talking to me again.

"You know, it's good I ran into you, Everly. I could really use your help with something with my sister, but I don't really want to talk right here." He looks back toward Adam. "Do you mind if I steal her for literally two minutes out front? Then I'll leave you two alone on your date."

I look over at Adam, who I can tell is debating if he should let me or not. He's usually not a jerk when other people are around. Everyone thinks he's such a great guy, but they don't know him in private. He always tries to please everyone else.

"You know, we really don't have long, so I'd prefer if I could spend the little time I have with her. You understand, right?" Adam says, trying to be nice, but definitely not willing to let me out of his sight.

Declan laughs. "Look, I promise it'll be for two minutes. You won't even be able to finish your slice of pizza."

Adam looks at him and back at me before saying, "Sorry, man. No."

Declan's smile fades. I don't think he thought Adam would really say no. "Really, *man*?"

"I hope you two can catch up some other time," Adam says, still trying to be pleasant, but not willing to give in.

Declan shakes his head. "Well then, I suppose the pleasantries are over. Adam, I'm going to need you to let Everly go and never contact her again. I'm going to make myself clear here. If I find that you contact her, I'll make sure that you pay."

Adam's demeanor changes quickly, and he smiles wickedly. He smiles! Is he seriously not afraid of the man in front of him, who clearly has a gun?

Adam leans forward. "I figured Everly wouldn't come alone without telling anyone. It was a dumb move, really." Adam looks over toward the table of four men and nods. All four of them make their way to our table and hover over us.

"I think these gentlemen want to take you out back to have a talk. Would you like to join them?" Adam asks like it's an invitation to a party.

Declan smiles now. Now why is he smiling? It's four against one. "I'd love that."

Declan looks at me with the don't go anywhere stare and then walks out the door with the men. I don't see where they go, but I'm sure it's around back to the alley. Crap.

Adam puts his hand on my shoulder and shakes his head at me, making a tsking sound. "I warned you Everly. Now his blood is on your hands."

I look at Adam with tears in my eyes and start pleading with him. "Please Adam, don't hurt him. It's his job to follow me and protect me. He didn't know."

He shakes his head. "He must have known enough to pretend like that and then to threaten me. Did you tell him too?"

I lower my eyes and don't answer him. He lifts my chin to look at him, but I look away.

"Everly, I asked you a question. Did you tell him too?" he asks angrily.

"I didn't have a choice, Adam. You don't understand," I say quietly.

He shakes his head again. "You always have a choice, Everly. And unfortunately, this choice led to his death. Let this be a lesson for you."

I don't even notice that I'm shaking until I move my hand to my lap. Please Declan, be okay. Please be okay. If anything happens to him. God. I can't even think about it. What do I even do now?

"Alright Everly, I'll tell you what. I think you've learned your lesson. I was going to suggest you come back to my hotel with me, but I think you need to get home. You're not looking too well. Unblock me and I'll send you another text with where I'm staying. I expect to see you there tomorrow morning. Then, after our nice time in the hotel room, we can have lunch at another restaurant here before I head home. How does that sound?" he asks, but I know it's a demand.

I nod my head, but I'm still shaking.

"Good, good." He puts some cash on the table and stands up. "I'll see you in the morning, babe." He leans down and kisses the top of my forehead.

This time, I can't contain it. The moment he walks out the front door, I run into the bathroom and throw up in the stall. I wait until I stop shaking and crying before leaving the stall and washing myself up. I stare at myself in the mirror, and I look horrible. Tears start streaming down my face again because I may look horrible, but it can't be as horrible as Declan. He's probably lying in the alley, dead. What do I do? Do I call my dad? Do I call my other security? Mr. Crawford? James? No... I can't call anyone because then they will be in the same position Declan is in. This is my fault. I need to just go home and pretend nothing happened and think about what to do.

I shake my head and start full on sobbing. No. I can't just do that. I can't leave Declan wherever he is. I'm going to find him first.

Right before I'm about to leave the bathroom, my phone rings, and it's from Declan. My heart stops in the hope that it truly is him and he's alive.

"Hello?" I answer, still sobbing.

"Where are you?" Declan asks.

I let out the breath I was holding. Holy crap, he's alive. He's okay.

"I'm in the bathroom," I say, and moments later, the door flies open.

Declan barges in and comes right toward me. I look at his face and he has a swollen cheek, black eye already, and a cut, swollen lip. Oh Declan...

My sobs continue, actually worsen at the sight of him. He comes over and hugs me. I cry in his chest for a moment, and he doesn't let me go. "I'm so sorry Declan. I'm so sorry."

"Shhh. Don't be sorry. It's okay. You're okay," he says, trying to calm me.

What? No. I don't even care about myself. I look up at him and say, "No. I'm sorry for you. You're hurt."

He smirks. "This is nothing. There were only four of them and it was fun."

Fun? What?

"Come on, let's go," he states while leading me out the front door, down the street, and into his car.

He starts the car, and I place my hand over his before he can drive off. "Declan, are you okay? Seriously, should we get you to a doctor?"

He laughs. "Seriously Everly. I'm fine, this is nothing. Let's go home."

We're silent for the first ten minutes of the car ride home. He finally forces me to tell him what happened. I explain the text from Adam and everything he told me in the restaurant.

That reminds me to unblock his number. I pull out my phone and feel nauseous as I unblock it, but I don't have a choice. It doesn't matter anyway because, clearly, he will just contact me from other numbers if I don't.

"He told me he's going to text me his hotel to meet him at in the morning," I tell him.

"Well, you're not going, but you are going to tell me when he texts you. I will be the one meeting him there," Declan says sternly.

"Declan, you're already hurt. I can't let you do that," I say, putting my hand on his arm.

He looks over at me and then back toward the road. "Everly, I'll be fine, I promise. I'll bring backup too. We need to deal with him to make this stop. I promised I would protect you, and I will not fail you again."

I don't know what to say, and I know that I can't deal with this on my own. I'll be in the same situation that I was in all last year if I try to do this on my own. I want to protect Declan, but at the same time, I feel like I'm in too deep and I don't even know what to do anymore. I'm just a kid. I can't do this on my own. I should've asked for help last year. I'm not going to make the same mistake again. Declan is okay. He obviously knows what he's doing.

Chapter Nineteen

Adam's text comes the next morning, just like he promised. He sends me the hotel information he's staying at and wants me to meet him there at 11 am. I feel nauseous just thinking about what's going to happen when I don't show up and Declan does instead.

I spent the night in James' room after explaining to him what happened. At first, he was angry with me for going alone and not telling anyone, especially him. When he saw how upset I was about everything, he quickly consoled me. I slept comfortably in his arms through the whole night, and he only laid kisses on my forehead and temple. He knew exactly what I needed from him last night.

"Let's go ziplining today," he says when he sees that I'm awake and texting Declan.

"I don't know that I'm up for it," I say, sighing.

He rolls over, partially on top of me, pushing back my hair from my eyes. "It'll help distract you from whatever is happening today. Let your security team deal with Adam. We don't have much more time. Let's have fun." He smiles down at me.

How can I resist that? He's right. I need the distraction, otherwise I'm going to be lying in bed all day thinking about what's happening or going to happen.

"Alright, let's do it," I say, smiling back up at him.

He leans over and gives me a quick kiss on the lips. He pulls away too quickly for my liking, so I grab the back of his neck and pull him back to me. He puts his arm on the other side of me to support his weight while he continues to kiss me.

He barely pulls his lips from mine because I have a death grip on his head, keeping him there. He smiles against my lips and says, "Everly, I need to text the group if we want to go ziplining today."

I ignore him and lift my head to kiss him again. He laughs. "Seriously, let me text the group."

He isn't going to give up, so I let him roll onto his back and send the text. When he puts his phone down and sits up, I roll on top of him and kiss him again.

"I think I have a better idea than ziplining to distract me today," I say against his lips this time.

He raises an eyebrow. "Oh yeah?"

"Yeah. We could stay in bed all day," I say seductively.

He laughs again. "And what would we do in bed all day?"

I smile down at him and start moving my hand down his chest, over his stomach, toward the waistband of his boxers while saying, "I can show you."

He grabs my wrist to stop me and brings my hand up to his mouth. "Everly, let's get ready to go."

Ouch. Did he just reject me? I know we haven't talked about what this is between us yet, but I thought we liked each other. The rejection hurts. I roll off him, grab my phone, and don't say a word as I leave his room to go get ready.

I immediately jump in the shower to clear my mind. James and I really need to talk, but I'm not in any state of mind to do so right now. Or maybe ever. Now I'm just feeling embarrassed about what just happened. Well, at least that was a good distraction from Adam and what's going to happen today.

I throw on some short shorts and a tank top. It's hot out today and we're going to be in the sun for a while. I pack a little backpack with some sunscreen and a first aid kit. I've never been ziplining before, but I'm so clumsy as it is that I feel like I may need it.

When I take out my phone to look at all the missed messages, Declan sent one, reassuring me that everything is going to be okay and that we will talk tonight. I don't know why he says tonight. Maybe he has something that he needs to do afterward. I'm nervous for him and for everyone, really. I don't know what he has planned, and I just hope whatever it is, that it is enough to keep Adam from hurting anyone.

I relax a little when I look down at our group messages.

James

Ziplining today. Leaving in two hours, who's in?

Jake

Heck yeah!

Ben

I'm in.

Bash

Why not.

I'm busy today.

Jake

What better do you have to do today?

Maybe I have a date.

James

With who?

With four super hot guys apparently going Ziplining.

Jake

Good one. Who's the hottest? Me right?

Ben

You think I'm super hot?

Bash

I'm interested to know the answer to Jake's question.

James

Me too.

I'll answer after spending the day with you guys.

I smile at the exchange we just had. I don't know what got into me to flirt with all of them, but it's fun. I also know it's going to be a fun day filled with flirting because they are going to want me to name them the hottest. I try not to think too much about it, but I'm pretty sure I'm doing this because of James' rejection earlier. Do I want to make him jealous? Yep. Am I going to really flirt with each of them in front of him? Hell yes. If he doesn't want me, then fine. He can enjoy watching me flirt with his best friends. I'm comfortable with that because I also know none of them really want me either. Well, maybe Jake. I don't know, he's hard to read since he flirts with everyone.

After eating breakfast and getting into the car with the boys, I send a quick text to Declan telling him to be careful. I sit in the back seat between Ben and Jake while James drives, and Bash sits in the passenger seat.

James and I haven't said a word to each other since I left his bedroom this morning. The longer we go without talking, the more pissed off I'm getting. What am I to him? He clearly cares about me, right? He let me sleep in his room last night and comforted me. Okay, maybe that could be considered like a big brother thing, but he willingly kissed me this morning. I know he kept pulling away, but he seemed to be enjoying it when I brought him back into the kisses. Or was it because he didn't want to make me feel bad? I should've taken that as a hint in the first place versus pushing for more. He was already rejecting me nicely before outright rejecting me. I feel myself blush at my stupidity.

I didn't realize how lost in my thoughts I was or that I'm bouncing my knee up and down until Jake puts his hand on my knee.

"You okay?" Jake asks me.

I look over at him and give him a weak smile. "Of course."

He doesn't smile back, and I know that he can tell something is bothering me. Now I'm also feeling worse because what's bothering me is James and being rejected by him. I haven't even been thinking about what Declan is going to be walking into in less than an hour. I glance at my phone to see if he responded, and he hasn't.

Jake asks again, "What's wrong?"

I continue to give him that reassuring fake smile. "Nothing."

He moves his hand up my leg a little more, leans in, and whispers in my ear, "I can distract you if you like."

I shiver at his touch and breath on my ear. A good shiver. My body still reacts to him and it's wrong. Isn't it? I've admitted to myself that I'm in love with James and it's true. James kissed me.

So, shouldn't I just be concentrating on him? Oh, that's right. He rejected me and is now ignoring me.

I look back over at Jake and put my hand over his to stop him from raising it further. At least someone wants me. "Mmm. That's tempting."

Jake laughs and pulls his hand off my leg. I glance up and catch James' gaze in the rearview mirror. He looks annoyed. What is he annoyed about? I was honestly hoping he'd look super pissed off, which would mean that he's jealous, but I guess not.

I stop myself from thinking about James for the rest of the ride. It takes only forty-five minutes to get there. The conversation between us is normal, except for a few extra flirtations from Bash and Ben. Jake is expected. They all really want the title of the hottest in the group. Except James, of course. He still hasn't spoken to me once, at least, not directly.

While everyone is trying to get out of the car, I take another look at my phone. My heart sinks to see it's past eleven and Declan didn't respond to my text at all. I take a few deep breaths to try to calm my nerves about the situation. Declan's going to be fine. He took on four big guys by himself and only had a few marks on his face. I'm right that he will be fine... right?

But then my mind goes to what if he isn't? What if what I thought happened to him yesterday happens today? What is Adam going to do since I set him up? Even if Declan comes out of it okay, what is going to stop Adam from harming my friends or father? Or from making my life miserable still?

I'm pulled out of my thoughts when Ben leans through the car door and asks, "Are you coming?"

I don't say anything, but nod. I scoot out of the car and close the door behind me. I follow the boys to the booth to check in for the ziplining. I've never done it before, so I have no idea what to expect. We're brought over to an area to put on some harnesses and given instructions of what to do and not to do while ziplining. To be honest, I didn't pay attention to anything the girl said, and I probably should have, but it was difficult when watching James. Everything James does is so sexy and now I'm getting angry again. Why am I so angry? Today is supposed to be fun. I need to forget about him and ignore him like he's doing to me.

We do a couple of small ziplines to get used to it and I have to say this is exactly what I needed. I was nervous for the first one, but excited for the next ones we did. When going down the first time, I had trouble relaxing. I was holding on with my arms and basically trying to pull myself up and tensing. Once I was able to relax, I really enjoyed the wind in my hair and the adrenaline that started to pump through my veins. I felt free. Sadly, it only lasted a few seconds.

"Alright, I don't know about you guys, but I'm ready for the Screaming Eagle!" Bash says, clearly enjoying this the most out of all of us.

I laugh. "What is the Screaming Eagle?"

Ben looks over at me and asks, "Have you really not heard of it? You're in for a treat."

I'm a little nervous from the way Ben said that, but I'm down. I've really enjoyed these other ones, so it can't be that scary.

Okay, so this looks pretty scary. I'm reading the information on what we are about to do, and I'm not sure that doing just a few small ziplines has prepared me for what's about to happen. We're going to cross a 600-foot-long suspension bridge that's 100 feet above a creek. Then we ride a zipline back across the creek that's 1,000 feet long. Then we will climb a 100-foot tower and ride down the Screaming Eagle that's 2,500 feet long. Okay, cool. So, I can't really picture exactly how big those lengths are, but I can definitely imagine how fast I'll be going, which is 70-75 mph! Are they trying to give me a heart attack?

Bash comes up beside me as I'm reading the information. "Don't worry Everly. I promise it's going to be a lot of fun. You enjoyed the others and the adrenaline rush this provides will feel amazing. It'll clear your head for a while."

I look at Bash and he looks at me like he knows that I need this distraction. Does he know what's going on? Did James tell him? I shake my head. No, I don't think he knows about Adam. I hope. Either way, I appreciate his words of encouragement. I think he's right, though. I really enjoyed the adrenaline rush of the others, I'm sure I will, here too. I love roller coasters, so it can't be much different. Plus, the view is gorgeous. The creek is beautiful, and all the trees and nature are amazing.

Yeah, I start to question my sanity as we step onto the suspension bridge. Look, I know that I'm attached to a rope here and I'm on a bridge, but what if the rope snaps? Then I'm doomed to fall 100 feet down to that creek. I'm fairly certain no one is surviving that. I didn't even think about the fact that the zipline itself could snap. Okay, this feels like a dumb idea. Why did I agree to this?

My heart is pounding out of my chest, and I feel nauseous. I go to turn around after only taking a few steps onto the bridge, but Ben is right there.

"Where do you think you're going?" he asks, knowing exactly what I'm thinking.

"Ben, I can't do this. It's insane. We're going to die!" I state, panicking.

He laughs. "Everly, it's perfectly safe. No one has ever died here."

That doesn't make me feel any better. "Well, with the luck I have in my life, I'll be the first. It'll be all over the news of the poor seventeen-year-old girl that fell to her death while four super-hot guys watched."

Ben continues to laugh, and I hear Jake join him. I didn't realize that Jake came back for me. I'm behind him. James and Bash are already halfway across the bridge while I'm holding these two up at the start.

"Everly, I promise nothing will happen, and this is going to be the most fun you've had all summer. Come on." Jake holds out his hand for me, and I take it.

"What if it does break, though?" I ask, still nervous.

He smiles. "Then it'll be on the news that a sexy seventeen-year-old girl and a super-hot guy fell to their death together."

I laugh way too hard at what he said. I don't know if it's because I'm so nervous or what he said really was that funny, but my stomach starts to hurt because I can't stop laughing. I see Bash and James both stop and look back. They are probably wondering what is taking us so long. I feel bad for holding them up.

"Thanks Jake. Let's go."

I held his hand for a bit as we crossed, but once we made it halfway, I let go. It was difficult to walk like that, but holding onto him did calm me. Ben stayed close behind me too and I knew it was because he was trying to make me feel better by being between both of them. Not that either of them could do anything if this thing snapped. We'd all just fall to our death together.

I sigh with relief when we make it across. I'm not nearly as nervous doing the zipline back down. This one is so much larger than the ones we did before. Jake is still in front of me, and I watch him go down it. He has his hands in the air and yells "Woo-hoo!" the whole way down. I can't help but smile.

Once I'm hooked up and ready to go, I take a deep breath and don't think before pushing off. My stomach turns as I get started and my heart is racing again, but the feeling of the wind in my face and hair... it feels amazing. I can't help but laugh most of the way down. It feels so scary but so amazing at the same time, and I love every second of it. For the short moment I'm in the air flying, I don't think about anything.

We take a short break before climbing the tower because it's really hot outside. I reapply my sunscreen and drink a lot of water. Bash comes over and leans against the wall beside me.

"You looked so hot going down that zipline." Bash winks at me.

I laugh. "Thanks Bash. I'm sure my hair whipping around like that was a huge turn on."

Ben joins in. "Actually, it was."

I roll my eyes and continue laughing. "You both just want me to say you're the hottest of the group."

They both shrug their shoulders, and I can't help but smile. I really feel like this is a competition for them. I never really thought about the fact that I would have to pick one of them at the end of the day. Oh well, that's something to think about later.

So, we climb the tower, and I'm out of breath by the time we get to the top. I feel like I shouldn't have been, but I really am out of shape. I need more training with Declan and to start running again. My stomach churns as I think about Declan. I really hope that he's okay. I didn't think to check my phone before climbing up here.

I look down at the zipline and am now regretting this. The last one was fun, but this one is just so much... more. I watch Bash go first and he's having the time of his life screaming all the way down. I couldn't see him past a certain point, and he just keeps going and going. This is going to be a long one.

James goes next. He's the complete opposite of Bash and Jake. He was silent the whole way that I would think he didn't enjoy it at all if he didn't look so relaxed going down it. How can he look so relaxed? And hot? The wind in his hair... Ben wasn't lying. It is hot.

It's Jake's turn next, but he turns around to face me before going. He grabs my face and looks me in the eye. "Hey, you got this. Look at the beautiful scenery and enjoy the moment. Let yourself be free and enjoy living." He leans forward, looking like he's about to kiss me. He's close but pulls back and pats me on the shoulder. "See you down there Everly!" He pushes off and screams just as his brother did.

I can't help but smile as I watch him. It's my turn, but I'm hesitating. I'm scared, and I know that because my heart is pounding out of my chest, but I do want to do it. But I don't. I just want to be able to enjoy it.

I feel Ben put his hand on my shoulder behind me. I turn to look at him. "Don't think about it, just go. It'll be worth it."

Yeah, I know it will. How do you not think though? Just when I was trying to get the courage to go, Ben pushes me. I gasp and yell, "BEN!"

I hear his laughter behind me, but I can't concentrate on that. My stomach feels like it's in my throat, but I continue to scream and then laugh at the same time. This really is the best feeling in the world. The cool air hitting my face and just the feeling of falling... I don't even know how to explain it other than it truly is amazing.

Once I make it to the end, everyone except Ben is waiting for me, clapping me on the back. I'm thankful they pushed me to do this. It was worth everything.

On the way back to the car, Jake asks, "So, who is the hottest?"

I roll my eyes. "Are you guys really going to make me choose?"

Ben laughs. "Yeah, that was the deal. Come on, we all know it's me, anyway."

They all stand in front of me while I tap my finger to my chin like I'm thinking hard about it. As much as I don't want to say, I'm going to have to choose who I will always choose in this situation.

"James." I shrug.

James has a smirk on his face as he continues walking toward the car.

"Aw, come on Everly. I thought we shared something once." Jake gives me his pouty face.

"Sorry, he was the only one that didn't try to flirt with me today to try to get me to pick him." I shrug my shoulders again and follow James to the car.

I feel them all sulking behind me, but they are the ones who wanted me to pick. I get settled in the backseat and try my hardest to not think about what happened today with Declan and concentrate on the fun I had with the boys.

Chapter Twenty

T he five of us walk in the front door of the Crawford house, still laughing and high from the fun day we had. Our laughter stops the moment we see Mr. Crawford, my dad, and both of their security teams waiting for us. I know this isn't good, but I decide to break the tension by running up to my father and giving him a big hug. His demeanor completely changes the moment I'm in his arms like his little girl again.

"I've missed you, daddy," I say hoping that whatever trouble I'm in would be lessened.

He lets out a breath and says, "I missed you, too."

I let go of him and don't say a word, waiting for an explanation of why he is here unannounced. I don't think I need an explanation, though.

"What's going on, dad?" James walks toward his father, knowing something is up.

"We're just having a meeting and need to talk with Everly. Sounds like you guys had fun today. Where were you all day?"

he asks, like he generally wants to know what we were doing for fun today.

"We just got back from ziplining," Ben says, stepping forward.

"Well, that does sound fun. If you would excuse us, we'll catch up in the morning, okay?" Mr. Crawford says to James and Ben.

They both nod and the security team walks off toward Mr. Crawford's office. My dad puts his arm around me and leads me that way as well. I know what this is going to be about, and I don't like it. Declan hasn't made eye contact with me at all since I walked into the house. He betrayed me.

My father leads me over to a chair and he sits right next to me. Mr. Crawford sits behind his desk and the whole security team is standing around the room in different spots. Some are leaning against the wall with their arms crossed and some are just standing there. Declan is against a wall to the left of my father and his eyes are trained on the floor. I will him to look at me, but he doesn't.

My dad puts his hand over my hand that's on my knee. "Everly, we need to talk about what happened with Adam."

I cringe at the mention of his name. My father knows that I was dating Adam all of last year, but he obviously didn't know the nature of our relationship. I stay silent, not willing to give up information that he might not know.

My father looks sad as he looks into my eyes. "Everly, I need you to tell me the truth when I ask you questions, okay? Everything will be fine, I promise." His voice breaks on that last part. He knows.

He clears his throat. "Everly... Did Adam... rape you?"

I flinch at his words, and I can't say it aloud, so I just nod. There's no use keeping it from him anymore. Adam knows that people know. I've fallen so deep down this hole, there's no way I can dig myself out of it.

I can't look my father in the eyes, so I look down. I see him for a second when I nod, and I hate the look on his face.

"How many times?" he asks, and I can hear it in his voice. He's usually so good at keeping his emotions in check, but this is impossible for him.

I shake my head to indicate that I don't want to talk about it anymore. I was so happy earlier and now I'm fighting back the tears.

"Everly, I need to know everything. I know this is hard for you, but please," he pleads.

"I... It was a lot. I don't know how many times," I respond.

I hear him take a deep breath. "Can you take a guess?"

Honestly, I could tell him exactly how many times it happened. I kept count. Why? I don't know. More of a way to torture myself. Or maybe to hold it against him in the future and fuel my hatred for him? I didn't tell Declan or James because I didn't want them to know. I don't want my father to feel bad either, but I also feel like I owe him the truth.

"Forty-nine times." Yes, forty-nine. Almost fifty. If he had his way today, it would have been fifty times. I didn't want it to get to fifty. Part of me wonders if Adam had kept count too, and that's why he came back. He wanted to make it halfway to one hundred. I feel sick to my stomach the more I think about this. I don't know why fifty seems like such a big deal, but it does.

I'm brought back to reality when I hear my father's chair screech against the floor as he gets up quickly. He's muttering to himself, and he's so angry. Tears stream down my face as I realize how much my father is hurting. It's not his fault.

Mr. Crawford stands up, rounds his desk, and puts a hand on his shoulder. "Thomas, take a deep breath."

My father snaps at him. "Don't tell me what to do! My daughter was fucking raped forty-nine times while I was doing what? What was I doing? Where was I? Not fucking protecting her." He looks at Declan and the other security guards. "None of you were fucking protecting her!" He looks like he's about to go beat each of them up. "I should fire you all!"

My heart tries to jump out of my chest at the realization that he may do just that. I stand up. "Dad! It's not their fault, please. It's not your fault. It's my fault. Please don't be mad at anyone else. They didn't know. No one knew..." My voice starts getting smaller.

The anger on his face fades as he sees me breaking in front of him. He wraps his arms around me as I cry in his chest. I don't cry loudly. I barely let out a sound. I hate crying about Adam and what he did to me. I want to move on. He's rubbing my back and making shushing noises. I pull back and look up at him.

"Daddy, I'm okay. It's okay, I promise." I try to give him a reassuring smile.

He has tears in his eyes now, and he shakes his head. "It's not okay, Everly. This never should have happened, and you never should have kept this a secret from me to protect me or anyone else. Promise me. Promise me that you will never keep a secret like this again and will always tell me, even if they threaten everyone you know. Promise me."

How can I not make this promise? He's so defeated, and I did that to him. "I promise." He hugs me again before letting me go and leading me back into the chair. Mr. Crawford sits back down behind his desk.

Mr. Crawford clears his throat. He's able to control his emotions well, but I can tell he's struggling, too. I barely see him while I'm here during the summers, but I know he considers me a daughter.

Mr. Crawford says, "Everly, we are taking new security measures to ensure that he will never get near you again. There is a lot going on right now, more than just Adam, so we ask that you take at least one security guard with you when you go out with the boys. If you're going out alone, then you need to take two. When you attend school, they will be on campus in case you need them, but they won't be following you inside. If anything happens or if anyone makes you feel uncomfortable, I need you to notify them immediately. Do you understand?"

"Yes sir," I answer.

He nods and then looks at my father. Neither of them is saying anything else. I'm not going to argue about the security team. I brought this upon myself. I do have questions though if they aren't going to willingly provide the information.

"What happened today with Adam?" I ask, looking at my dad.

He sighs. "He was warned about contacting you or approaching you again. His father and I had a talk, and he ensures me that he won't be bothering you again."

I nod. What more can they do? I don't even bother asking if they went to the police because I already know that answer. Adam's family is rich. Too rich. For something like this, he would be able to get out of it before he was even handcuffed. I'm pretty sure that even if he murdered me, he would get away with it. I don't want to think about that, but speaking of murder, I wouldn't be surprised if my father tried to murder him. He most likely wouldn't get in trouble with the law, but I know Adam's dad. It would not end well.

I put my hand on my father's. "Daddy, please don't blame yourself and please let it go. I wanted to protect you, so don't make that in vain by killing him. Okay?" I give him a small smile, trying to make it seem like I'm making light of the situation, even though I know perfectly well what my father is capable of.

He shakes his head. I'm pretty sure that means he's still thinking about it. "It's not worth it and I'm fine, I promise. I'm happy and safe here. I want to just forget it ever happened, okay?"

He kisses me on the forehead. "Okay, sweetie. I want you to go to bed now. I have to leave early in the morning, but I'll say goodbye, okay?"

I nod. I look over toward Mr. Crawford, saying, "Thank you, Mr. Crawford, for keeping me safe and always taking care of me like your daughter. I just wanted you to know that I do appreciate everything you do for me and my father."

Mr. Crawford's gaze softens as he looks at me and nods. I look back at my dad and say, "Goodnight daddy, I love you."

I walk out the door and immediately upstairs to my room. I open my door and see James sitting on the edge of my bed, waiting for me. I don't have it in me right now to discuss this with him. I just feel numb.

"What happened?" he asks.

"They know what happened with Adam. They've taken care of it and added extra security precautions. I'll need to take security with me every time I leave the house. Adam won't be bothering me anymore. He's been warned." I say, hoping that this will be the end of it, and he can leave now. I usually want him to comfort me, but for some reason tonight, I don't.

James shakes his head like he's angry. "That's it? He's been warned?"

"Yes, that's it, James. What more do you want?" I ask.

He stands up off the bed. "I want him rotting in jail or, better yet, dead."

I gasp at him actually saying the words. The thought has crossed my mind many times too, but to say them aloud is different.

"James... You know he will never be kept in jail for this. And don't say that again. You're angry, but not a murderer," I say.

He doesn't move his gaze from mine. "I'm not as good as you think I am, Everly. I do mean it. I want him dead."

Was that a promise? Because that felt like a promise, and I don't like that at all.

"James, promise me you won't do anything to Adam," I say seriously.

He doesn't respond.

"He's no longer a threat. Promise me!"

He sighs. "Fine. I won't go after him."

I let out the breath I was holding in and nod. Good. I don't know what I would do if James killed him. Or worse, got killed himself. I don't need this right now.

James comes over to me and puts his hand on my shoulder. "Everly, do you want to spend the night in my room?"

For a moment I consider it, but at this moment I don't want to. I'm still hurt by his rejection, and I still don't know where we stand. He barely looked at me or talked to me today. Tonight is definitely not the night to talk about all that, though. I have someone more important to talk to.

"I need to be alone tonight." I step out from in front of the door so he can leave.

He doesn't look too upset about my rejection, which oddly hurts. "If you change your mind, you know where to find me," he says as he walks out of the door.

Well, that hurt even more. No good night. No kiss. I guess this is it. He must have just been trying to see what we could be, kind of like Jake and I did. Clearly, he thinks a relationship with me would go nowhere and he probably regrets it all together. Why do I feel like this is over before it even started?

I shake the thoughts out of my head and pull out my phone to text Declan.

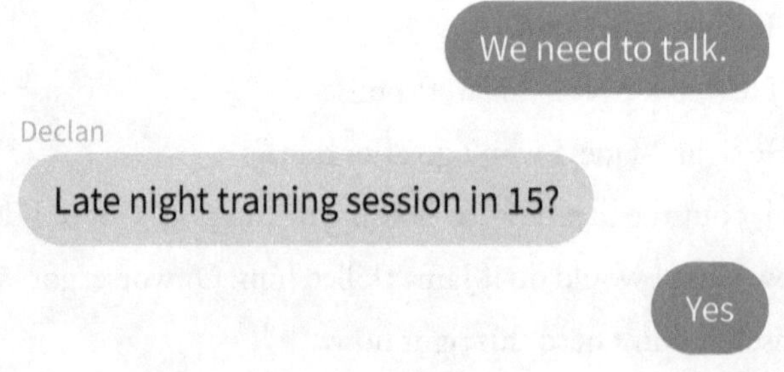

I throw on some workout clothes and meet Declan in the training room. I was just going to come down here to talk to him, but then I thought it might be a good idea to get out some of this anger. I don't know how I go from being upset, to numb, to angry in less than an hour, but I do.

We begin stretching. "What happened?" I ask.

Declan understands what I'm asking as he immediately responds. "I'm sorry. I didn't have a choice. Things weren't going as planned during my meeting with him, so I needed to involve your father."

I nod and don't say anything. What is there to say?

After warming up, Declan wants me to fight him. Obviously, I've had barely any training, and he could beat me in two seconds, but I don't think that's his plan. He wants me continuously to throw punches at him as he blocks me. I gladly do. I, unfortunately, can't seem to lay a single punch on him.

We don't say a word as I continue to try to beat up on him. I'm sweating, and he is hardly out of breath. That makes me even more angry.

My punches are sloppy, and I'm stumbling over my feet. He doesn't say a word or try to correct me at all. I know he sees everything I'm doing wrong, but he still doesn't correct me. He wants me to take my anger out on him.

Only when I stop throwing punches to catch my breath and get a drink of water does he say something. "Do you want to talk?"

I stare at him as I gulp down water. "What is there to talk about?"

"That you're angry at me. That I broke my promise. That I couldn't protect you," he says it all with a straight face, but I can see the pain in his eyes.

I'm so exhausted, physically, and mentally, that I just don't have it in me anymore. I sit down on the mats and just stare at him for a moment. He sits down in front of me.

"Declan... I'm not mad at you. You did what you needed to do to keep me safe, and I don't blame you for that. That's your job. I don't think I can tell you any secrets that I want to keep from my dad, but again, you're my security guard. I shouldn't be doing that, anyway. And as for not protecting me, I've told you before that it's not your fault. I don't blame you for that either," I say, hoping that this can be the end of the discussion because I'm just so tired.

"Okay," he says.

"Okay," I repeat.

He stands up and holds his hand out to me. I take it and as I stand, I throw a punch right into his stomach. He stumbles back for a moment and when he looks up, he has a wide grin on his face.

"Sorry. I couldn't leave here without getting at least one hit on you. Now I feel better," I say as I walk out the door and back to my room.

Chapter Twenty-One

I t's a girls' day! I love the boys, but I'm badly in need of a girls'
day after everything that's been happening. I understand
they care about me, but they all have been a little more moody
than normal, and protective. I appreciate them, but I need to
get out.

Ashley and I have been texting almost every day and met
up for coffee the other afternoon. We decided it's time to get
Lauren out of the house too, which is apparently difficult to
do with her parents. I haven't asked much about her situation
at home just because I don't want to be that nosey person. I
appreciate it when people don't pry into my life. If she wants to
tell me, I know that she will.

Declan and Barry are driving us to the mall. They are both in
the front seat while the three of us are sitting in the back. It's a
spacious SUV, so there's plenty of room.

"I can't believe you're going to be sneaking into a club! Are
you sure your fake ID is going to work?" Ashley asks while
looking at the ID I just showed her.

"The guy James got it from is a professional. It looks exactly like my normal ID, just the age is obviously different," I say while shrugging my shoulders.

"Do you think he can get us some?" Lauren asks the question just like she would ask what we want for dinner.

Both Ashley and I stare at her and then glance at each other like we are making sure we both heard her ask it.

"You want a fake ID? Lauren, what would you do with a fake ID?" Ashley asks her seriously.

"Oh, I don't know, maybe go to a club..." Lauren responds.

"What would your parents do if they caught you sneaking out and going to a club?" Ashley continues asking.

Lauren shrugs her shoulders. "It can't get much worse than it already is. I'm rarely allowed out, anyway. At least I would have one fun night doing something normal teenagers do."

I laugh. "I'm not sure normal teenagers have fake IDs and go to clubs, but I suppose they sneak drinks at least."

Lauren sighs. "I'm so jealous of you, Everly. It's like you can do whatever you want to do."

I shake my head. "I have more freedoms, but I wouldn't say I can do whatever."

"Everly... You're going to a club and drinking underage. You went to a cabin for two nights with four teenage boys and went skinny dipping and got drunk. Do I need to say more?" Lauren asks while looking like she's ready to list off the other things I've done this summer.

"Okay, fine. I have a lot more freedom than a normal teenager does, but I wouldn't be allowed to do anything I want," I respond.

"List one thing," Ashley chimes in.

I take a moment to think it over. What wouldn't I be allowed to do? I mean, Lauren's right. I was allowed to spend a couple of nights in a cabin with four boys. That's crazy. There has to be something I wouldn't be allowed to do.

"I don't know, but there has to be something," I say while looking in the rearview mirror for Declan's eyes while he's driving.

As if he knows that I'm looking at him, he looks back in the mirror and smirks.

"Declan, what wouldn't I be allowed to do?"

He shrugs. "Lauren has a point. You're allowed to do whatever you want to do."

I gasp. "Declan! You're supposed to be on my side. I know there are things. Like... going on a road trip, right? Say I wanted to drive to California for a couple of weeks."

Declan shakes his head. "No, I'm pretty sure your father would think that's a great idea."

I roll my eyes only because I know he's right. I'm not going to get into why he's right with them, but I'm sure my father would prefer that I'm across the country after everything that has happened with Adam. Regardless, this isn't going the way I want it to.

"Well, whatever. That's only because I have you guys for protection. It's not like I'd be allowed to go alone," I state.

No one argues that point.

We finally make it to the mall and the first stop is to find a dress to wear to the club. Ashley and Lauren are on a mission to find me the perfect dress that's going to make it so James can't keep his eyes off me. With the way James is acting toward me, I could be naked, and he wouldn't even glance my way.

I do try on some modest dresses, but they just aren't club material. Lauren has been picking out long dresses with barely any cleavage showing, while Ashley is picking out dresses that I would hardly consider to be more than a rag.

I walk out in one of Ashley's picks and immediately decide this is the dress. It's a short, strapless, sparkly black dress. It's perfect.

I do a twirl for the girls. "What do you think?"

Ashley has a huge grin on her face while Lauren's mouth is hanging open.

"Perfect!" Ashley yells.

"Are you sure?" Lauren asks, looking like she's not approving.

"Yes. It's sparkly and perfect," I say.

Ashley is gushing over it and telling me how hot I look while Lauren just continues to stare. It is short, but I'm going to a club. That's the whole point, right? I need to look good.

"No," Declan says as he walks closer to the fitting rooms.

"What?" I ask, shocked that Declan is having an opinion.

"You are not wearing that to the club," he states with authority.

"Why not?"

He stares at me like he's trying to choose his words wisely, but he decides against saying anything.

"Declan, I'm going to a club. Isn't this what girls wear?" I ask.

"Yeah, if... never mind. Look, I think you would be better off wearing one of the dresses Lauren picked out for you," he states.

I laugh. "No way. Declan, didn't we just discuss in the car how I'm allowed to do pretty much whatever I want? You're proving my point that I can't."

"You can wear whatever you want, Kid."

I roll my eyes. "I will."

So, despite Declan's objections, I buy the dress with some sparkly black flats. I was having second thoughts considering I wouldn't be able to bend in this dress and it honestly isn't the most comfortable, but I'm feeling petty right now. Plus, I do look really good in it.

"Where should we go next?" Ashley asks as we walk out of the store.

"I'm good for whatever," Lauren answers.

"Want to get some lunch?" I ask.

"Sounds good," Ashley and Lauren both say at the same time.

We decide to go to a restaurant right outside the mall. I've never been, but they say this place has the best cheesecake, and I do love cheesecake.

Right before opening the door, I hear my name. "Everly!"

I smile as I turn around, knowing that voice. I find Jake and Ben heading our way.

"Jake! Ben! What are you guys doing here?" I ask.

"We have a few things to buy at the mall, but spotted you on our way," Jake says, and Ben just looks toward the building past me.

Okay, why does Ben look guilty?

"Want to join us?" Ashley asks a little too quickly.

She looks excited as she's looking between them both. I can't help but shake my head. I haven't known her long, but she seems like she's boy crazy. We head in and grab a table together. Ashley places herself between Lauren and Ben while forcing me to sit on the opposite side of the booth with Jake.

We make small talk about our day as we look over the menu. I can't help but notice Lauren seems to be looking anywhere but at the boys. She looks so uncomfortable and has been silent the whole time since they showed up.

"So, what are you shopping for?" I ask, looking over toward Ben.

"Just some school stuff," he replies.

I tap my fingers on the table because this seems so awkward. The tension with Lauren and then the boys acting weird is getting under my skin. Ashley seems oblivious to it all, as she is just talking with Ben.

"You ready for our last bucket list item?" Jake asks me.

"Yep, I just bought a dress today for it," I say.

"Can I see?" he asks with a gleam in his eye.

I laugh. "No way! You'll see when we go."

The server comes over with our food, and we're mostly silent as we begin eating. I got the chicken alfredo, and it's amazing.

I'm about to break the silence when Lauren stands up out of the booth and says, "I'm going to the bathroom."

She runs off without a response from anyone.

"Is she okay?" Jake asks.

"I don't know," I say while looking at Ashley.

She shrugs her shoulders and continues eating. Well, if she's not concerned, then I guess I won't be either. I like Lauren. She's kind and fun to hang out with, but her personality differs from mine and Ashley's. She's shy and timid. She acts like she's constantly looking over her shoulder like whatever she's doing she's going to get in trouble for. Maybe her parents are super strict and don't want her hanging out with boys.

The tension has disappeared since Lauren left for the bathroom, and everyone is talking again. I watch Ben as he's eating and notice that he hasn't been using his right arm, which is weird because he's right-handed.

"Is your arm okay?" I ask Ben.

"Huh? Yeah, of course. Why?" he asks nervously.

I grin. "You're not using it."

"Yeah, I am," he says while shoving his face with more food.

"No, you haven't used it the entire time you've been here."

I can see Jake's shoulders shaking beside me and then hear him laugh uncontrollably, like he's been holding it in forever. Ben glares at him.

"Ben, what happened to your arm?" I demand an answer.

He sighs, raises his right arm, and lifts his jacket sleeve. I did find it odd he's wearing a jacket in the middle of the summer but thought that maybe he was just cold from the air-conditioning. Then I notice a shiny silver bracelet hanging from his wrist. No, it's not a bracelet, it's handcuffs.

Ashley chokes on her drink as she sees the handcuffs and touches them. "Ben, these are like real handcuffs. What happened?"

"Nothing," he states quickly.

"Ben! Did you get arrested and escape?" I ask jokingly.

"Of course not!"

"Then what happened?" I continue to ask him for an answer.

"Nothing. I'm not telling you," he says, while pulling his sleeve back down.

I look over toward Jake, and he puts his hands up in the air. "Not my story to tell."

Of course not. I can't help but laugh. I'm curious about what on earth caused Ben to have handcuffs attached to him, but I know he's not going to give up the story. He always gets into the weirdest situations that I just don't understand, nor will he tell the story about how or what happened.

We finish up our meals and order some cheesecake when I remember that Lauren went to the bathroom like fifteen minutes ago. "Should we go check on Lauren?"

Ashley's eyes go wide. "I completely forgot about her. I'll go check."

Ashley gets up from the table and walks toward the bathroom. We all watch her as she disappears inside and then comes out just a few seconds later and back to the table.

"She's not in there," Ashley says.

"What?" I stand up and follow Ashley back to the bathroom to double check.

Sure enough, she's not. Ashley walks toward the front of the restaurant, and I walk out back to check for her. I open the back door and step outside, running right into her, literally.

"I'm sorry!" she says as she takes a step back.

I steady myself and look at her. I see a guy walk around the corner of the building, but there's no one else around out here.

"What are you doing out here? We were worried about you," I say.

Her face is red, and she's not looking at me when she responds, "I just needed some fresh air."

I nod and open the door for her to go inside. I don't believe her when she says she just needed fresh air. She's a terrible liar, but I'm not going to push it. Like I said before, if she wants to tell me, then she will.

After eating the best cheesecake I've ever tasted, the girls and I head back to the mall to continue shopping. We went our separate ways from the boys because it is our girls' day, after all. We spend most of our time in the bookstore and I buy a few books that have been on my list to read.

Once I get home, I relax with one of my new books in my room. It was nice going out today, laughing, and enjoying myself. I'm hoping with them as my new friends, we'll have a good senior year together.

Chapter Twenty-Two

There's less than two weeks left of summer break, and we have one item left on the bucket list that we're going to check off tonight. Going to a club. I've had time to convince Declan to let me go and have him stay outside since James promises he won't be drinking. I'll be riding with the boys, but he will be following closely behind.

We get into the club too easily. They look at our IDs and let us through without a second glance. We've only been here an hour and a half, and we are all, minus James, drunk. I love hanging out with the boys, but I do wish my new friends were here. Being the only girl can be exhausting. Unfortunately, James couldn't get them a fake ID in time. I didn't realize how much I missed the company of having another girl around until I started hanging out with Ashley and Lauren.

I dance with Ben, Jake, and Bash multiple times and I'm sweating. James never asks to dance with me, and I don't bother asking him because he seems to have no interest. We still haven't talked, and we've barely seen each other since the day we went ziplining. His father took him away for business for a bit, and he didn't even bother to text me once. I want to say that I'm over him, but clearly, I'm not. I'm just so confused about what happened. One day we're making out and the next we're barely on speaking terms.

I sit back at the bar and order another Sex on the Beach. These are amazing. Ben slips into the chair beside me and orders himself another drink as well. He's already more drunk than me.

"Do you want a pet?" he turns and asks me.

"What?" I ask, confused.

"Do you want a pet?" he repeats his question like I just didn't hear him over the music.

"No, I heard you. Like a cat?" I ask.

"Yeah. I was wondering what type of pet you'd want if you wanted one." He stumbles on his words a little. I'm not sure he really needs this next drink.

I think about it for a moment. "Um... I guess I'd like a kitten at some point."

He laughs. "I could see you with a kitten."

I smile back. "So, do you want a pet?"

"I want a chinchilla," he says seriously.

This time I laugh. "A chinchilla? Why?"

Before he has the opportunity to answer, Bash sits in the chair next to me. "Dude, why would you want a chinchilla? You can't get them wet."

I look at Bash and say, "Huh? You must be thinking about gremlins, not chinchillas."

Both Bash and Ben laugh.

Bash argues, "No, it's definitely chinchillas. Besides, you're thinking of not being able to feed gremlins after midnight, not that they can't get wet."

I shake my head. "No, it's definitely a rule for gremlins. You can't feed them after midnight, you can't get them wet, and you need to avoid bright lights."

Bash pulls out his phone and looks it up. "Huh, you're right. But it says that chinchillas also can't get wet, though they won't multiply like gremlins."

Ben finally interrupts us after continuously laughing. "Guys, gremlins aren't even real. I don't want a gremlin. I want a chinchilla. And... hold that thought. Jake's calling me over. He has a couple of girls over there..."

Ben walks, or more like stumbles, toward where Jake stands. He's talking to some girls that don't look much older than us. They must be at least twenty-one, though. I go to turn back toward Bash, but he's also gone. I didn't even notice him get up.

I scan the room for James, finding him at the other end of the bar, alone, and staring in my direction. Has he just been sitting there the whole time watching out for us? How boring. I get off my chair and climb into the empty seat next to him. Once I sit down, I remember I left my drink over there. Oh well, too late now.

"Hey," I say as I get comfy on the chair.

"Hey," he replies without even looking up at me.

Seriously, how has he not looked at me? I'm in a strapless black dress that's sparkly and barely covers my butt. Doesn't he realize I wore this for him? Crap. I don't like drunk me and my admittance. I said I was wearing it for myself to feel good and it had nothing to do with James. Yeah, who was I kidding? It has everything to do with James.

"Come dance with me," I say, hoping that he'll take me up on my offer.

"I'm good," he replies, still looking down at the bar.

"Seriously? You come to a club and barely drink, don't dance, and just sit here. You're not even having fun. This is our last bucket list item," I say, hoping to convince him to at least dance with me once.

He shakes his head. "I'm the DD. Of course I'm not drinking much."

I shake my head this time. "James, you know we can get someone else to drive us home. Declan is right outside."

"Well, he's outside, not in here. So, if I get drunk, there's no one to watch out for you or those idiots over there," he says, nodding toward our friends.

I laugh. "They are so drunk."

"You're not far off," he smiles at me.

God, that smile. It's so sexy. I've been looking for that smile for a while now, and it's done a good job hiding. I just want to kiss him so bad.

What the heck, why not? I lean forward and kiss him. He immediately pulls back.

Wow. Again? I thought maybe a rejection wouldn't hurt as much if I was drunk, but clearly, I was mistaken. What am I doing? How many times does he have to reject me for me to realize that he doesn't want me? I quickly stand up and walk away before he can see the tears forming in my eyes.

I was certain there was a back door this way, but after passing the bathrooms, it's like a maze back here. I didn't realize how big this club was. It looks like there are a bunch of offices around every corner.

Right when I decide to head back, I turn the corner and run into someone's muscular chest. He steadies me by gripping my shoulders, and I push back off him.

"I'm so sorry," I say, still looking at his chest.

"Hazel?" the man asks.

"Huh?" I look up at the gorgeous man. By gorgeous, I mean he literally is gorgeous. His hair goes just past his ears and is a dark brown, but like mine, with a hint of red. At least in this lighting. His eyes are a stunning green and his facial features are perfect. Like someone handcrafted this man.

He snaps me out of my drunken trance as he says, "Oh, pardon me. You look very similar to an old friend... Are you alright?"

That's the question of the century, isn't it? "Honestly, I'm just wanting to get out of here. Like, not going out the front entrance."

He laughs. "Well, you missed the turn to the back door that way. Why don't you come sit with me and I'll get you a drink."

"Okay." Wait. Why did I say okay? I'm drunk, but I don't really want to be sitting down with a stranger right now, but for some reason, I let him lead me back toward the bar area. Instead of sitting at the bar, he leads me to a private booth, and the music isn't as loud over here. I can hear myself think again.

I slide in one side of the booth, and he slides in the other. He smiles down at me. "I'm sorry, I didn't catch your name."

"Everly," I say, holding my hand out for him to shake.

"Asher," he replies and shakes it.

"It's nice to meet you Asher, but I've had too much to drink, and I really should be going. I'm not sure why I came back here..." My mind is foggy.

"Here, have some water," he says as he passes me a glass of water. Wait, had that water always been there? I didn't see a server come by.

I take a few gulps like it would counteract what the alcohol is doing to my system. I can't believe I keep drinking so much this summer.

"So, why were you trying to leave out the back door, Everly?" he asks with that smile still plastered on his face. God, he is seriously gorgeous. Like, I feel like it hurts to look at him.

"Uh, yeah, I really don't know why I'm sitting here. I really should be going."

Since I met him in the hall by the offices, he probably works here. If he finds out that I'm only 17, I'm going to get in trouble and so will whoever let us in.

He puts his hand on mine. "I just want to help. Talk to me for a bit and I'll help you get out of here and home. I promise."

He looks like a man of his word. Honestly, why not? My friends are still getting drunk somewhere having the time of their lives. Why not talk to this gorgeous stranger who I would never see again?

"You really want to know all my drama?" I ask and laugh.

"I asked, didn't I?"

I grin. "Alright, sure. This summer was supposed to be fun, but it turned out to be one bad decision after the next. After a year of hell, I started new here and decided sleeping with one of my best friends would make me feel better. Spoiler alert, it didn't. I mean, maybe for a minute, and it didn't end badly, it was just a dumb mistake. Then I played a prank on an ex-best friend, which ended poorly as well. My ex-boyfriend, not the best friend I slept with, was still threatening me and causing issues. Everyone is mad at me and the decisions I was making to keep them safe. The guy I'm in love with wants nothing to do with me and I just want to go home, go to bed, and pretend the last couple of months never happened. Or maybe the last year and a half. That's probably better."

Asher gives me a sympathetic look. "I feel like there's a lot missing in there, but it sure sounds like a lot of drama. So, let's start with the most recent thing in there. The guy you love wants nothing to do with you. Why do you say that?"

I sigh. "Well, at first, every time I tried to tell him how I feel, he'd push me away and tell me I'm drunk. Then we kissed a few times, but now he's just rejecting me or ignoring me. I kissed him before I ran into you, and he rejected me again."

"Have you talked about your feelings when you weren't drunk?" he asks.

I look down at the floor to think for a moment. Have I talked to him when I wasn't drunk? Huh, maybe not. I kept thinking we needed to talk about what we were when we started kissing, but I kept putting it off. We kissed when I wasn't drunk, but we didn't talk about it.

"I guess I haven't."

He smiles. "Well, there you go. Tomorrow, when you're no longer drunk, why don't you tell him again and see what happens?"

I lean back and sigh in relief. It seems talking to him might not have been a bad idea. Maybe I made at least one good decision tonight. "I'll try that, thanks. But I think I have more courage right now than I will tomorrow."

"Try writing yourself a note on what you want to say and how you feel. Then in the morning, read it and see if you still feel that way. Convince yourself to have the same courage if you do," he says, passing me a pen and a pad of paper.

Wait, was that pen and pad of paper always there? I don't remember there being anything on the table. There's definitely nothing else on the table other than my empty glass of water, right? I look around and don't see anything else. I look at my water to find it full. What? I swear I just finished drinking that... I did not see anyone come to refill it.

"Okay, I'm really drunk. Did you always have that pad of paper there? And... wasn't my water just empty?"

His smile is glued to his face as he leans back. "It was. It just got refilled and now you have paper and a pen to write yourself that note. Go for it." He nods down toward the pad.

I take the lid off the pen and put it on the pad of paper. Hang on, he didn't answer my questions. Oh, whatever, I don't know what's going on anymore. I take a few minutes to scribble down how I'm feeling about James and what I want to say to him right now. I also give myself a message for the morning to make me talk to him this time. I hope I can read this in the morning.

When I finish, I hand him back the pen. "Thank you for your kindness and advice. How can I repay you?"

He's staring at me for a little too long, like he's trying to figure me out. "Tell me about yourself. How old are you?"

"Seventeen." What?! Crap! Why did I just give him my real age? How drunk am I?!

He laughs. "I figured you were young. Fake ID?"

"Yes." What?! I was saying no, I swear no was coming out of my mouth before it changed to yes. What is happening?

He smirks and pushes his hair from his eyes behind one ear. I can't help but stare at his ear. It's so... pointy.

"Has anyone ever told you that you have pointy ears?" I ask and immediately my stomach twists. Why did I just comment on his ears? That was so rude.

He looks shocked for a moment, and his hair falls back over his ears. "I can't say that they have."

I think the alcohol is starting to hit me again because now I'm laughing. I've really never seen anyone have pointy ears like that before.

"Are you an elf?"

He looks offended. "I am certainly not an elf."

I can't help but continue laughing at his reaction. "Are you sure? You're so gorgeous and have pointy ears. Isn't that like an elf trait?"

"What do you know of elves?" he asks, leaning forward on his arms on the table.

I laugh even harder. "I'm sorry, this is silly. Obviously, there's no such thing as elves. I was just kidding."

He eyes me skeptically. "Of course."

He clears his throat. "Well, Everly, it was very nice meeting you, and I hope that everything works out tomorrow morning. If you find yourself needing to escape or wanting more advice, don't hesitate to come and find me here. Don't bother with your ID. Just tell them you're here to see me."

Is that really all he wanted from me? This was... interesting.

Before he stands up, I ask, "I don't know anything about you. You know my name, age, and drama. At least tell me how old you are and what you do here. Do you work here?"

He keeps that same smile as before on his face. "Something like that. Age is just a number, it doesn't matter. That's why I don't care that you're 17 and getting drunk."

I guess he's right. He seriously can't be more than 25, though. He looks young. "Alright, well, you promised you'd help me get out of here."

He looks over toward the side of the room and says, "If you still want me to, I will, but it looks like someone wants to talk to you. You can find me in the third office to the left if you need me."

We both stand up, and I see James come my way. Asher walks off before James makes it to my side and puts his arm around my shoulder. "Are you okay? What were you doing with him?"

"Who?" I ask, trying to pretend like I wasn't just with anyone. Clearly, he saw us both get out of the booth.

"The guy you were just sitting with…" he states, annoyed with me.

I roll my eyes. "Nothing James. We were just talking. I'm going home now."

I push his arm off my shoulder and start walking away. I guess I'm going out the front this time because that's where I'm heading. Should I go back to find Asher? Ugh, I just want to get away from James. Again.

"Everly, wait." James grabs my arm.

I feel the tears welling in my eyes again. I can't do this. This was supposed to be a fun night. I can't keep doing this.

"James, just let me go, please."

He lets go of my arm just like I asked. Why does he have to be a gentleman?

"I'm sorry. I just want to go to bed. I'm tired."

He nods. "Let me take you home."

"No, Declan can. You can't leave the others, they're drunk. Don't let them do anything stupid. I'll see you tomorrow," I say, walking away and texting Declan at the same time.

Why was I looking for the back door earlier when I could've just walked out the front and texted Declan? I need to stop drinking. My brain cannot function like this. Once Declan pulls the car up, I hop in and neither of us says a word.

CHAPTER TWENTY-THREE

W aking up nauseous and with a headache seems to be a common occurrence this summer. I want to say it was worth it to have fun the night before, but was it? Yeah, I guess I had a blast with the boys, and it is nice being numb every now and then. Some annoying emotions kept peeking through, though, so maybe I didn't have enough to drink. At least Declan was nice and said we can train this afternoon versus this morning.

I open my eyes and roll over into a body. Wait, what? I swear I went to bed alone last night. The room is dark from the black-out curtains blocking out the sunlight, but I could make out James' figure next to me. I suppose I can't see him clearly, but I definitely know the feel of his chest.

I try not to stir as I recall the events from last night. The last thing I remember is Declan bringing me home alone. I remember taking my clothes off and just throwing a t-shirt on. Did I even put underwear on? I explore below the blanket to find that I indeed had no underwear on and only a t-shirt. Okay, so after that, I jumped into bed. It was definitely my bed I laid in last night. So how did I end up in James's bed?

I try to slowly roll off the bed gracefully, but the combination of my headache and the dizziness I feel makes me stumble and literally roll off the bed onto my side. Ow. I pause for a moment to try to calm the pain in my skull and get my breath back that's knocked out of me.

"Are you okay?" I hear James lean over the bed to try to look at me.

Well, this is embarrassing.

"Fine…" is all I can get out.

He gets off the bed, but I force myself up quickly before he can help me. I don't need his help.

He opens the curtains slightly to let in enough light to be able to see each other clearly. That little bit of light is like a knife to my forehead. I sit back down on the bed and groan.

"I don't remember how I got here last night. I swear I went to sleep in my own bed," I whisper.

"You don't remember anything from last night?" he asks, trying to see if I'm telling the truth.

I shake my head. "Well, I remember everything other than how I got into your bed."

He nods and says, "You came in, in the middle of the night. You looked pretty out of it."

"So, you just let me insert myself beside you in bed?" I ask with a small laugh.

He smirks. "You have a tendency to do that."

I laugh because he's right. "Well, I've never done that with only a t-shirt on and nothing under it. I'm sorry I bothered you. I'm going to go now."

His eyes grow wide for a moment at what I said and then they narrow as he looks me up and down. I have no idea what he's thinking.

Before I can open the door, he grabs my wrist. I turn around to look at him and he doesn't do anything but stare at me.

The silence and pounding in my head are deafening, so I say, "James..."

He interrupts me by kissing me, hard. Harder than he ever has before. I kiss back, but only for a second. I'm so confused. I can't keep doing this with him. I want to keep kissing him, but I also need to know what is happening with us.

I pull away from the kiss. "James, I'm so confused. One second, you're pushing me away and the next you want me. What is this between us?"

He lets go of my wrist and rubs his hand through his hair like he's in pain and deep in thought. I think he is going to walk away from me, but he swoops in and pushes me against the door, his body against mine. His breath is on my neck as he runs his nose up it and to my ear.

He bites my earlobe and says, "Everly, I don't know what you're thinking half the time, and I keep saying this is a bad idea. I try to stop myself, but then you do this." He reaches down and touches my thigh, dragging his hand all the way up my leg, stopping at my hip while my shirt is pushed up over his hand.

"Coming in here with nothing on but a shirt. I can't resist you Everly."

"Then don't," I say, breathier than I wanted it to come out.

He groans and rubs his hand over my stomach and comes so close to my breasts but stops just below. "I need to resist you, Everly. This is a bad idea... We shouldn't do this."

"Why?" I ask, frozen.

"We won't work out. We can't," he says, just as breathy as I am.

"Take the future away. What do you want right now?" I ask, hoping he will answer truthfully.

He groans and kisses below my ear and down my neck. "I want you... so bad."

I gasp at his admittance. "Then take me James. We'll worry about the future later. I want you. Take me."

I thought he would put up more of a fight, but surprisingly, he doesn't. He immediately starts kissing me everywhere and finally moves his hands to my breasts and squeezes. He captures my mouth with his and lifts me up, bringing me back to bed. He sits me on the edge and forces me to lie down. He continues to kiss me as he pushes my shirt all the way up, revealing my naked body below him.

He stands back for a moment and admires me. "Beautiful. So damn beautiful."

I feel the goosebumps rise on my body from just his words.

He kneels at the end of the bed and spreads my thighs. Oh my God, is he going to do what I think he's going to do? No one has ever... Ah!

He strokes me with his tongue and feasts on me ravenously, like he can't get enough. It feels so good, and I don't know what to do with my hands. One hand clenches the sheets on the bed while the other grabs his hair and pulls, yet pushes to keep him going. Just when I think it can't get any better, he enters two fingers inside me and stretches me. It doesn't take long for me to be so close. I'm seconds away from reaching my climax when he gently sucks and sends me over the edge.

"James!" I yell, way too loudly. I can't help my moans as he continues to feast on me through my climax.

When I finally finish, he crawls on top of me and kisses me. I can taste myself on his lips.

"You taste so good, Everly. I've wanted to taste you for longer than I'll admit," he says.

I don't know why that's so hot, but it is. I've thought about having him inside my mouth on more than one occasion, even though I've never done that before. Thankfully, Adam never forced me to do that, he always just wanted to be inside me.

As he kisses between my breasts, I say, "I want to taste you."

Heat swirls in his eyes as he looks at me, trying to comprehend my words. He stands back up for a moment to take his boxers off, and I sit up and stand next to him. I push his chest to indicate for him to sit, and he does. I kneel before him and grab his length with my hand and rub it for a moment before putting him in my mouth.

I feel nervous because I have no idea what I'm doing, but his moans give me courage to keep going. I swirl my tongue around his tip and then lick the length of him. I put him in my mouth as far as I can without gagging. He grabs my hair and helps guide me at the pace he wants.

"Fuck! Everly, I'm not going to last," he pants.

I keep going, knowing what he's trying to tell me. I've always thought it was gross how girls can let a man come in their mouth, but at this moment I don't even care. I don't want to stop. I love doing this to him.

I quicken the pace, and I can feel him tense. "Everly, you have to stop..."

I don't stop and I think he gets the hint because he keeps his hold on my head, and he tenses. I feel his cock twitch in my mouth, followed by spurts of salty warmth going down my throat. I suppress a gag and allow it to fill my mouth instead. Once he finishes, he pulls out of my mouth, and I take a few gulps as I swallow it down.

He watches me intensely. "You have no idea how hot that was."

I give him a wicked smile and stand up. I wrap my arm around the back of his head and kiss him.

"Lay down with me," he says while pulling me back onto the bed.

I do what he says and follow his lead, laying back in bed with him. I curl up next to him, facing him, and he wraps his arm around me.

He kisses my forehead. "Everly, I'm sorry."

"For what?" I ask, hoping he's not going to say he regrets what we just did.

"I shouldn't have…" he pauses for a moment and his voice becomes strained. "I shouldn't have let it get this far."

I stiffen. "Do you regret what we just did?"

He doesn't respond. His silence indicates yes.

I get angry. "Well, I don't James. I can tell that you don't feel the same about me, but I'm done with this game. I'm going to be honest with you. I'm in love with you, James. I've loved you for a lot longer than I wanted to admit to myself. If you don't feel the same, then that's fine. I get it. But I don't regret what we did. In fact, I want more. I want all of you. But I'll take whatever you will give me."

He stiffens this time and sighs. He's still silent, and I start to get nervous. Maybe it wasn't that he didn't like me, but he didn't like what I did to him. It was my first time.

I have to ask, "Was it… not good? I'm sorry, James, it was my first time ever doing that…"

He rolls over onto me and gets inches from my face. He pushes some hair behind my ear as he says, "No. God, no. You were amazing. Wait, that was your first time? Never mind, it has nothing to do with that."

"Then what does it have to do with?" I whisper.

He rolls off me, sits up, and sighs. I sit up too and lean against the headboard.

"Everly... You and I are not a good idea. We just never will have a happy ending."

That's not what I was thinking he'd say. "What do you mean?"

He stands up and grabs my shirt off the floor, handing it to me. I feel embarrassed for a moment because I didn't even realize that I am sitting here naked. I quickly put it on over my head as he puts his boxers on and sits back down next to me.

"You're still in high school, and I'm leaving next week to go back to college. We'd have a long-distance relationship which never works out. Then once I graduate, I'm going to be working for my father and I'm not going to have any time for you. You deserve to be with someone who can make time for you, and I can't do that. I'm going to be preparing to take over his company one day and that means my life revolves around work. You deserve someone that will put you first." His voice sounds sad.

"James, I'm not high maintenance and need someone to be with me twenty-four seven. I'm used to being alone. I love being with you, and I love you, James. I meant what I said. I'll take whatever you can give me," I say sincerely, hoping that he understands it.

He rubs his hands through his hair again. "That's just it Everly. I can't give you much at all and you deserve the world. Fuck, with everything you have been through... you deserve so much more. I can't ask you to wait for me through this next year and then only have pieces of me after that."

I shake my head. "James... Shouldn't it be my choice? I understand what you're saying, but right now I just really want to be with you. Can't you let me choose? I promise that if I'm not happy down the line, then I'll let you know. If it doesn't work out, then it doesn't, and I'll walk away, okay?"

He looks me dead in the eyes and says, "That's the problem, Everly. Once I have you, I don't think I can let you go. I'm barely able to let you go right now and if we go any further with this..."

I think I understand what he's saying. Are we both willing to live a life of heartbreak? If we continue this and I do walk away, then he would be hurting. I don't want to do that to him. If I stay and I do need more than what he can give me, then I'd be hurting. But what if it is all enough for us? Isn't love worth the risk of all the pain that could happen? For the hope of a happily ever after? Does that exist though?

I take his face in my hands and stare into his eyes. "James, I'm all in. I need you to know that I. Am. All. In. I love you and I am willing to risk this ending horribly for the chance that it doesn't. All I know is that every time I'm in your arms, I feel safe and like I'm home. When I walk into the same room as you, I can't stop staring at you. When I see you smile, it makes me so happy, and I can't help but smile. When I kiss you... the world fades away. You are everything to me, James and I want to be with you regardless of the risks. If you don't feel the same, I'll

walk out of this room now and never look back. But if you do...
If you love me and are willing to take the risk with me..."

He doesn't let me finish and kisses me hard. He lays me back down on the bed and continues kissing me. Our clothes quickly come back off and, in this moment, with us kissing, he doesn't have to say his answer. I know his answer is that he's willing to take the risk, too. And while he hasn't said out loud that he loves me, this moment right here tells me everything as he kisses me and makes love to me for the first time.

· · ● ● ● · ● ● ● · ·

ALSO BY

Are you ready to continue Everly's story? Check out the next book in the series, fALLINg into Senior Year!

After a summer of romance, friendship, and chaos with four insanely attractive boys... reality's about to hit hard.

My boyfriend James and his best friend are off to college, leaving me to survive senior year with their younger brothers. Between the reckless antics and the friendships we built over the summer, it almost feels like everything might stay perfect.

But nothing stays perfect for long.

Just when life feels steady, my past comes crashing back, bringing fear and danger with it. Suddenly, keeping my friends safe and keeping myself afloat feels impossible. I'm determined not to let the darkness win. But then something unimaginable happens... and everything begins to spiral.

Senior year was supposed to be unforgettable... just not like this.

If you'd like the inside scoop of upcoming books and releases,
join my Facebook group:
www.facebook.com/groups/snchristensenreaders/

Follow me on TikTok
@authorsnchristensen

ACKNOWLEDGMENTS

There are so many who I want to thank for the success of writing and getting my books out into the world. First, and foremost, to my Lord and Savior Jesus Christ who died for my sins so I may have eternal life.

To my biggest supporter since I was little, Aunt Karen. Not only have you always been supportive of my writing and every dream I've had, but you also spent countless hours editing my books and listening to my story ideas. These books would hardly be readable without you.

To my husband, who read my stories as I wrote them, listened to every crazy idea that I had, and bounced back ideas. For taking care of the kids and allowing me to dedicate time to writing. For being understanding and taking on whatever role was needed when I was exhausted and stressed.

To Kelli, who was my first reader of these books and for being invested in the story and my characters. For understanding me and my anxiety by being there for me and texting as many times as I needed to support me.

To all my friends including Ashley, Wes, Sydney, Wendi, Jordin, and Kelly for believing in me and being excited for me to write these books. For continuing to support me through my writing journey and allowing me to share my excitement with you.

To my children, who have been patient with me and never once making me feel bad for spending time writing instead of time with you. To Amara, who constantly asked me how my book was coming along and being proud of me for being a writer. To Aiden, who graciously allowed me to go write and made me smile every time I finished for the day by being excited to see me again.

To my mother and father, who both believed in me from day one when I said I wanted to write a book. For always encouraging me to write the moment I said I wanted to be an author when I was little. For being excited and proud of me for my accomplishments.

And finally, to all my readers. I wrote these books because it was something that I'm passionate about. When I put them out there, I never expected anyone to actually read them. So, thank you for taking the time to read my stories and for getting invested in my characters. I can't wait to continue the stories of the characters and see where they take us.

S. N. Christensen

ABOUT THE AUTHOR

S. N. Christensen lives in a town outside of Atlanta, Georgia. She holds a BA in English and MA in Secondary Education. From a young age, she has dreamed of being a writer. She loves writing in the fantasy, thriller, and romance genres.

When she is not writing or reading, she can be found teaching at her church preschool and serving at her church. When she is at home, she loves to spend time with her husband and two children playing games and crafting.

9 781965 818015